"Joel Rose is a writer—increasingly rare these days—who has both technical proficiency and heart. His book is not only a pleasure to read; it is a literary event."
—David Black, author of
*Murder at the Met* and *The Peep Show*

"Wildly hilarious, but the reality of Avenue A is terrifying. Joel Rose is one important novelist."
—Reinaldo Povod, author of
*Cuba and His Teddy Bear*

# KILL

## the
# POOR

# KILL
## the
# POOR

**Joel Rose**

**The Atlantic Monthly Press • New York**

Published simultaneoulsy in Canada
Printed in the United States of America

Library of Congress Cataloging-in-Publication Data

Rose, Joel.
  Kill the poor/Joel Rose.—1st ed.
  ISBN 0-87113-260-5
  I. Title.
  PS3568.07634K55  1988    813'.54—dc19    88-15417

Designed by Julie Duquet

The Atlantic Monthly Press
19 Union Square West
New York, NY 10003

First printing

*For Catherine*

# Acknowledgments

Chapters from KILL THE POOR, some
in slightly different form, appeared in
these magazines: "Señor DeJesus" in
*Confrontation*, "Money" in *Bomb*, "I Am a
Dynamo," "Spike and Mazie," and
"Fire" in *Between C&D*.

I wish to express my appreciation to the
National Endowment for the Arts for its
generous support.

I wish to thank Gary Fisketjon
for his editorial advice.

Kill, kill, kill the poor!
Kill, kill, kill the poor!
Kill, kill, kill the poor!

Tooooo-niiiii-yi-yighttttt!!!!
—Dead Kennedys


What they're saying is: "Don't kill white people."
—Michael Daly
New York *Daily News*

# Contents

# 1

# Señor DeJesus

My daughter goes to daycare directly across the street from where I live. Three doors away is the temple where my grandmother married. Six doors away was my grandfather's tailor shop. Across the street is where my mother was born. The building is no longer there. It's burned down. The temple—where my grandmother hoped I would reclaim my grandfather's seat—has been looted, its roof caved in, windows smashed, the front door padlocked. My grandfather's shop, where he pressed the pants of Louie Lefkowitz, future big shot New York State attorney general, is an apartment building with a green brick front out of which drug dealers push junk. "Red Tape," they whisper as you hurriedly walk by.

"Grandma, what's happening here?"

"Oh, it's terrible, Joe! I came to America in 1903 from Hungary, but this is no America I know."

I've come back, Grandma.

That's the truth.


My grandmother moved from Manhattan to Brooklyn in 1937 to get out of the ghetto. My mother moved from Brooklyn to the suburbs, Lynbrook, Long Island, in 1951. So many people were making that move that they didn't bother thinking up a new name. They just reversed what they had. Brook-lyn. Lyn-brook.

So now I move back. Here I am on Avenue E.

It's coming to eat me. The junkie says, "Hey, man, you, young man, you got change of a quarter for the washing machine?" He is standing outside the laundromat on the next block, holding up a coin that glints in the winter sunlight.

I reach in my pocket and pull out a handful of coins, but they're all quarters and pennies and only two nickels. The junkie thanks me anyway, and asks the next passerby, "Hey, man, you got any change for the dryer?"

Washer? Dryer? Who's cleaning up Avenue E, Grandma?

DeJesus's gym is on East Fourth Street. He's the man with the biggest gun, the fastest fist, the quickest wit.

"Fook you, motherfooker!" is what he wrote on the wall after the fire destroyed his fifth-floor apartment in our building, after we paid him to get out, off my block. "Fook you, motherfooker, old man homeowner."

"Carlos's got Indian blood," I'm told by Attila, the Puerto Rican man who comes with DeJesus and pretends to be his lawyer. What kind of Spanish name is Attila?

DeJesus's got bodyguards with him. Three hard boys who all partake at the Conquistadores, the gym. One's telling me, muscles rippling under his polo shirt, he's been on tv two weeks previous. Three professional bodybuilders, two professional wrestlers, and Juan LaPorte who once fought Eusebio Pedroza for the lightweight title.

I tell them, "Man, my mother was born on that block. My grandmother came to that street in 1903."

"And you want it back!" snaps DeJesus's cousin, who's known as Shorty. Shorty is not short. He may not be tall, but he is not short. "You don't want nobody but white people."

"Who, me?"

"You're prejudice against Puerto Ricans."

"Hey, I didn't say that. Anyway you're prejudice against white people.

"Man," I say, "I'll tell you something . . . "

My grandmother came to Avenue E in 1903. She worked as a maid in Harlem, commuted all the way uptown in a horse-drawn bus. When she was seven years old, just before she came to America, a fortune-teller in Hungary told her she would marry a very handsome man.

My grandfather's last name was not Greenfield. His name was originally Whimmer. He took the name Greenfield because when he escaped the army and fled Hungary, he ran across the green fields to freedom. I always thought that he ran away because he didn't want to fight the Cossacks, but no, my grandmother said it was because the army didn't serve kosher food.

My grandmother never thought of herself as a great beauty. It thrilled her to marry my grandfather, whom she took as the personification of the Hungarian fortune-teller's prediction.

The main criminal on the street in those days was Ike the Woodrobber. People said Ike was once a great lawyer, but now he lived on the street in rags. His mind had snapped after a tragic love affair. All the rich women on the block (there were not many) would let him into their homes, and all the gossips (they were plentiful) marveled it was only when the rich women's husbands were not in attendance. So what was the wood Ike was robbing? Whose home fires were burning?

DeJesus looked at me from across the table at Leshko's, and I saw that these were not the questions on his mind.

My neighborhood reminds me of South America, not North. The brick tenements are steamy tin shacks. Yesterday I noticed that a shantytown is being constructed on Sixth Street. Where the city knocked down all those abandoned buildings and dope houses, now people come with cardboard and tin and build huts, and aren't those *frijoles* being sold on the street? Look over there on Avenue C! Doesn't it say *Carnicería?*

"Wait!" I say to Annabelle, grabbing her arm. "Isn't that the place reported in the *Post* . . ."

"Reported in the *Post* for what?"

"For selling human meat."

"Human meat? You're kidding? Are you trying to be funny? Zho, your sense of humor . . . What were they selling it as?"

"Barbeque."

"Oh, Zho, the *Post* is a rag."

"It's terrible what they did!" Attila says. "Inciting people. Others have to make a living too. Don't they realize, we have to stick together?"

The last time I heard that line, I was with a Biafran. I was visiting a friend who was attending university upstate. The Biafran's father was chief of his Ibo tribe, making this guy a prince. The whole village pooled their money, sent him to school in America during the Biafran war to save his ass, and he had never gone home. I met him at an off-campus bar and we were soon drunk on tequila. I dropped my keys and reached down to pick them up, then couldn't stand up. He helped me to my feet, put his arm around me and helped me up the stairs, all the while chanting in my ear, "Eet's al right, mon, we have to stick together. Eet's all right, mon, we have to stick together." He repeated it over and over again. "Eet's all right, mon, we have to stick together. Eet's all right, mon, we have to stick together. Eet's all right mon . . ."

There's a place on the corner here that sells pot out of a storefront. They sell nickels, about three skinny joints worth in little brown envelopes. They stamp each five-dollar envelope with an ink pad. GET YOUR HEAD TOGEATHER, it says, making a case for marijuana abuse and remedial spelling in school. How long has this place been in operation, sandwiched between the grocery store and the tailor who sells cocaine?

The other week, eight o'clock in the morning, I was running to the bodega to get milk for Constance's bottle, and the cops were busting the marijuana store. They'd closed it down in the past, but now they were closing it down for good. Three cars came, and they dragged away the furniture and fixtures. "No more selling pot here, boys."

*"No más hierba aquí*, motherfooker."

So much for *togeatherness*.

The schools are miserable. That's why it was such a relief to find this daycare center. Velma's Play School, it's called. Otherwise, where were we going to send Constance? Into the projects with all those disadvantaged kids? All those poor kids? All those black kids? All those Puerto Ricans?

No, no sense in even considering those, they wouldn't even let us in. No white man *aquí*, motherfooker. We chose Velma's lily white.

"Stop it, Zho! Be fair. You're so bitter."

Annabelle is right. Yolanda is black. She helps Velma with the school. And Sequina, she's black. And Vanessa, she's brown, half-and-half. And Milo, he's Italo-American, like canned spaghetti. And Tana, Portuguese and Uruguayan. Mara is Latvian. And Mr. Ben and Mr. Hans and Tao and Jenny, and on, and on, and on . . . all American.

We're all Americans.

The Puerto Rican I'm talking about, that DeJesus, he's an American.

If we're going to fight a war in Latin America, will DeJesus go?

I've asked him. Not to fight his *compañeros*, he said.

Perhaps, if made general. Generalissimo DeJesus! I could pose the question to Attila.

"Oh, no, impossible."

"He'd be given a nice uniform. One with five stars."

"You're cute, Peltz, funny, but you know who kept the junkies out of your building?—Carlos DeJesus, that's who. When they came in the middle of the night to shoot up, he went into the halls with a flashlight and a baseball bat and chased them away."

On Fourth Street, where the gym is, he did the same thing. Some of the biggest dealers hung there. DeJesus said, "Get out!" and they got. They know who he is. He hates dope.

Now don't get me wrong, but isn't that Carlos's daughter, the one with the hat, chases you halfway up the block shouting, "Red Tape! Blue Tape! Black and White! What I'm going to do for you today, brother?" Then calls you names when you tell her to go stick it up her ass.

That's her. And her brother—shooting out the window at poor old Yves when he's rebuilding the retaining wall where the bulldozers knocked the original one down after the junkies burned the building behind ours and the city had to come demolish it. He throws the garbage out the window, that one. Rice and beans and rolling papers.

But shooting at Yves? There's no excuse for that.

Don't tell Yves that. Yves is scared. DeJesus scares him. He scares all of us.

Rightfully so. You know what I told DeJesus during our

negotiations, after he said I set the fire? "I got a kid myself," I told him. "I know what could happen in a fire. I don't fuck around like that."

"What if Carlos's kids were home?" Attila asks me.

What if? What if? Obviously his kids weren't home. Carmencita took them to the doctor for checkups that day. DeJesus knew that. He's the one who set it. Ask him.

"Someone comes and cuts a hole in the roof and pours gasoline down and lights it."

"Horrible," I tell him. "I can't even bring myself to think about it."

DeJesus growls, "I know the one. I'll get him." Then he says, "I want five hundred dollars for my losses."

Later he reconsiders, "I want a thousand dollars for my losses."

And still later, "I want two thousand dollars for my losses."

How much more, *señor?* How high will it go?

DeJesus says, "I want eleven thousand dollars to give up my rights to my apartment, my home for eleven years. This is a fair price. A thousand dollars a year. It is my apartment."

"I have no argument. It is yours."

"I'll keep it forever. When the junkies were here, who came out in the middle of the night? I faced their needles with a baseball bat and flashlight."

"You are one tough *hombre, señor.*"

"Damn right. And now someone has come like a dog and bitten a hole through the roof and poured gasoline down the hole and lit it. Who set fire to my apartment?"

You did it yourself, *señor.* "Not me."

"No, I know the one. The *maricón!* The one who walked naked in the hall in front of my family. The one with the beard. The one with the cats. The one who worked on the roof. The old one.

"I'll make a list," DeJesus says. "I'll show you everything I lost and how much it cost, and for my mink coat, an extra one hundred dollars."

*Caramba, señor,* must have been one hell of a mink!

This morning when I was leaving the building to take Constance to daycare, I saw a rat run downstairs into the basement. I thought if someone's getting off down there, the rat'll scare the shit out of him.

"Annabelle, you know who I saw on the block today?"

"A rat. You already told me."

"No, besides that. You know who I saw?"

"I have no idea. The mayor?"

"Paul Newman."

"Paul Newman. You're joking! In this neighborhood! What was he doing here?"

"They're making a movie. You know, at that bar, Vazac's, where they put up that scaffolding, and we thought they were redoing the facade. No, they're making a movie."

"Paul Newman! And you saw him?"

"Well, to tell you the truth, not exactly. But I asked one of the technicians, and that's what he said. DeJesus was there. He said they were gonna give him some sort of bit part."

"He's going to be an extra?"

"You can say that again. He's going to be superfluous."

He was gnawing on a rib. When I passed by he saw me. He wiped barbeque sauce off his mouth with the back of his hand. He said, "What about the other eight hundred seventy-five dollars?" I said, "You already signed papers, my man." I said, "If you weren't satisfied with the settlement,"—which was very fair by the way—"you shouldn't have cashed the check." He said, "What papers?"

The guy's an animal! Why can't he subscribe to the same standards of civilization that we do?

My daughter goes to daycare across the street from where I live. The butcher shop around the corner was closed down for selling human meat as barbeque. Paul Newman is filming on the corner. All over the neighborhood, homesteaders are rebuilding shells of buildings that have been abandoned by their landlords. No one likes poor people. On the corner heroin is sold for ten dollars a bag. Red Tape. Blue Tape. Eighth Street Express. The M14 bus runs up Avenue D, the toughest street in America, according to the *New York Times*. At Fourteenth Street the bus makes a left and goes crosstown. One day there will be a link between the rich section of town and the poor. My grandmother said they were saying the same thing when she first moved here more than seventy-five years ago. But she doesn't live here now.

# 2

# The Boy
# with Green Hair

My name's Joe.

I'm taking a bath. I just come home from work, it's seven o'clock in the morning, and I can't sleep worth shit.

I wake Annabelle up by accident and she's pissed. Pregnant and pissed. She throws an overcoat over her kimono and leaves.

I'm a terrible man.

She comes in from the outside. The front door opens into the kitchen. She's holding the *Village Voice* and the baby's showing, has been for about a month.

The tub's in the kitchen. I ask her why she's buying the *Voice*, I'll bring it home from work tomorrow morning.

She ignores me, sits down at the kitchen table and starts turning pages. For a moment I hope maybe she'll come over, fish around in the bathwater, find my cock, get me off.

I ask her what she thinks she's looking for. Not in the water—because she hasn't made a move—but in the real estate pages where she's looking. There's nothing she's gonna fuckin' find. What does she know? Damn foreigner.

Not a word out of her. She just keeps turning pages.

"Nothing in there," I tell her again. "New York's a lock, and we locked out. No apartment, no nothing. Girl, there ain't no such thing as a good place to live in the big city unless you got the dough-re-mi."

"I always have good luck with apartments," she says. "Good luck with places to live."

"Yeah, like right now? C'mon, wise up."

We live in a little three-room hole over the Ukranian Home for the Blind on Second Avenue. All those poor blind bastards, rolled out in their wheelchairs, sitting in the chilly spring sunlight, silently waiting on the sidewalk. For what? For those homeless assholes from the shelters to stumble up, offer them a swig of whiskey, a pull of wine, wheel 'em into the street so a taxicab rushing down Second Avenue can cream 'em.

"Luck for places to live," Annabelle says eyeing me. "No luck for men, *peut-être,* but luck for places to live."

I guess she ain't gonna give me that handjob. She fingers the scar on her face.

"There is something, Zho," she says. "E Avenue. You know where this is?"

"Avenue E?"

Yeah, I know Avenue E. Little strip of urban highway, used to be a regular big avenue, but then Jacob Riis or some like-minded social reformer built housing projects for the poor to the left and housing projects for the incorrigible to the right, leaving one little island of it, right in the middle, only a few blocks long between East Third and East Tenth streets. Yeah, I know Avenue E—Spanish neighborhood now, once Jewish. On the edge, full of tough guys, drugs, danger, decay. "Perfect place for us. Just your speed,

Annabelle. Just what you French love," I tell her. "Yeah."

"You know it?" she asks again, losing patience. "Zho, do you know it?"

"Yeah, I know it," I says. "My mother's from there. Avenue E. Sure. Lower East Side. Used to go there when I was a kid, but that neighborhood's changed, Annabelle. They call it by a new name now."

Loisaida.

Alphabet Town.

"Zho, answer me?"

No place for you, white boy.


One day, after we bought the apartment and I'm living right there on Avenue E, I go under the stoop and there's a guy shooting up down there and he's just about to put it in his arm and I come down the front stairs under the stoop, leading to the basement, and he's torn, seeing me, between sticking it in his arm and getting up and splitting, and I say, "Ahh, shit, go ahead," and he jabs it in and I turn away. Jesus Christ, under the stairs! Dank, filthy, smelly. People shit down there. Can't you even wait to get back to the crib, bro?


Listen up. This is a song I'm gonna sing to my kid soon as she's born:

> East side, west side,
> All around the town,
> The block is ring-around-rosie,
> Brooklyn Bridge is falling down.
>
> Boys and girls together,
> Me and Mamie O'Rourke,
> We'll skip the light fandango
> On the sidewalks of New York . . .

"Zho?"

"Yeah?"

"What's that mean—'skip the light fandango on the sidewalks of New York'?"

Whisper these words right after me. And I'm not talking to Annabelle, I'm talking to you now. Go ahead, mouth 'em:

**E.T.! Red Tape! Dom Perignon!**

Oh, you hear them, and sometimes you just want to say, need to say, okay, all right, do me up, sell me a bag or two of that there "Executive." I'm carrying. I'm loaded. Give me a deck, b. Fork it over here, this way, and a set of them works too.

Are they new? I'm asking.

"Still wrapped in cellophane, my frien'."

See? There you have it. Fresh gimmicks. That's all I'm asking, dude. Keep it sanitary. Kiss you on the lips, black bean. Don't want none of that contagious AIDS shit, hear?

You ain't gay, is you, Joe?

Gay-shmay, no way, but it don't matter. Haven't ya heard?—and I quote from newspaper headlines—AIDS is a real and present danger to all IV drug users if not to the entire general population at large. So there.

For the last twenty-eight years, my mom and dad and my uncle Yitzhak have run a newsstand in front of a strip joint on Broadway at Forty-ninth Street. Three ex–ghetto rats, happily fled, but not escaped. I walk like them and I talk like them and I think like them.

My old man saying, "Now don't that beat all—Avenue E." He got his finger on the ad, his mouth working as he reads the copy:

APARTMENT FOR SALE
AWARD-WINNING BLOCK
PART OWNER OF BUILDING READY
TO SELL THEIR INTEREST
TERMS TO BE DISCUSSED
$15,000 DOWN

Uncle Yitz comes over. My mom ain't working today. My uncle's my father's partner. He's my mother's oldest brother. Never made good. Pop grumbles I take after him. The only bad blood on my old lady's side of the family and I got it. Like a scourge. *Que será será!* Right? Whatever will be will be. Pop says what other explanation is there for my meshuggeneh ways. He don't know, I ain't telling. My father calls him over.

"Hey, Yitzhak, come over here."

It's fucking cold, even though it's May. Yesterday it snowed. A cold snap. WINS radio says first May snow since 1937. It's melting now, but the Yitz's breath is turning to vapor in front of our eyes. His gloves got the fingers cut off them. (I've seen the same on the cover of a book by George Orwell, *Down and Out in Paris*.) Figure one day I try cut off my fingers, gloves and all. Maybe I already have. He looks down at the paper.

"Award-winning block?" the Yitz says with a snort. "What award that block win? Shit Hole of the Year Award?"

I tell him, "Hey, Unc, Annabelle talked to the people who own the place. They say the apartment's beautiful."

"Beautiful?" he snorts again, like some fucking racehorse in the paddock at Belmont Park. No Secretariat, though. Uncle Yitz is a plug. He says, "Boool-shit! Beautiful? How can that be? I grew up there, remember? Don't bullshit a bullshitter, Joey. There ain't nothing happening down there in that neighborhood. Never was. Not even when we lived down there. It's always been a hellhole, and it's a hellhole today. Mark my words. Your grandmother worked her whole life get the family off that block."

"So the kid takes a look," my old man says. "Can't hurt. Joe's doing all right for himself, he's in the family way. Right, Joe?" He gives me a bony elbow in the ribs. "He knows what's good for him."

My father likes Annabelle, the way she treats me, the way she talks to me, the way she don't let me get away with all my bullshit. Tells me she's good for me, knows I made the right move marrying her, cut my losses with all those Jewish American princesses who rubbed my face in it. And her blond hair, and those good tits, he was outraged when Leonardo cut her that way, "But you come out the winner in the end, right, Joe?" he says to me.

"I know where I'm going, right, Pop?" Me, Jo-Jo Peltz, with a high-class French girl?

"Yeah," Uncle Yitz says. "Right to Avenue E. Wait till your mother hears about this! Right back where she was born. Hey, Joe, check it out, the old temple still there?"

I walk with Annabelle hand in hand. The bombed out buildings, derelict, decrepit. Her eyes are bugged. She says the baby's kicking. I point out the shooting galleries. The Black Door. Blue Door. The Toilet. Places I used to run when I had a habit. On the corner of East Eighth and C, two guys I think I recognize, either from the old days or from their pictures in the post office, says, "Executive? E.T.? Black and White?" Now that was my brand, that E.T., and later on, Yves says he was looking out his apartment window and there are two guys sitting on the back stoop, the two of them sitting in the sun, and they share a couple of bags and a needle, then one guy takes out a gun and blasts the other guy in the head. Boom. Like that. And I never see my two guys again. And I wonder was it them who Yves saw?

And there's a guy in my bathroom getting high.

Annabelle screams, "Get out of here. Don't do that

ever again!" and that French accent driving him, me, crazy, "Zho, promise, you can't be this way, not when the child comes."

Annabelle's camera clicks.

There's something I got to tell you right now. Annabelle's going to tell it to you for me because I'm incarcerated in the penitentiary.

"He's scared."

But I'm not scared. I'm not scared of nothing. Nothing, you hear! Not DeJesus, not nothing.

She bought me a dress once. You fucking believe it? What do you want me to say? It was a beauty? It had style? Let me ask you something—Would you wear it?

So she bought me a dress once. A designer opened up a couple of blocks away, calling herself "East Village," and started sporting these dresses for men. Annabelle thinks she's gonna make me over. She says dresses for men are popular. All the rage. I tell her, I'll show her rage. She wants me to go to a meet with a hard boy like DeJesus in a tutu? What do you think this street man's going to think?

She says, "You have a satin jacket. You're not embarrassed to wear that. Green satin."

*He wore green sa-tin . . .*

She's right. It has *Passaic DeMolay* stitched on the back, the name *Drew* stitched on the front. Bought it on the street for four bucks.

"Zho, you got that fur coat."

Genuine Korean mouton, full length. Used to wear it after I got off for the night from the newsstand, used to go downtown to the after-hours clubs. Every time I'm on the street some black dude comes up to me, asks me if he can buy it. Think I'm a pimp.

I ain't no pimp, motherfucker!

But what you think, you see a bird like me on the

street? Move across the boulevard. Mama, this guy up to no good.

You a righteous dude, bro. Wear your collar up, your pants down.

I like your threads, blood.

Ought to offer that coat to DeJesus, and I will, he comes in with his lawyer, Attila—Atilla the bum, I call him—and he say, "You done it, motherfucker. You done it to me, and you will pay."

Annabelle takes me to see the apartment on Avenue E.

We can't get in the building. The door's locked. I bang and bang, nobody answers.

How long I'm gonna stand here? "Wha'd they say?" I ask her.

She says take it easy, they'd be down.

I'm sick of waiting. "I ain't waiting no more," I tell her. Maybe she got the wrong address. There's two dykes across the street, sitting on a stoop. Maybe it's that building. That one looks okay. Three story Federal. This building we're at is a piece of shit anyway. Some old law tenement, a hundred and twenty years old if it's a day, in piss-poor shape. "Go ask them if they's the ones got an apartment to sell," I tell her.

I watch Annabelle cross the street Avenue E, an avenue no more. Just a poor, pathetic little stretch in the middle of nowhere. It's my mother's block though, *that* tickles me.

They used to call it the Doctors' Block, an oasis with sixteen doctors and lawyers living here. Always one of the most beautiful blocks on the Lower East Side. I guess, in its way, it's been preserved. A fucking lot less devastation here than elsewhere, but still . . .

Annabelle comes back. No, not them. They don't know nothing. *Rien.* They don't have an apartment for sale, and they don't know any that are.

Annabelle says she can call from the corner, she

brought the paper with the number, so we go to the corner of Seventh Street and Avenue D. There's a pharmacy there with a bunch of phones outside. Three of them are torn out, but one seems to be working. A line of drug salesmen are working the site. A girl in a watch cap. Rapping at the prospective customers. Annabelle rummages around for the number, takes out a paper. I give her a dime, say I'm dropping it, the dealers look at me and spread out. A guy with green hair comes by, says, "Hey, you looking for an apartment?"

I say, "No, we ain't lookin for an apartment." Guy with green hair! We ain't gonna live in any apartment some asshole with green hair recommends. Annabelle gets an answer. The people say they'll be right down to let us in.

# 3

## Money

Money makes the world go round!
The world go round!
The world go round!
Money makes the world go round—
with such a happy sound!
Money, money, money, money. . .

Get this! This is gonna make your hair stand on end: Every
day of Annabelle's life, since day one, she has a picture taken
of herself. Including today, a Polaroid, before we come over
here to see this apartment on Avenue E. Eleven thousand,
three hundred and sixty-eight, so far, all laid out in front of
her. "Look, Zho, this day one thousand eighty-two. I am
thirteen days short of *trois ans.*"

"Gorgeous," I say.

This was all her mother's idea to begin with. Third kid,
but the first born alive; two stillborn in the maquis during

the war. Then it was a long time coming, the conception of delicate Annabelle. Now to make sure, record every day of her precious daughter's life from the day Annabelle hotfoots it out of the womb up there in Normandy. Every change, every nuance. Annabelle says it just struck the old lady, came to her out of a dream or hallucination, camera ready:

Annabelle? Annabelle? Look at me, sweet thing. There, there, Pittou. Say *fromage* . . .


Let me tell you how we can afford to buy a place on the Lower East Side, no matter how cheap:

We got some money from an incident that went down at the Gotham, where Annabelle worked as an exotic dancer.

"Say what, Zho?"

Ahem . . . Bite my tongue. Rather, *Annabelle* got some money from an incident that occurred at the Gotham dime-a-dance strip joint where she worked just to pay the rent. She didn't really like it.

Stay with me here. There's a certain mentality today—moneywise. Do you agree or what? Every fat fuck on the make. Not that Annabelle didn't deserve the money Leonardo wound up paying her. Not to mention, otherwise, we'd still be living over all those blind people, hearing the squeal of brakes, those horrific screams . . .

Right after I was born my old man used to sell his papers off a standpipe sticking out of a building on Seventh Avenue and Forty-seventh Street. Right outside the hottest strip joint in New York City. That's how I remember it when I was a kid. Me and my sister. My father in earmuffs, his nose red.

One night, nothing personal, Leonardo, the Gotham floor manager, who has the same basic shape and size as a mirror armoir, cut Annabelle's face with a bottle opener. He claimed he lost control. Didn't know what it was about, didn't know why he did it. High on something. Smoking crack. Cut her one hell of a slice right across the cheek, hooked her lip and tore it pretty good. When I go inside people are backed up, looking. I push some away, step in front of him. Blood running down her face, but no tears. I tell him, "Leonardo, put it down, bro," and he laughs at me, and says, "Listen, you little Jew! . . ."

Later he apologizes, repeats that he didn't know what came over him, this mindless violence. He smiles, pays her thirty thousand bucks to keep her mouth shut, no cops, no authorities, keep his business open, keep his liquor license. He arranges to have the cut stiched up by a customer he claims is an "A number one" Park Avenue plastic surgeon. Later, I swear, I see the guy advertising on tv, looking at me through the void, the voidoid, "A number one," saying that you too can be all you ever dreamed and more, me thinking, looking back at him, watching him at his table, drooling over the girls, the spittle running down his chin, pulling his six-dollar Beck's that much closer across the table, my folks calling me in the bedroom, six months after my sister died, saying, Jo-Jo, we been talking, you seem depressed, would you like a nose job, the guy looking at me out of the screen, his eyes saying, we can do a number on you too, sir, me thinking, man, you can kiss my skinny white ass . . .

Annabelle looks at me, blank, no comprehension, and asks me what kind of doctor advertises on television. "I'm not an American. I never heard of such a thing. In France doctors don't advertise. . . ."

I say that's exactly the point.

Fucking Leonardo. She fingers the scar, says she'll hold a grudge till the day she dies, longer. She'll get him back, no matter when it is. This man, the size of a deep freeze, with a heart like a pint of Häagen-Dazs deep in its cavity.

So, listen, I'm telling her, my gal, all is not lost, you got me out of this deal, right, your Zho-Zho, your baa-by, your American, girl, remember me? I run to your aid when you're in danger, my own physical welfare be damned, not to mention the long green that comes to bear, the thirty thousand to the better we're going to make work for us.

In the end, I got the dame to boot, so who says justice is not mine? Me, just a regular guy, the star of no novel or motion picture, I got her, a sexy beautiful girl, French like I say, *mon mec*. That's America, right? Land of opportunity.

Annabelle laughs, unimpressed. "Zho, you sick."

I ask myself, has anyone ever said my name better?

Yesterday I showed her this story I tore out of the paper and brought home from work, some woman in Harlem wins sixty-five million bucks because a hospital refused to treat her after she ate—get this—a bad chicken wing and got food poisoning. Then we saw her on the six o'clock news. Crying, says she lost her husband because of what had happened, her health was a mess, some kind of terrible infection spread to her spine. Her life was over, she said, but now the hospital was gonna pay, she'd teach those people a lesson! Annabelle says, "What lesson?" Nothing's gonna change. Those people don't care. They won't remember. They see another poor black woman come in, they gonna run to her, grovel, say, "Yes, ma'am, what can we do for you today?" Or even provide decent health care?

Annabelle shakes her head. No way. She says this country is fucked! Racially, classically, economically, politically. Fucked.

We're sitting on the stoop outside the building on Avenue E.

I wouldn't mind having sixty-five million dollars. Even half that, sis.

"What are these people asking for the apartment?" I ask her.

"I don't know."

"Well, we'll talk 'em down, no matter what . . ."

"Let's see it first, okay, Zho?"

Sure, sure, okay, understood.

"Don't fuck it up."

She looks at me. How?—beseechingly. The neighborhood makes her nervous, scares her to death. Rightfully so. The pushers barking, C & D, coke and dope, coke and dope. The addicts is about. Shifty, skinny, gaunt, cruising the street in their low-riding Chevys, slouch hats down over their eyes, lining up for the buy.

Behind us the door opens.

Building, I'd say, built somewhere between 1870 and 1890. Old-law tenement, which only means it's got a little air shaft in the center for ventilation. Soiled badly on the outside, facade crumbling, cornice falling down, look up, jagged edge of torn tin, a sword dangling over our heads, but hey, dude, I'm willing to be open-minded. That's cool! Live dangerously. Annabelle swears the lady on the phone said wait'll you see the apartment, you won't believe it, so don't prejudge.

The block I know. Did I tell you my family's from this block? The same block I sit right now stoopwise, my grandmother came to in 1903 when she arrived in America from Hungary. The block my mother was born on. Always a good block. "A good block, Joe." I remember it from when I was a kid, when we came to the temple, came to the doctor, came to the nurse, came to see the lady with the alligator purse. To visit my mama's friend, still there, ensconced, long after my mama and her family got out. And now I see the little skinny soldiers of chaos and anarchy creeping about in those low riders and beat autos, you see them in the street, they look you right in the eye, sitting on the stoop, and their gaze is cold, b, their gaze is fucking freezing.

I follow a white broad inside, says her name is Betty, just call her Beneficia. Got a gut on her. She looking at me like I'm from a different planet, but I'm not, I'm from the Earth. Just like you. It's only my eyes, they're from Mars.

"Are you all right?"

"Sure, sure."

"He's always like that," Annabelle says pleasantly, and they go inside, chatting like they've known each other for the last hundred and fifty years.

Down the hall I trail, little boy lost, see the building crying, crying, save me, save me, Joe, ragged around the edges, but coming back, no question. Annabelle looks back down the long hallway at me, her eyes asking what do I want, please behave.

Hey, this ragged-ass building don't bother me. I'm used to it. I've lived in worse than this. The world's ragged around the edges and I don't condemn it for decrepitude. I notice the stairwell is marble, still square. Run this by you real quick, carpenter lingo: *The stairs is plumb*. See? None of them is at an angle or falling down. None of the kickers gone. They's all there, no treads missing, though worn smooth, concave like a bowl, a million feet having trudged up and down these stairs, hiking to some promised land, high in the heavens. Probably five hundred thousand of those feet belong to junkies, prodding and jabbing needles, even between their toes, taking that long hike, all within the last ten or fifteen years. And I see all the old plaster is knocked off the walls, and the bricks is clean and the glass is all neat and trim in the hall windows, not a shard showing, nothing knocked out or busted. No graffiti. No filth. Surprising for this neighborhood. Pretty nice deal. People do a job like this, people like this Betty, this big white Betty, this Beneficia, they should be proud of themselves, the shit holes I've seen down in this neighborhood. Woman deserves a medal!

Somewhere up above, she's into her rap. "What you see is the sweat of collective labor," she says. "What you're buying into here, why it's so cheap, is the sweat of our collective brow, all the brows who live here. A decent place to live. We've done it all ourselves," she crows proudly. "Bought this building, and the one next door, from the landlord three years ago for two thousand dollars, some back oil bills, and fourteen thousand in scofflawed parking tickets.

Since then we're putting it back together ourselves. Independent of all bureaucracy, all city agencies. No contractors, no city inspectors, no codes, no intervention. Only hard work, just build our houses, just build our homes." She's finished. Nothing to do but follow her on up, me huffing and puffing, look up her skirt, see yards of cotton billowing, her white underwear covering her big butt. Beneficia climbing the stairs like a mountain goat.

I take a break, Annabelle and Beneficia going ahead. Directly below me, on the first floor a door opens. I see an eyeball in the crack. It opens no further, just an inch, the eyeball peering up at me. I peer back.

"Hey, how far up?" I call to Beneficia.

"Four floors."

I sing to myself, "I'm a lone cowhand, on the Rio Grande . . ."

My shape ain't so good, standing around at the job all day. La grande madame and la petite mademoiselle leave me far below in their wake. Huff, huff and climb. Huff, huff and climb. "Hey, up dere!"

"Door's open," big bad Betty calls down. "Just come on up when you're ready. Take your time."

I hear Annabelle say, "Oh, eet's beautiful," the accent grating on me. *Oh, eet's beautiful.* Huff, huff, doo-wop, catch my breath, sit down, light a cigarette. Below me, the guy who was peeking out his door steps out into the hall. He cranes his neck and looks up into the stairwell.

Hey, here I am! Hey you, monkey-face! What do you want? Mind your own business! Pleasant guy—I y'am, I y'am. But I don't say this. What you think I am? One got to know how to live in the big city, though you shouldn't believe everything you read. Things are changing in this country. Used to be, you know, you could trust everybody, everybody's normal, everybody's like us, you and me, your neighbor and your pal. Nowadays who's gonna argue about convention, it's all up for debate, ain't that right? This guy looking up into my puss. Me breathing hard trying to catch a second wind. None of his business. "Hey, buddy, you live here?"

He says nothing, pallor of gray face, slinks away ratlike under the stairs. I hear a door slam.

Above me a man's waiting, dark skin, dark hair, dark eyes, looks like an American Indian—*How, keemosabee* . . . —and takes my hand when I say, "I'm Jo-Jo Peltz."

"Proud to make your acquaintance," he says. "Beneficio Gomez." Half the size of his wife.

Annabelle's sitting on a couch in the living room. She says, "Eet's lovely, Zho. Eet's beautiful, no?"

Sure, sure, the place is a veritable wonderland. A palace. Versailles. What can I say? Beneficia gushes, jumps right in, tells me how once, before the Flood, it was six apartments, now incorporated into one stately, majestic, phenomenal space. She tells me how their group of homesteaders took the building over from the landlord. "There'd been a fire, it was on the verge of being abandoned." The place was being overrun by junksters. A group of people from other buildings on the block got together try to rescue the building. In a way these two buildings, situated in the exact middle, anchor the entire block. "Stability was essential. The only legitimate tenant here was a guy named Ike, who lived in the basement. He's still there."

"I think I saw him," I says.

"He can't be missed," Beneficio quickly ventures, sitting up straight. "But he's harmless."

"I wouldn't say that," interjects his wife, her voice acidic and I look up, hmmm.

Beneficio gives me the Cook's tour of the premises, shows me how they opened up the apartments. Originally, there were three apartments on each floor. A small, square four-room unit in the front and another in the rear connected by a narrow three-room railroad apartment in the center. At one point, when plumbing came indoors, there was a shared water closet at the center rear on each floor.

He shows me where the hall was and the side-by-side front doors that opened into either kitchen.

"The apartment's not quite finished yet," he apologizes, "but all the heavy demolition is complete," and if there's no sink in the bathroom and the sheetrock's up but not taped, so be it. There's a monstrous wooden scaffolding over the stairwell leading upstairs, no railing on the rudimentary staircase, the dirty, splintery floors covered by a hideous mustard-colored rug, but there's no describing the charm, the space, the expanse, the pink brick walls, the warm light. This is the Lower East Side. This is the neighborhood where twenty million immigrants settled when they first arrived in America. Nothing has changed. On the streets outside the open window, we hear jabbering, and a car alarm going off, the waves of electronic noise sounding to me like: CAR-TOY CAR-TOY CAR-TOY CAR-TOY CAR-TOY CAR-TOY . . .

"Somebody turn that off!"

Beneficio leans out the window. "It's that damn Dagmar's car again."

He says the guy's got one of these cheap alarms goes off every time the garbage truck goes by or somebody breathes too hard.

Annabelle is sitting quietly, breathing deeply, trying to suss the place out, gather her impressions. Conversation dies, the siren finally stops, Beneficia sighs, "Thank God." Annabelle forces a smile, says she loves it, but, frankly, she has some concern. Not the apartment, the apartment's a stunner, *incroyable,* but the neighborhood, says if it were just *her* . . .

Beneficio and Beneficia look at me like it's me holding her back, my fault. I got to explain, Hey, I'm a street dude, born and bred, my family's from this neighborhood, I can take care of myself. It's not me she's worried about, no way. I walk the streets of any neighborhood in this city. I tell them Annabelle's pregnant. She's worried about navigating the highways and byways of urban America with our little helpless offspring, you understand? Their faces light up. "A baby!"

"The neighborhood?" Annabelle pleads. "Is it a danger?" Did they ever have any problems?

They jump on it. "Oh no." This isn't a bad neighborhood. It looks so much worse than it really is. They've got two kids. This is a *family* neighborhood. Sure, the drugs are on the street, but nobody likes drugs, most of all the people who live here, the Puerto Ricans are just as worried about their kids as any of us, drugs proliferating . . . But the violence, that's between the junkies. Beneficia says she comes home late at night, never had an incident. They call upstairs and their son comes down to prove a point.

He's fifteen or sixteen, face like a tomahawk, wearing army fatigues. "This is Benny," Beneficio says.

We shake hands. The kid's got one of these vise grips, crunch up your bones. I say, "Hey, watch that! I'm a concert violinist."

Beneficia says, "Are you really?"

Then the sister comes down. Her name's Gloria. She's maybe fourteen, with a little baby fat, but she's gonna be a beauty when she grows up, almond eyes, dark skin. Slinking down the stairs, watching.

I ask Beneficia what an apartment like this one costs, what are they asking?

She says to tell the truth, they already had it sold. Beneficio works for IBM, who's transferring him down to Boca Raton, Florida—do I know it?—growth capital of the world, gateway to the new Southern Kingdom. "Lovely," she says. "We bought a house down there and sold this one, to an Italian fashion designer. But the designer went home to get some details straightened out in her factory, and left power of attorney with her lawyer, and he came down here, took one look, and said, 'Sorry, in good conscience I can't.' "

"Say what? Good what? Can't what?" I ask.

"He's doing his job. Frankly, we're not entirely legal. But slowly we're working on it."

"Meaning what?"

"There's no two ways about it, you're taking a gamble. There's no denying that. The building's not exactly kosher. This can be your home, but it's not just sitting here all perfect, you're going to have to work at it. Hard. The building has a vacate order. The city claims it's unsafe. There's been a fire here. No one was living here except for Ike downstairs. There were no systems, no water, no gas, no electricity. No roof. Slowly we've restored what was here, but officially the building's still classified U.B., unsafe building, and there's no C of O—that's your certificate of occupancy—so no one can legally live here, even though we do, of course, that's because after we bought it . . .

She says a lot of buildings on the block are done the same way. Almost all of them. Some have had a dispensation from the state attorney general's office, but that's because Louie Lefkowitz was from this block and made a special case.

She says when people started the corporation—that's what she called it, *The Corporation,* EAT CO, E Avenue Tenants' Corp.—it was five hundred a unit to buy in, a unit being one original apartment. "We have six," cost three thousand dollars. "But the building's not what it was when we started. It's come a long way. It's a little rough in the wintertime, but by and large . . .

"And we put in seventeen in materials, not to mention our own labor, and we contracted an electrician and a plumber. . . ."

Somebody appears at the top of the stairs. "Oh, Mewie," Beneficia exclaims, like it's her long-lost cousin, back from the Amazon after a lifetime living with the Yanomami.

Meanwhile, Benny's lost interest and split. Went upstairs, came down with a plastic machine gun and left. Now this skinny bird's standing up there, bearded, his Manson-eyes gleaming down on us.

"Who's this?"

"Our next-door neighbor, Mewie Cotton."

How'd he get there? Beneficio gave me the tour of the house, didn't see *him* up there. Spooky. Unless he'd been hiding in the closet.

"That's one thing we haven't gotten round to," Beneficio says sheepishly. "Closets."

Beneficia says this Mewie character climbs over from his apartment in the adjacent building. She shows us the well window, overlooking the air shaft, five stories up, between buildings. "Climb over?" I say. "That's dangerous. He could fall."

"Nah, it's easy. No problem." He sits down, smiles. "Don't mind me!"

Suddenly Beneficia jumps up with a brilliant idea. Maybe Annabelle would feel better if she talked to another woman who lives here, someone more her age and inclination. She throws open the window and knocks on the fourth-floor window across the well. "Don't let her appearance distract you. She's very nice, a very smart girl."

The girl arrives at the window sporting a red mohawk with black tips. Beneficia takes Annabelle's arm, steers her over and makes the introductions: Scarlet B, Annabelle Peltz.

But Annabelle says, "No, not Peltz. I use my own name, not Zho's."

They lean toward each other. Annabelle and Scarlet. This is the old neighborhood. I see it now. Strong. It freezes me. Annabelle pregnant, holding her belly, standing by an open window in a tenement on Avenue E, the block my mother was born, chatting with a red-and-black-headed punkette named Scarlet.

The skinny bird, this Mewie, leans closer, says something to me.

"What's that?" I says, turn to him, look into those red eyes.

He's grinning at me, pats my knee, says, "Hey, I hear you're pregnant. Congratulations!"

# 4

## Meet Me at the Meeting, Mary

"It's so sweet that you're pregnant," Beneficia says to Annabelle, a big lopsided grin on her face, "and I'm so glad you're interested in purchasing our apartment. . . ."

"Fuck that," Annabelle scoffs later, as we're walking home, west, the spring sunlight finally warming the city streets. "How maternal can you get! I don't take that crap from my own mother."

A battered panel truck is stopped at the light at the corner of Seventh Street and Avenue B. Hand-painted above the blinking left-hand turn signal is the legend EL PASO and opposite, above the right, SUICIDE and in the middle, across the back doors, EL SMASHO.

Beneficia told us if we truly want the apartment, what we really get is shares in the corporation and a proprietary lease on the space for ninety-nine years, and that we have to come to a meeting, meet the other members of the corp, see if we like them, they like us, and so it goes. "Won't be any problem," she says. "Can you come back seven-thirty tonight? We don't have much time."

I sit on the stoop, waiting for my honey. I tell her, "Meet me at the meeting, Annabelle." I'm still waiting. She has this habit of being late, says she likes to be late. I say I like to be on time. She says that's what makes horse racing. I say horse racing, that's a fuck of a thing to say. Doesn't sound particularly French to me. She says what's the matter, you can't stand another American? Someone more American than you?

Annabelle's big obsession, like I say, is taking a picture of herself every day of her life. Her mother's brainstorm originally, now just a bad habit. Annabelle claims it's a record, the record of a life. If it just happens to be hers, what can she do? Every day, click. Here she is thirty-one and change, she has eleven thousand three hundred sixty-eight snapshots of herself. Annabelle says it's an important document. You be the judge.

Then, looking around, she gets a new idea, maybe document the neighborhood, hard boys on the corners, teenage girls with their babies hanging outside buildings, brickwork coming down, junkies lined up, old men hanging out windows listening to the street sounds of salsa, the big box, the ghetto attaché, the pothole traffic, the Kool Man ice cream truck, the Chihuahua dog, it's all there, and I say, yeah. "I ever show you the picture my grandma was in, a Jacob Riis photo taken on the corner of East Sixth Street and Avenue C? She's hurrying around the corner, a tight skirt, a turn of ankle, the men from the pushcarts' eyes on her, one man in the gutter, resident *bummerleh*, homeless, looking, longing. Did I ever show you? No? Remind me, okay?"

While I'm waiting on the stoop, looking up the block, down the block, for any sign of lovely Annabelle, another couple comes by. These two are the new you, just the ticket, the new society, matching pink shirts, white baggy sporty pants. You're not excluded, Joe, don't worry. I don't say a thing. Who are they? What do they want? They don't belong, not like me, not like my gal, we, we, *we* are the new you! Not them. I don't know, I can't imagine, but pretty soon Beneficio comes out and says hi to them and hi to me, and he asks where Annabelle is, and I tell him she's late but she'll be here, so he says, "Joe, I hope you don't mind, but I'll take these other people in, because everyone's there for the meeting and I'd like to get started."

I say okay, sure, what am I supposed to say? But after he ushers them in, I grab his arm, and say, "Hey, what's the story with these people? I thought you were selling to us, remember?"

"Don't worry," he says, "you're number one on the hit parade, but we need a backup, a safety valve. Look, we already got screwed once by the Italian. If something like that happened again . . . What if you decide you don't want to go through with the deal, or if the corporation doesn't give their approval?"

"Don't give their approval?" First I heard of that. What's the matter with us? "You think that's a possibility?" I ask him.

"Joe, excuse me, please, I got to get things going. Don't worry."

"Annabelle'll be here any minute!" I call after him.

Looking out at the street, nothing happening, Tuesday night, a couple of people walking by jabbering in Spanish, I pick out a few words, a pretty girl, I smile, nod hello. A kid comes up and yells, "Carmencita!" Tough, wiry, he looks at me sitting on the stoop and says, "One way or the other, bro." I slide over. He steps past and goes into the building. A little while later, Annabelle arrives.

"Where you been? You're late."

"I'm always late," she says. "I believe in being late."

She don't have to tell me. I know, I already told you. Maybe I'm not upset about her being late, maybe I'm upset about something else. Maybe I'm always upset. "Another couple's inside," I tell her. "At the meeting."

She shrugs. "We'll get our turn."

"Beneficio was down here. He said we're number one. Top of the list. I hope so. I don't want to lose this place."

"We won't lose it," she says. "I have the luck, the good stars." She sits down with me, watches Tuesday night pass by on Avenue E.

"How you feeling?" I ask her.

She rubs her belly, puts my hand on her stomach. "I felt the baby kick this afternoon," she says. "Wanna feel?"

I don't feel a thing, only her warmth. It makes me feel hungry, her heat always does, gives me a stir in the groin. Her pregnancy is sexy, full, hot, rampant. I lean over, nuzzle her, look for her mouth, soft lips wide, wider, engulfing mine. Her tongue licks me.

Above us the door opens. Beneficio comes out leading the pink shirts. He smiles, shakes their hands, thanks them for coming, tells them he'll let them know.

The pinkos are eyeing us, the competition. They don't like us. *They* don't approve. Two slutty lowlifes kissing in public. Get that shit off the street, bro!

"I like your shirts!" I say cheerfully.

Beneficio has a big hello for Annabelle. Very solicitous, this man, trying to be so nice. Maybe he thinks Annabelle's easy. She apologizes for being late, says she had a fit of nausea. Oh yeah, he nods up and down vigorously a few times, man must do aerobics, that good neck movement, no stiffness there, he knows what that's about—morning sickness. It's his specialty at IBM, he explains. " 'Course, my wife," he says, "that's a different story. Betty weathered every conceivable storm. Never gave in for a minute, and let me tell you, Benny was never easy. Never. His labor for her was a human abomination, just gritted her teeth and went on, and on, twenty-seven hours, wouldn't let it affect her. After Benny was born, they kept him in the hospital six weeks recuperating from the ordeal, but Betty was home in four days."

From the looks of the son, maybe he never recuperated.

"It's what I've come to expect of her," he says. "No matter what anybody tells you, it's because of her these buildings are standing today. No matter what anybody tells you!"

"Why would anybody tell us different?"

"Oh, she's had some problems with some of the people here. She's a strong woman. People react against that. Especially"—he clears his throat—"some of the men."

He pushes open the door and we go inside. This building's not what the other building is. This side's decrepit, a real slum tenement, to come in here a dark cold night puts the chill of fear in your bowels. The hall light is busted, dim or missing. Only a single bare bulb illuminates a swatch of graffiti on the wall, APRIL FOOLS written in blood letters, the floor tiles broken, one front apartment door twisted a quarter off its hinges. The plaster on the ceiling crumbling, other apartment doors battered. The stairs broken, the struts missing from the bannisters, water dripping from broken pipes, and the stench, the horrible ammonia smell of cat piss.

"Don't mind this—it's all going to change. We have some problems, but they'll be solved."

A guy is standing under the stairs. He takes a puff on a cigar and grunts at Beneficio.

"You coming, Dagmar?"

"Just think I'll attend to my car."

The meeting is held in an apartment on the third floor. The apartment is basically one half of what Beneficio and Beneficia have, but little work has been done save the demolition of walls, ceiling, floor. We walk into an empty, eerie space and all heads turn toward us.

"Joe, Annabelle, this is the corporation . . ."

They are sitting on folding chairs and on foam cubes and they turn in unison to look at us, all males, all grungy, in need of shave, turn, say how do you do or hi, names scooting by us, Yves, Ike, Mewie, Negrito, Spike, the guy with the green hair from the phone this morning. I nod. Annabelle says something sweet like *"Enchantée,"* something that makes me laugh, most of them mumble back, 'ello, but Negrito, he says, *"Salut,"* with a perfect accent, and Annabelle looks at him and smiles and I know this a cakewalk, we have them eating out of our hands, Annabelle's charm, but then her eyes go fiery and she turns to me. "Where are the women?"

Beneficia steps forward. "Don't worry, dear."

"Where are the women?" Annabelle repeats. "Don't any women stay here?"

"Why of course there are . . ."

The male eyes on us, hard unrelenting.

Voices grunt, hands show us to seats. Inquisition. We sit down, and they start in asking us questions. Where we live, what's our philosophy, what we feel about homesteading or do we know anything about it, the land rush, Oklahoma Territory 1858, for example, do you think that applies, where you live, the Lower East Side, what you know of the neighborhood, speak!

You willing to work? You ever done construction before? What do you think your input to a building like this could be?

I tell them as far as construction goes, I've never done any, but I'm good with my hands and my mother's from this block, my grandmother came to this block from Hungary in 1903. I tell them it's important to me to move back, the connection, my roots, to live where my family lived, to walk the same sidewalks, to pass the same buildings. I got eyes, I see what's happening to this neighborhood. Things are changing. The neighborhood went as low as it could go, but it's poised—

"Then you're willing to work to bring it back?"

"I'm willing to contribute. Work, yes. What does it take?"

They say they don't have much money. They do everything themselves. Once a month they get together have what they call a work party, but it ain't no disco, it ain't no Mudd Club, it ain't no foolin' around. Everybody pitches in, helps to accomplish a task. I got anything against that? They all look at me.

I grin, "You boys ain't communists, is you?"

"We all work in harmony, that's it."

"That's it. I understand. No, I don't have anything against that." These boys aren't Reds, they're the Seven Dwarfs. Yeah, and I can smell it now: Beneficia, grinning at me, she be Snow White.

Does the corporation have any more questions?

"You seem responsible, capable people—"

"I don't understand the animosity," Annabelle says. "What's this undercurrent I feel?"

"*Tabarnak*, not against you, dear," this old codger in a watch cap, introduced as Yves, some kind of a frog, protests. Quebecois, I later learn. He smiles at Annabelle, an even, perfect smile. "*Pas contre toi, chère amie.*"

"Perhaps I ought to leave," Beneficia says. "Obviously, what Annabelle is picking up is directed against me."

"Perhaps you ought to." The monkey-face guy I saw standing under the stairs gets to his feet. "Maybe you should take Beneficio with you too. You're not board members anymore. I think you should leave these people with us."

He looks me in the eye, and holds me as Beneficio and Beneficia slink out. After they're gone, he says, "Look, my name's Ike. I lived down here on the Lower East Side my whole life. For the first time I got something. I'm not looking for nobody to fuck it up."

"I don't blame you," I says. "Is there some kind of problem?"

"Not now there's not."

"No?"

"Understand me, Peltz, I won't give it up."

"Hey, I'm telling you, bro, I'm in full concordance."

"So I got only one question for you, bud," he goes on, not missing a beat. "You gonna be a help to us or you gonna be a hindrance? Which will it be?"

"Oh, well spoken, Mary!" Mewie claps. "Well said.

Joe, Annabelle, let me introduce Ike, our new president! Too bad, what a shame you made Beneficia leave before hearing such a resounding speech, Commandante! I'm sure it would have stirred the cockles of her heart. Why don't you ask Joe if he approves or disapproves of embezzlement or does he have any strong feelings against arson, for example, or, for that matter, murder?"

"I still don't understand," Annabelle complains. "What exactly are you trying to do?"

"We're trying to survive. You don't seem to realize, we're in the face of it. This neighborhood's like the Wild West a hundred years ago. Cowboys and Indians, treacherous, murdering savages, life in hand, homesteading in hostile environments."

I tell them cut the melodrama, Annabelle can take care of herself and I've been here before. I grew up in this city remember? Here or hereabouts. I know what it is to live on the streets, weather the gangs, fight it out, survive. They talk like they're the first heroes ever, the first to walk these mean streets.

I tell them I made my choices. This apartment's important to me, living in this neighborhood is important to me. I won't be denied. There's history on this street for me, meaning. I want to bring my family here, raise up my kid. It's my right.

I know how it is in the streets, getting worse every day but, at the same time, getting better. They're doing a good job, they can be proud of it. If everyone doesn't exactly coalesce, so be it, they never do in a group. Just make the best of it and go on.

We all look at each other. Those with the power, the approvers and the approvees. "We all understand what it is today," I says. "The streets they're rough. Everyone around you is a danger."

They all grunt their approval, except Annabelle, who burps, pats her belly and says, "Oh, excuse me."

# 5

# Floor Plan

Now I'm going to present a floor plan of how we lived in these buildings on the Lower East Side at numbers 310 and 312 Avenue E, New York City, New York 10009, USA.

Originally when these buildings were constructed there were three apartments on each floor of each building. A square four-room apartment in the front, an identical four-room apartment in the rear, and an extremely narrow three-room railroad apartment extending between them.

The year was 1872. The area along the East River had been swamp and lowland, but the city government had seen fit to use landfill to cover up the marshes. Most of the city's feed warehouses for horses and livestock were housed here. The mosquito population in the area thrived.

Enormous waves of European immigrants were streaming into the Lower East Side, and many, many more were poised to come. Lower Manhattan's rancid tenements could no longer hold the swells. For health reasons tenements were being built with center air shafts, or wells, with intentions that each and every tenement room have a window for ventilation. Unfortunately, the new, progressive, right-thinking law did not work because ignorant immigrant people tossed their garbage out the well windows, and the resultant stench wafting up from the damp swamp-fill rot was fierce and terrible. The mosquitoes liked it fine, however.

By the way, just a brief aside, they're still here, the mosquitoes, but there's this new product on the market that's really wonderful called Bite Erase. It comes in a container that looks like a fountain pen. The mosquito bites you, and then really quickly you just apply this liquid . . .

In 1872 the toilets were in the backyard, but they eventually came indoors: a shared W.C. off the public hallway on each floor, a cramped, claw-footed bathtub in each apartment kitchen, gas jets for light, little grimy men selling tiny quantities of coal out of basement storehouses for cooking and heat.

Modernization in 1912 brought a bathroom into each immigrant apartment, and electricity, wire wrapped in paper, strung and embedded in the plaster walls.

"Don't put your finger in that socket, Shavey! Not while you're in the bathtub. Now listen to Mommy, darlink, if you want to live to see your fifth birthday."

In the building at 310 Avenue E, the people who now live here are:

FIRST FLOOR:

Ike, junior established himself many years ago and occupies all three apartments on the first floor. Because of the entrance hallway and stairwell there is no feasible way to connect these apartments without infringing on public space, which is strictly forbidden by the corporation bylaws. The front north is combined with the rear apartment to make one living area. The third apartment on the first floor, the south, is retained by Ike as a storage facility for all the artifacts, detail work, plaster moldings and assorted rubble he collects from scavenging the street and abandoned buildings. Ike is the son of the scourge of Joe's mom's youth, Ike the Woodrobber, and he has been an apt pupil, learning well at the dirty hand of his infamous father.

SECOND FLOOR:

Spike, an up-and-coming gallery artist with international design, and his girlfriend, Mazie, the East Village doyenne, own the entire second floor. Using the fruits of Spike's smarmy labor, they also own:

THIRD FLOOR:

Two apartments on the third floor, the front apartment and the center interconnecting railroad. They've duplexed up with a majestic wrought-iron spiral staircase. Quite elegant.

The Quebecois, Yves, owns the rear apartment, but doesn't live in it. He has an arrangement with a young Puerto Rican boy named Negrito, whereby Negrito pays the apartment's maintenance fee to the corporation and a small sum to Yves, whereby Negrito will eventually assume ownership of the space, and become himself a legitimate shareholder in EAT CO, the E Avenue Tenants' Corporation.

FOURTH AND FIFTH FLOORS:

Annabelle and Joe own all six apartments on these two floors, which they bought from Beneficio and Beneficia for thirty thousand dollars, the entire settlement or bribe money or payoff received from the oily Leonardo to save his skin and liquor license. The twenty-two rooms of the original apartments have been reduced to twelve and the two floors are connected with a simple pine ladder staircase. This gigantic space, the largest in the buildings, was readily accessible because of the fire in 310 that burnt off the entire fourth and fifth floors and ultimately led the original landlord to abandon the buildings and eventually sell to the corporation for two thousand dollars, plus assumption of debts (including fourteen thousand dollars in unpaid parking tickets). When Beneficia owned this apartment she affectionately called the space "her kingdom," as in Thy Kingdom come, Thy Will be done . . .

In the building at 312 Avenue E:

NOTE WELL: 312 was never abandoned. The building has continuously been occupied since its completion in 1872. When the corporation took over ownership it assumed responsibility for all residents, some of whom still remain, be they rent-controlled or rent-stabilized.

FIRST FLOOR:

Dagmar and Delilah live in the rear apartment. Delilah is the daughter of Pandora, who lives on the second floor. Delilah was born in this building and has spent her entire life here. Dagmar, the one with the car and cigar, is Delilah's husband.

Fausteen O'Grady lives in the center railroad, although she's in prison at Dannemora at present for receiving stolen goods without a license.

Mewie Cotton owns the front apartment, but does not live here, and has not touched the space. He says he just likes the "idea" of ownership.

SECOND FLOOR:

Paco and Pandora live in the front space. Their apartment is rent-controlled, and they receive their rent check from the New York City welfare department. Pandora, who is in her late fifties, has lived in this building, in this apartment for more than thirty years. Paco moved in with her seventeen years ago. Paco is not the father of Delilah.

A pottery maker from Toledo named Dana owns and occupies the center railroad, but she stays to herself and rarely attends meetings or participates in corporation business. She says she's shy, likes only clay.

In the rear second-floor apartment, Howard Kumundga lives alone. He is not a member of the corporation, but a renter. He pays three hundred and fifty dollars a month for his apartment, a questionable fee in some people's minds for what is tantamount to a cold water flat. The rationale, however, is that Kumundga's from a wealthy family so fuck him. Three hundred and fifty dollars is the most paid by anyone for rent. Maintenance fees are ninety dollars per unit. Kumundga was originally a friend of Mewie's from the gay nightclub where Mewie works. It was Mewie who first told Howard Kumundga about the vacant apartment and brought him over here. Unfortunately, since then, he and Mewie have suffered a falling-out, and now are engaged in an ongoing feud.

THIRD FLOOR:

Butch Olson occupies the front apartment, which he sublets from Yves. Butch is a Ph.D. candidate in social work at the New School, and is from Minnesota. Butch regards these buildings as a laboratory. He considers himself a radical progressive and claims he's had just about enough of what's going on here in these buildings and the exploitation of tenants. As a direct result, he has organized a rent strike, enlisting Howard Kumundga and Fausteen O'Grady to his side. He has also tried to interest Scarlet, Paco and Pandora and Carlos DeJesus, but has been frustrated in his efforts.

Yves owns the other two apartments on the third floor, but does not live in them. They are vacant. Eventually, he says, he *will* live here, but right now he has a comfortable apartment in Chelsea, and he's scared of DeJesus, who has made blind threats against several members of the corporation, although never against poor Yves in particular.

FOURTH FLOOR:

Scarlet B lives on the fourth floor in the front apartment. Scarlet rents her apartment from the corporation, although she has been invited to buy. She has painted all the walls black and covered the windows with tin foil.

A middle-aged Puerto Rican man named Huaquero lived in the back apartment, but he went home to P.R. and has never returned. His fate is still unknown. His apartment is padlocked and remains vacant. The corporation could rent it, but already there has been so much trouble with renters that they are reluctant.

The center railroad is one of the rent-stabilized apartments and was occupied by a black woman named Mary Johnson until her untimely death over this past winter from pneumonia. Social Services took her two children. The apartment remains unoccupied for the same reasons Huaquero's does.

FIFTH FLOOR:

Mewie Cotton, resident loudmouth and know-it-all, owns the front two apartments, and lives in them with his fifteen cats, Boy 1 through 15.

Carlos DeJesus and his family occupy the back apartment. DeJesus lives common-law with Huaquero's daughter, Carmencita. They have two children, Fidelito, seven years, and William Guillermo Morales DeJesus, age three. Also living with them is Carlos's daughter and son from his first marriage, Nubia, age seventeen, a local drug runner, and Segundo, age fourteen, a real cocksucker.

# 6

## So the Fat Fuck, He Backs Off

What have I gotten into? I ask myself. Why move here? I hate the work. I work too hard, and now I see there's only a hard core who work hard too. The other corporation members fuck off every chance they get.

Annabelle is disgusted, and she doesn't want to come around the building. "Zho, you think we made a mistake?" she says. "Zho, why do you rag me all the time? I didn't do anything. When I come you just pick on me."

"Annabelle," I say, "I don't mean it."

"I'm pregnant."

"Fuck you," I say.

Deep in my heart maybe I think I don't want Annabelle around anymore. She ain't doing nothing for me except whimper and complain. So fucking negative. She say it's hormonal. She wants to stay on Second Avenue until the baby's born. But I say, "Why don't you move in down here?"

"Why don't you move back with me?" she says. "We need to make love more often."

But I can't, not right away, not that night. A couple or three times a week you gotta stay at the building all through the night, sleep in the basement, make sure the junkies don't loot the place.


I'm working in the halls one morning with Yves when Mewie shows up and says, "You know what they did last night? They stole all the pipe I spent the day installing!"

Yves throws his hat on the floor and stomps on it.

"I told you so," Mewie whines. "Joe's too too new."

I slept here, I didn't hear a thing.

Yves says we got to buy and install a decent steel door, keep the junkies out once and for all. We need DeJesus to stand guard all night with his baseball bat. Yves says he'll pay for the door, and the corporation can pay him back when it has the money.

"Yeah," I say, "That's what we got to do, keep the junkies out."

Mewie says he doubts I could keep mice away much less hard-core junkies. He don't think I'm formidable enough, says I got to toughen up my act, suggests I wear studs and black leather. "Junkies are scared of black leather," Mewie says. "At least when the right person wears it. They don't like when you look too weird." He looks at me. "I never been robbed," he says. Then he adds, "Joe, give us a real mean scowl."

I think Mewie's never been robbed because he has fifteen cats in his apartment, stinks of their piss, and looks like one of those homeless men who sleep in the park. I'm frank, and tell him that.

He shrugs. "You might be right."

Today we put in new beams under Scarlet's apartment. When Yves goes to remove the floor into her bathroom, he drains and unscrews the toilet and breaks it by accident because he works too headstrong, and then he tries the bathtub, but the fucker weighs a ton and he begins to get mad and shouts, "Maybe I ought to smash this fucking thing once and for all!" and suddenly with a sledgehammer he does. And crack, this cast-iron piece of shit falls apart.

"Can you beat that?" he says as he tosses the pieces into the kitchen, and Scarlet says, "Now what am I going to do?" We look at the pile of jagged enameled cast-iron pieces and Yves says, "What the fuck, send Ike, he can get you new fixtures out of an abandoned building." Proud of himself, he laughs, and smashes the sledge down on the biggest pieces left.

Then Dagmar the fuck from downstairs comes up to complain about all the noise Yves is making, and Yves shows him what he's doing, how the leak rotted the floor, and how all the beams will have to be replaced, and the fat fuck says, "Well, can't you hammer softer?"

Yves looks at him incredulous now. "What the fuck's wrong with you? How can you hammer softer? If you did one ounce of work around here, you'd know you *cannot* hammer *softer!*"

So the fat fuck, he backs off.

# 7

# Who's Pregnant Now?

A guy come over to me on the street. He says, "I know you. I know who you are. You one of those white boys move in over there . . ."

"Is that right?" I answer. Is it? He's waiting. "Yeah, that's right. I be the white boy."

On the crosstown bus home I was listening to two Puerto Rican women having a conversation. One says: "Carmencita's sick of that shit. She gotta face it! Jesus's blood's against her."

"Poor thing!" the other one says.

What is it to have Jesus's blood against you? I ask myself. Is his blood against me? Is it against Annabelle? Constance? And if it is against me, is it because I'm Jewish? Jews didn't kill Christ. Romans did, and they already paid the piper. Their language is dead as a doornail.

In the back of the *Voice* an advertisement catches my eye. JEWS DO BELIEVE IN JESUS, it says. CALL THE CHOSEN PEOPLE.

See? You see?

I'm on my way to pick the kid up. Six months old we put her in daycare. How's that gonna harm her? My old man says I'm crazy. "What's a matter wit you?" he says. "She's too young. Why don't you have Annabelle take care of her?"

"Dad, kids need kids. Left to their own devices they form their own society, and Annabelle isn't really interested in babies, not even her own. . . ."

Constance doesn't know who I am. Do any of these kids know their parents? I walk into Velma's. A little boy waddles up to me, grabs me around the legs. Looking up into my face, he murmurs, "Mama!"

I look down. "You're confused, kid," I tell him.

He doesn't pay any attention.

"Mama!" Persistent little bugger.

Off in a corner somewhere Constance begins to cry.

Today, in my mind, I look back to when Annabelle first talked about having a kid. "Count me out," I said. "Count me in, okay, but count me out. I don't know a thing about kids."

"Zho," she said, "you're the one who brought it up, not me."

"Annabelle, I'm not maternal, and neither are you, or maybe I am."

"Still . . ."

We were sitting on a rock in Central Park. A five-year-old gypsy kid came by. "You wanna buy a flower?"

Annabelle was worried about Immigration. One of her friends from the Gotham got picked up by the authorities. They showed up at the club and carted her away. Annabelle says a kid helps convince them. Just like that (snap of fingers) you're legit, on the up-and-up. "We're married, we love each other," I said. "That's enough."

"No, it's not," she said.

It was a beautiful day, cool air, blue sky, sun. The gypsy kid was working for a living. Annabelle said when she was in Algeria she saw kids three, four years old working.

"Sure," I said, "why not us? Rescind the child labor laws." I'm for it, sis. Bro, stop coddling those *enfants!*

"Zho . . ."

"Sure, Annabelle, it's *l'amour.*"

Sometimes you come around. A girl sitting on your lap, her hands behind your head, looking in your eyes, talking in a French accent. She kissed me. I felt her breasts against my breasts, felt myself getting hard.

"A child?" I said, he said, Zho said. "A child?"

"Mmmmmmm."

Maybe it was my idea, like she said. She says the way I remember it is bullshit. She said I was talking about *Little Big Man,* the Dustin Hoffman movie. It's the one he plays a cowboy lives forever, rubs elbows with all the right people, Buffalo Bill, Wild Bill, Sitting Bill, Electric Bill. Little Big Man knocks up his Cheyenne wife. When it comes time for her to give birth, she walks off alone into the wilderness. Little Big Man watches her but doesn't move, doesn't go to help, hadn't been to birthing classes. Alone, squatting in the brush, his squaw, her haunches begin to quiver. Tough woman, she endures, labor comes to an end, she delivers the baby herself, bites the umbilicus, gobbles the placenta, and returns to Dustin and the rest of the tribe as they continue their trek across God knows where.

In my case, the Lower East Side.

I told Annabelle, "Okay, you want to have a kid. Keep in mind what I tell you. Concentrate on Dustin's wife. You're always saying how independent you are. Prove it."

Annabelle is the kind of woman who needs a challenge, takes to it. You just don't come here to America, leave everything you knew, an immigrant in this tough-ass country. Her family in France is pissed that she's here, her old man outraged, thinks she married beneath her, far beneath her, American heathen, the man calls me *Zho-Zho, le sauvage Commanche!* If he ever knew . . .

What? Knew what?

Knew where I am right now. He'd turn over in his grave.


I wake up in the middle of the night and there's a ghostly specter hanging over my bed. I blink once, twice, then recognize the presence. My sister, Maddie, dead all these years! She's standing over my bed, her M14 army issue rifle clutched in her hands. She tries to say something. . . . No, that was just sleep in my eyes. Now I really recognize the ghost. It's Annabelle.

"What's the matter?" I ask.

"I'm scared," she says, trembling violently.

"Scared? Scared of what?"

Since becoming pregnant, she's always worrying about something, always kvetching. She is the most maddening woman, bro. I kid you not. I had explained to her about Dustin Hoffman and *his* wife. Why did she insist on not listening? What does she want?

She points out a small round damp spot on the mattress. She says she thought that maybe she might have broken water. "Bullshit," I say. "You probably pissed yourself." I ask if she's sure that she's broken water or if she just thinks she might've.

She begins to cry, says I was right. She probably had only wet the bed.

I came around. I mean, don't believe everything I say. I'm not so mean or macho. "Annabelle . . ."

*"With Zho, it's all a pose."*

So, at three o'clock in the morning, Annabelle and I found ourselves poring over our notes from Consejo birthing class, trying to figure out if the water Annabelle was passing was urine or embryonic fluid. I smelled the stuff. Who knew? Suddenly I didn't feel as smart as I thought. She sneered at me, "You never been smart. Oh, Zho . . ."

"My belle, Anna-belle."

In this modern day and age (check my watch, it's June 16, 198–) I refused to be one of those fathers who escapes down to the neighborhood bar, the White Horse would be a good one in some people's minds, Vazac's in others, to tie one on while his baby is being born, and his wife is enduring that gut wrench and all that other who-knows-what.

During Annabelle's pregnancy something came over me. I began to feel like I wanted to share everything. I wanted to feel as pregnant as she. I didn't fool myself. I knew I would never blow up, never carry the baby in my womb. Not unless science had been working overtime, and hadn't notified me that men could now get pregnant. I went to the public library before work, pored over the medical journals. Had certain sudden steps been taken? Steps that I was unaware of, that had been kept silent, gone unreported by the leading scientific researchers . . .

Dear Dr. Frankenstein,
It has come to my attention . . .

I wanted to stay by Annabelle's side. Our relationship has started as one thing—a girl running away from a gangster who wanted to keep her enslaved as a stripper in a midtown dive—to another, a girl running away from immigration authorities who wanted to return her to the country from which she had come. What do you say to something like that? A girl comes up and says, "Help me stay in the country, please! Please, I beg you!"

Do you say, Good riddance!?

Boot her the fuck out?

America for Americans, fool!

Annabelle needed my support and she gave a mean blowjob. Believe what you want to believe. I love her. I was waiting for the kid. Our kid.

It's so much easier for a man when it comes to children. If he does anything he's a hero.

So shoot me.

Anxious. Annabelle reached for me. She needed me to help her breathe, help her concentrate, relax. Feed ice chips in her mouth. Now, the bed soaking, I felt overwhelmingly part of the birth process.

She grasped me (we're in Saint Vincent's Hospital), hung on to me, and we were both pregnant, and in labor, together, and ready to deliver. The birth of my baby, little Constance, was the highest high I ever experienced. No shit. I went back to the junkies, "Man," I said, "that Red Tape, that Executive, that E.T., bro, that shit ain't nothing!"

It startled me when I broke away from Annabelle's side to grab a quick piss. In the Father's Waiting Area the room was crowded with chain-smoking men, laughing nervously at bad jokes.

Why are the steering wheels on cars in
    Mexico so small?
So they can drive in handcuffs.

Why's the Puerto Rican constitution six hundred
    fifty pages long?
It's spray-painted.

So why aren't all these dudes with their women? I wonder. "Hey, why don't you guys go out, smoke a joint, come back, see your babies being born?"

They say, "Marijuana makes us paranoid."

I say, "Cool out, dudes." They look at me like I'm nuts. So I smiles. "Take off your coats, your ties, your brogans, boys, relax, I'll tell you a real good joke." I look at the time. "I've only got a second so let's hurry it up.

"The pope was going to Nashville, right?

"On the plane the stewardess comes up to him, says, 'Welcome aboard, Elvis.'

"The pope says, 'I'm not Elvis.'

"The plane lands at the Nashville airport, all the city dignitaries are waiting. Everybody goes, 'Hooray for Elvis!'

"The pope goes, 'I'm not Elvis.'

"The pope is escorted to his limousine, the driver holds the door, says, 'How do you do, Elvis?'

"The pope says, 'I'm not Elvis.'

"The driver takes the pope to his hotel. The clerk says, 'Your room's waiting, Elvis.'

"The pope says, 'I'm not Elvis.'

"The bellboy shows the pope to his room. The pope slips the kid a buck. The bellboy says, 'Gee thanks, Elvis.'

"The pope says, 'I'm not Elvis.'

"Three gorgeous, naked groupies are waiting in the pope's room. Seeing him, they screech, 'Elvis!!!'

"The pope sings, 'One for the money, two for the show . . .' "


The delivery room was crowded. Now remember, I'm recalling all this. The delivery room was crowded. Our doc, two nurses, a student physician from Downstate Medical, a hospital observer, all helping Annabelle and me work, bring our baby into the world, bring her back to her heritage, to Avenue E. One of the nurses spreads Annabelle's legs to mark the baby's progress, calls me over.

"Look," she says.

Five centimeters away, down a dark tunnel, ill-lit, I saw a little curly head coming toward me.

"Annabelle!" I shout. "Annabelle, you can't believe it! I see it. I see it! I see the baby."

Annabelle was pushing too hard to even know what I was talking about, but tears welled in my eyes.

The baby was beautiful.

Everybody said so. Scarlet, Yves, my mom and pop, Mewie, even Spike and Mazie. What perfect features! And a mouth, a mouth like Brigitte Bardot. Must have come from her mom.

"No," Annabelle says. "Your mouth, Zho. She has your mouth."

She was so tiny, her little fingers and toes. And everything worked, all greased and ready to go, that was the amazing part. Even the hardcase nurses, probably the same ones who ignored that woman who ate the bad chicken wing, would come into the room to play with her, my kid, and I could tell they were not simply going about their jobs with that accustomed ho-hum drudgery. They dug her.

My mother-in-law called from France. She said she just wanted to check on one thing—what was the baby's nose like? She said a nose like mine was okay for a little boy, for a *petit garçon*, but on a *fille* . . .

The saleswoman at Woolworth's on Fourteenth Street took a new interest in me. She knew me from before, thought I was a shoplifter, but now she helped me fumble through the bins searching for cotton crib sheets.

The Puerto Rican couple at the Avenue D pharmacy laughed when I told them how beautiful my daughter was. At the laundromat doing a bagful of soiled stretchies, I found myself in lengthy conversation with the old wino who spent the day sleeping on the sill in the front window. He blessed my child, he blessed me, he blessed Annabelle, he blessed his sneaky pete bottle and offered me a swig, which I politely refused.

When Annabelle was carrying Constance I used to imagine it was three of us making love, the baby being so close, merely a thickness of skin away. Now here she is, the poor little helpless creature that Annabelle had carried inside her so snug for nine months. I call her Milko because she looks drunk after she finishes suckling, but Annabelle calls her the Boss, and I guess that's more who she is.

Bigger than Bruce Springsteen.

Attila the bum, DeJesus's lawyer, standing in front of

me, puss to puss, saying, "Carlos would never burn down his apartment. What if his kids were home?"

And me saying, "I know, I got a kid too." One kid. Constance the Beautiful.

Before we decided to have her, I thought to myself, I have to be reasonable. A new baby, so be it, suck up the gut, and go about your business. No longer the fuckup, no longer the underachiever. Be a grown-up, Jo-Jo. Pretend to survive in the world. So I'm unhappy. So I'm depressed.

In all honesty, I knew I was the maternal one. It's no big thing, you understand, I'm confident what I got hanging between my legs. Somebody shoves a prick in my face, I'm just not the kind to gulp it down. Annabelle wouldn't let me get away with it. "You want me to be sexy," she said, "do the dishes." All right, it spread to the shopping, the cooking, the cleaning, the wash. Ike sneered at me. He said I was pussy-whipped. I said, "No such thing—it's the eighties, man. Share and share alike. Anyway, Annabelle does all right. You ever see a woman wield a hammer like she can?"

Ike said, "What's all those photographs she's taking?"

I told him I didn't know.

"It ain't her memoirs, is it?" he asked. "She better not be taking no pictures of me."

Why hadn't somebody warned me? I had no inkling, you see, no clue. How could I? The final question to the Hundred Thousand Dollar Pyramid: How much work could a baby be? *or:* How much wood could a woodchuck chuck . . . ?

Changing diapers, going to the laundromat, the supermarket, the drugstore, taking the kid for walks in her Snugli, taking her for walks in her stroller, taking baby to the doctor's, giving her vitamins, changing her clothes, wiping her chin, holding her in your arms when she's crying, flipping her around, entertaining her. Round-the-clock attention: talk to her, coo to her, agitate her, show her her teddy bear, back and forth, up and down, coo-coo, sing to her, use a variety of funny little voices, rock her, roll her, cajole her, say soothing things to her, all the time refraining from kissing her on the lips because she hates it.

"Some lover she'll make," I tell Annabelle. "Is this a French broad or what?"

One minute this sweet little creature, my daughter, brings tears to my eyes with her tiny little beatific smile, the next I could throw her through the wall. Colics? Now what's that? Why's she crying now?

"Shut up! Just shut up!"

I shake her, hard, then catch myself.

It disorients me. I find myself doing some little chore when suddenly it dawns on me: Men don't do this! Jo-Jo Peltz don't do this! No *way* he does this.

The other day I come home from running all over the neighborhood stores, up Avenue C, down Avenue D, searching for a box of superabsorbent disposable diapers. Anywhere you look you can buy smack, crack, chiba, coke, everybody saying C & D, but me, I'm looking for diapers with tucks, and I can't find them. I come home I find the baby asleep, Annabelle luxuriating in a hot tub full of bubbles.

I blow up.

She says, "What's the matter? Can't take it? Shoe on the other foot? The poor man's work is never done?"

She says, "C'mere, *viens,* " and she pulls me in clothes and all.

"Zho? Don't be glum." She kisses me. "You are perfect."

One day I'm at the newsstand talking to the Yitz and I tell him somebody should have told me how hard it was to have a kid, *so* much work. He thought that was a great joke. He laughed and laughed. It irritated me. I swear I almost punched him. What did he know? What had his part been in child raising? While he and my father were here at the newsstand, my aunt and mother were home taking care of us kids.

Curiously, when Annabelle goes, I go too. I find myself plunged into the depths of postpartum blues, just like her, Charlie Parker on the stereo. I accuse her of exposing me, allowing me to catch it as if it were some contagious disease like measles or mumps. I cry. I tell her I'm having trouble dealing with all the work and responsibility surrounding the baby. She says what do I think she's having? I kick myself. I am a fool. I thought it would be easy, and now I'm overwhelmed. Why have I done this? I ask myself. Where is that son of a bitch Hoffman? C'mere, Dustin! I got something to say to you, bro. Sometimes I don't know who I am, who I've become. Who is Jo-Jo Peltz?

When I give Constance a bottle she doesn't care who I am, who it is who's feeding her. If I'm the father, if I'm the mother. All she wants to do is drink. Who's giving it to her is secondary.

But at least Annabelle has a reason for feeling ditzy. The baby is eating her up, drinking her down straight from the tit. But me? I'm the one who feels like an empty shell.

"Zho, it's America. It's the building."

"What?"

The baby is not that difficult. The baby is not that difficult. She's no crier, no complainer. She does have those colics. What is that again? A bubble of gas?

"Doc, is that normal?"

"No big deal," she says. "Sure, normal."

Then why am I tempted to throw her through the wall. I love her, man. Don't I?

She sleeps through the night like a little angel and has since her first month. Still, I can't recover. I'm always exhausted. By four o'clock in the afternoon, time to go to work, I'm ruined for the day. I swear to God, seven-thirty, middle of the theater rush at the newsstand, and I'm dozing off. My father sticks around, says, "What the fuck, I'll give you a hand."

Annabelle suffers too. Her mind is cloudy, she explains, she feels mentally slow. I say, "Ike asked me today what you're doing, taking all those snapshots. He thinks you're recording the history of the building. He thinks you're going to use it against him."

"Use it against him?"

"I told him. I said you're recording my memoirs."

"Yours?" she says.

"What was I supposed to say? Yours? Immigrant girl dancing topless in the Deuce—"

"Hasn't he ever heard of Jacob Riis, social reformer, documented daily life on the Lower East Side? Tell him I follow in his footsteps. Social reformer. One day the projects be called Annabelle Bonpetit Memorial Subdivision for the Terminally Poor and Destitute."

Hey, my mind is as misty as hers, my self-control as nowhere. I try to buoy her up. I really do, sis. I want to help her. But what about me?

I find myself continuously at the refrigerator nibbling chocolates and cookies. Or running up to Nathan's on Forty-third Street or Popeye's right across Seventh Ave. Is this possible? Suddenly I'm recognizing myself in all those women's mags we sell at the stand: *New York Woman, Self, Working Woman, New Woman, Woman's Day, Woman's World, Ms., Ladies' Home Journal, Redbook, Family Circle.* You know the ones. I don't have to tell you. Before Constance, I looked at those things, I had difficulty understanding. I mean, what the fuck were they talking about? Now I'm poring over them, seeing how I can apply articles like "Baby's First Three Months" to myself.

When Constance was born, the doctor, a woman by the way, held her up. At the time, no fault of my own, I mistook Constance's swollen genitalia for a little boy's scrotum, I mean the kid had *balls!* Big fucking cahoongas! So when the doctor said, "It's a girl!" I said, "Bullshit it is! That's a boy if I ever seen one. My son!"

# 8

# Joe Hates Drugs

It's them against us, bro. What do you want me to say? That I hate drugs? That all of a sudden I've made a complete turnaround? Living down here on the Lower East Side. I was walking along the street, and a man, a real mean looking dude, come up to me. He says, "God bless your child."

I looked at little newborn Constance in my arms, and he says, "It's so small," and I say, "Yeah, blessed be. It's amazing that all the parts work." His eyes narrow. He says, "What?"

I said, "You heard me. *Works!*"

"Works? Two bucks," he says, and makes a little sign with his thumb and forefinger like a plunger on a syringe. He says, "You score the doogie, right down the block, bro. What you like, that E.T.? That Dom Perignon? A man of your taste. And for your little girl I got just the ticket. . . ."

His look says, Man, drugs suck, man, and you with a

baby on your chest. Ought to be ashamed of yourself. Don't be taking that stuff! Just say no.

So you can never tell. Maybe I run into this dude another time. Maybe this other time he tells me, he's back in the arms of God. Maybe he tells me he's happy now. Maybe he is.

The streets are so beat, so dingy where I live. How about your neighborhood? Hey, did I tell you my grandmother came here and she cried? Here I am, standing tall, and my grandmother cries like I let her down. Home is where the heart is, right? Annabelle says I remind her of a Jewish Gary Cooper.

"Coops," she whispers in my ear. "Sweet Coops."

"Say it again."

"Darling sweet Coops."

I thought the neighborhood looked pretty damn good, despite everything. The neighborhood . . . the neighborhood's in a state. Still, it's better than it looks. "Don't cry, Gram'ma."

My mama, when she heard I'm moving back to the old neighborhood, asked me, "What about Eighth Street? Is the bank still there? The herring factory? The theater on the corner of Avenue B?"

"The Loew's Avenue B!" I said. "Mom, that thing ain't been there in twenty years."

"Well, I ain't been there in twenty years," she said, hurt, insulted. "Longer!"

Once my mother told me when she was a kid she wanted to be a concert pianist. Only she didn't get to play the piano. Her brother, Yitzhak, got violin lessons, though. My mother says bitterly he never cared, never even practiced. He went into the meat-smoking business. I told him once, "Unc, it causes cancer." He told me to mind my own business. It's part of the Jewish heritage to smoke meat and eat it too! If I don't like it, too bad. But too bad on him, because he made a mess of it, my father had to take him into his newsstand business and now Yitz is standing behind the counter with me on Forty-ninth Street. "Will you look at her!" he says, pointing to a girl with deep décolleté.

My uncle asked about 369, and I said, "Fire." And he said, "What about 365?" and I said, "Fire," and so it went. Fire, abandoned, knocked down, etc., for all the buildings my family had ever lived in, and hung around in, and visited, all except my grandfather's cleaning store, and I said, "Yeah, it's still standing, it's the Good Lookin' Candy Shop now."

He said, "Candy? Good Lookin'?" and I said, "Yeah. The junkies have it."

"What the hell happened there?" my uncle wants to know. "It used to be such a beautiful block. The neighborhood . . ." and his voice trails.

So I tell him, Jew landlords, just like him, his blood cousins in crime, money hungry, don't care, more money, abandoned property, spit on the poor. "No need to run a scenario like that by you, right, Unc?"

He sells a paper, blows his nose, studies me, says he heard it was the Puerto Ricans coming into the Lower East Side, and not knowing how to live, living like animals, not caring for their own place to live, their own homes and apartments. He says he hears the old neighborhood is like the Wild West. "Is that how it is, Joey?" he asks, pointing his finger at me. "You playing cowboys and Indians like you did when you was a kid?"

"Yeah, that's right, Unc, only this time there's something a teensy-weensy different . . ."

I go to look at the rear apartment, where Yves is standing against the back wall. I scan Eighth Street and beyond. "Brother," I say, "will you look at that." A building on Ninth Street has fallen down. The tenement where Ike told me he went to scavenge his floors, and took his beams, and took the moldings and ripped up the floorboards, got Scarlet her new toilet and bathtub. That building. And Yves tells me a story he's already told me twelve times before, about the day when he was standing here at this window, and these two junkies are back there, and the sun's out, and they've just gotten off, and one takes a gun out and shoots the other guy in the head. And Yves looks across and there's DeJesus watching from his window, and Yves catches DeJesus's eye, and DeJesus holds his finger up to his head, and he cocks his thumb and he shoots himself in the head too.

My grandmother moved to this neighborhood in 1903. She worked as a maid in Harlem. After I moved in she insisted she come back to pay a visit. She saw what had happened and she cried. I brought a kitchen chair down for her from upstairs so she could rest on the way up. I carried the chair up to the second floor landing, then I ran back down, took her arm, helped her up. She sat. I waited.

"Joe," she said, "vhy you come back here. Vhy?"

"I like it, Grandma," I told her. "I really do. Hey, I still remember coming to the temple on the High Holy Days when I was a kid."

"You shouldn't be here," she said. "You shouldn't be vurking for your father. You should make something of yourself."

"Don't worry, Grandma, I can take care of myself."

"Can you? You know, Joe, I can remember all kinds of tings about this neighborhood. I remember vhen my father carried in the ice to save paying Ike the Voodrobber a nickel. My mother said to my father, 'Vhat are you doing? Vhy are you doing dis? Ike'll do it for five cents.' The ice came in a big block, my father lugged it in from the street, but before he could get it up the stairs, vhat does he do? he drops it. The landlord had just put in a new floor in the foyer with real marble from Italy, and the block of ice fell on the new marble, not even a footprint on it, and vhat do you think, it broke. *Oy*, the landlord vas furious. I remember it to this day. He made my father pay every penny, *zien mazel*, and it vasn't cheap."

She looks at me, her eyes shiny with tears. "Such vas his luck, Joe. You remind me so much of him, my father, your great-grandfather. You are just like him. I pray to God you are a better father than you are a son."

My old man says, "*Meshuggener!* So this is it. You got your work cut out for you. I wouldn't wish this on a rodent."

As she stepped into my apartment, my mother said she had to sit down, the smell hit her out of the past. She said she could smell the eels boiling in a pot.

I said, "What eels?"

She said when she was a girl, she used to come to this very apartment and babysit, and the woman who lived here was always cooking eels, every time she came. Then my mother said she remembered the first time she ever made money babysitting at this lady's house, she went out and bought a new dress. She remembers the dress to this day, blue linen with red piping. But before she had a chance to even wear it, her sister asked to borrow it. Then, when my mother wore it on a date, the boy she was with said, "Are you so poor you can't afford a dress of your own, you gotta wear your sister's dress?"

They sit there at my kitchen table swapping memories. Thinking back, mulling over, my mother crying, grandmother crying, my father staring off into space. Constance crying in her cradle. Annabelle jumping out of her chair, flustered, screaming at the baby, saying to me later, "What's the matter with you? Your family's here, you can't lift a finger? You can't help? Make me do everything. It's not that way when they're not around! Zho, usually you're so sweet.

Can't do enough. Share the work. Never an argument. I never even have to ask you. Zho, don't block me out. Are you listening? Zho-Zho . . ."

So I put my toe on the cradle. Rockabye baby in the treetop, when the wind blows, the cradle will rock—

—around the clock. Tonight.

Annabelle's mother, grandmother, great-grandmother, how many more lay in this cradle shipped over from France? On the phone Annabelle's mom explained how important it was to her, to the family, that Constance lie where every Bonpetit woman for four generations had lay. Her old man growling in the background, "Don't ask if you can send it! Tell him! Tell the *amerloque!*"

"Such history and tradition should not be denied," I submit when the frog contingent expect me to put up an argument. But it's not me, it's their daughter who wants no part of their precious tradition. I simply state, "A real American can sleep wherever she likes, *n'est-ce pas?*"

Before hanging up, Annabelle's mom says, "Take *la petite*'s photograph every day, just like I did for Annabelle. Annabelle, *tu entends?* Are you doing it? Annabelle, are you following my orders? Zho? Annabelle? 'ello? . . ."

Sitting around the kitchen table, my father, mother and grandmother discuss where my mother was born. Was it 312 or 318 or 327 Avenue E? My grandmother says she knows where every one of her children was born. My mother was born in 345.

"Three-forty-five's not there anymore. It's burnt down."

"Three-twelve's not there either," my mother says. She's noticed every house the family's ever lived in is no longer standing. "Must be some sort of coincidence," my mother says.

"Every house?" my grandmother says. "Couldn't be."

This building not there, that building not there. The

Democratic Club. Hymie the tailor, the pickle factory, the barber. "Every vun of these buildings had a little store in the front. People used to vurk out of their apartments. Your grandfather, may he rest in peace, he had his cleaning shop right across the street . . ." She gazes out the window. "Vhat's a matter there? Vhat's a matter vit the temple?"

"Grandma," I says, "the temple—"

"Mom," my mother butts in, "the temple's abandoned."

"No one vurships? Vhat's the matter with Jews today?" she says. "Don't anybody have no respect? Vhat's the country coming to?"

My mother and grandmother are crying, see. My mother wants to take a walk around the block, wants to have a look at some of her old haunts.

I tell her it's impossible. "Mom, you stay where you are, okay? Later, maybe, I'll take a walk wit' you, but you gotta leave your ring home, and dad's got to leave his watch, in case we get mugged. It's not safe." She opens the window and props her elbows on the sill like when she was a little girl. "Oh, I did this many times," she says. Then she gets up and gets a pillow.

So she cried on the windowsill. My grandmother stood and looked at the temple across the street. The facade was there, smooth and ornate, but the steps were broken, the front gates crooked, rusted and padlocked, the windows busted out, the roof gone, the entire building open to the weather. Pigeons flew in and out, crapping as they pleased. The old lady just stared, and that was before some cocksucker wrote his tag up and down the marble. SEGUNDO, it said in big black ugly letters, then BENNY scrawled across that, then I OWN YOU!

When we got out on the street my mother just stood on the stoop. My grandmother stayed upstairs. My mother, my father and me. We stood on the stoop and took a long hard look. I could see my mom was looking back on what was, and what was now.

"You know how many years it's been?" she said. "Jo-Jo! What ever possessed you to come back here? Your grandfather would die, him and Mom worked their entire lives ..."

I looked down the street. "I remember the street from when I was a kid," I told her. "I remember going to the doctor, and I remember going to the temple. All the women were upstairs in the balcony, I was downstairs with the men. I stood next to Pop and he was rocking back and forth saying his prayers, *davening.* There was a man with a handkerchief knotted at the corners of his skull, he had a tattoo on the underside of his forearm. He grabbed me by the elbow ..."

"That doctor, you remember his name?"

"Sure, Dr. Steingesser."

"That's right. Steinie we called him. He delivered you and your sister." Tears came to her eyes. "He was the one who wanted her to be a doctor. You too. Do you remember he said if you went to medical school you could have his practice? His office was right down there. 368, I think. That gray building." She pointed across the street to one of a line of Federal houses. "Yeah, there was Steinie in 368, Dr. Esner in 366, Dr. Feldstein, Dr. Hershkowitz, Dr. Schwartz, Dr. Hurtstein, Dr. Nuesbaum. Sixteen doctors and twelve lawyers on this one block, not to mention the politicians. Remember Louie Lefkowitz? He was a big shot on the block. Right, Yakov?" she said to my father.

"He was from this block, sure." The old man kicked plaster dust around on the floor. "Called this street the Doctors' Block."

"Your grandfather never let him go by without calling him in, say, 'Louie, how can a big shot politician go out with wrinkled trousers? What will people think of you?' and he'd make him take his pants off right there on the spot and he would press them for him. I can't tell you how many times

I saw the famous Louie Lefkowitz in his underwear, his skinny legs poking out. . . . The Democratic Club that was down the block, is that still there?"

My mother held on to the railing and guided herself carefully down the stairs. One of the building's problems was that the stoop was a structural disaster, the stairs broken, crumbling, the iron railing so wobbly you were lucky if you didn't go head over heels to the sidewalk below. The mailman refused to deliver mail up the stairs. My father almost tripped, cursed under his breath, then muttered behind me loud enough to hear, "Nice investment," in a lousy, sarcastic voice.

Then she saw that the yeshiva is a Pentecostal church. Immediately she turned back. "Yakov?" she said. "Give me the keys, I'll sit in the car."

"I wish you wouldn't," I said. "Mom, someone sees you in there, an easy mark . . ."

My father started telling me how it was, how it is now, but curiosity got the best of him and he asked to see the famous temple.

"Your grandparents were married in that temple. Your grandfather helped found it, helped buy the torah. Jesus Christ, what's that? It doesn't have a roof anymore?"

"It don't, no, sir."

He shook his head. "Will wonders never cease? How can they let this happen?"

"Times is tough," I said. "There's no more Jews here, Dad."

"You're a Jew," he told me.

"This neighborhood changed a long time ago. There's nothing I can do about it now."

"Who says I want anything done? I got a lot of memories, is all."

We walked down the block. All the grocery stores were called bodegas, but he knows that's happening everywhere. "Nah, just another immigrant group coming in. How about them? How about them P.R.'s? Do they like Jews, Joe?"

"They're a lot like us, Dad."

"When I went in the army nobody liked Jews," he said. "I don't know who they thought I was, but I swear to God I never told nobody I was a Jew. My friends called me Yakkie, so I told everybody call me Jackie—Jackie Peltz, you see? I don't know what they thought I was. I just guess it never dawned on them."

"Never told anyone you were Jewish?"

"Never did. I was drafted. They put me in with a bunch of guys from Minnesota."

"You thought they were all anti-Semites?"

"They were, Jo-Jo."

"All them years in the army and never told a soul?"

"I was in North Africa, Italy, France, Germany, Jo-Jo. They hated Jews. Most of them never even seen one before."

"Yeah, so?"

He didn't say anything more, except, "Yeah, I should have been a big shot like Louie Lefkowitz. If I'd gone to Vietnam, like your sister, I would've bragged how I was a Jew. Yeah, being a Jew was great in Vietnam. Look what it did for her."

I thought he was about to cry.

"I would have bragged how I was a Jew!" he went on. "Because of how Israel kept on beating the pants off the Arabs, Jews were fighters again, warriors. 'Course you had to be one dumb-ass Jew to be in Vietnam in the first place. And even stupider to be killed there! Right, Jo-Jo!"

"That's not even worth answering."

Why's he doing this? I wondered. My mother always said just let him be, it runs in the family.

"When *I* went to war, Joe, Jews were little meek guys with horns and circumcised cocks, but now ask anybody, the Jews are some of the fiercest fighters on Earth, and they got pricks, man, like prongs. They're tough. Just like you got to be, Joe. Keep your Annabelle satisfied. Joe, you know the story about the Indians are the lost tribe of Israel? Great fighters—annihilated. Let's not let that happen to us." Our eyes locked.

"No one's annihilating me, Pop."

"Don't let 'em ruin the temple, Jo-Jo. What's that they're playing—dominoes?"

"Pop—"

"Let's go home. I can't take this. What are all those guys hanging around that Good Lookin' Candy Shop? You know what that was? That was your grandfather's cleaning store!"

He knew. I didn't have to tell him.

He shook his head. "Dope dealers. So close to you. And you with a brand new little daughter. How can you stand it?"


We return to my mother who is waiting in the front seat of the car, sitting in the dark. Together, we went to the stoop and I tell her to watch her step up the stairs. I realize, then, I left my keys in the apartment. I yell up, "Annabelle!"

Nobody answers. Maybe the baby is crying, she can't hear. I yell again. Still nothing. I pound the door. I peer through the glass. At the back of the hall, I see that character Ike.

"Hey, open up!" I yell at him. "Remember me? I bought Beneficio and Beneficia's apartment."

Here's a man in his own world, but eventually he comes.

My mother takes one look at him and mumbles, "Oh, my God, it's Ike, Ike the Woodrobber!"

Then she goes down like a rock, faints dead away.

# 9

# I Am a Dynamo

Pandora says murky like moirky. "Moirky. It's all moirky. Nothing's clear. I don't understand," she says.

None of the tenants did, so it's no reflection on poor Pandora. Welfare pays her rent. It doesn't cost her a cent. Not a red one anyway. At least she has a place to live.

"Moirky," she says as she, Scarlet and I sit in Pandora's kitchen discussing the fact that the corporation will take her to court if she participates in the rent strike. Scarlet says Pandora often has a favorite word of the day. "It's all moirky. Nothing's clear."

"It's Butch's fault all right," Scarlet complains. "He did it. He organized the whole thing. Who does he think he is? Socialist? Do-gooder? All he cares about is himself."

"Where's he from anyway?" I ask. "He's not from this neighborhood."

"Get real, Joe," Scarlet says. "Not wit the way he talks."

\* \* \*

Paco loves the methadone program. Everything's the methadone program to Paco. He goes to the program every morning. When he comes back from the program, Paco is singing. "Pandora, I love you. Pandora, I love you. You is the most beautiful woman I know. I looooooove you!"

It's nice to see Paco happy. He skips down the street and jumps up and touches the branches of the freshly planted Japanese cherry trees. When he sees Butch, he says, "Butch, can I get you a cup of coffee?"

Butch is trying to organize the building, dig? Butch says, "The homesteaders are bad landlords." Butch says, "The homesteaders want poor people out. They want the apartment building for themselves." Butch says, "The homesteaders are trying to ruin the neighborhood. Hike up those rents." Butch claims, "The homesteaders want to get rid of the poor."

"That's Butch," Scarlet says.

"Where is Butch from again?"

"Butch is from Minnesota."

Scarlet says Butch is a funny fellow.

Butch makes Scarlet laugh.

"Ha-ha."

"Butch's pet peeve is no heat," Scarlet tells me. "Butch says he's cold all the time."

When I run into him in the hall, I tell him, "It's the same for everybody. We all live here together. Put your coat on, Butch."

Pandora tries to be nice to Butch. She brings Butch cabbage soup when he's shivering. Butch thanks her before going into his rap. "Pandora, you ever think about joining the rent strike?"

Pandora tells him she doesn't want any of that shit. "Welfare pays my rent, honey. I don't want to cause trouble."

"We're not getting any heat," Butch repeats, this time

loud enough that Pandora is sure to get the message. "I keep
a record. There's already been twenty-four days this winter
where we've been cold and it's only December. Can you
imagine by February?"

"Them boys say they're trying to fix the boiler."

Butch snorts. "Them boys say a lot."

"Don't go trying to get me in trouble," Pandora says.

But it wasn't Butch who got Fausteen O'Grady arrested. He blames it on Mewie Cotton and the rest of the
corporation. One day the police came and threatened to
knock down Fausteen's door. "Open up or we shoot," they
said.

"Who you gonna shoot?" Fausteen answered through
the plywood.

"You, motherfucker!" the police said.

They dragged her away in handcuffs. Fausteen has a
big dog. The dog went, "Woof, woof."

The dog's lucky the cops didn't shoot it.

"Who's gonna look after my dog?" Fausteen said as
they led her away.

Butch, just coming home from work, said he would, but
first he wanted to know what the fuck the cops were doing.
The cops told him they were locking Fausteen up.

Butch doesn't look after the dog the way Fausteen
looked after the dog. Pandora says Fausteen and the dog had
something more going than ordinary pet and master. Pandora claims when her brother got out of jail, she sent him
to Fausteen because everyone knew she was easy. But after
Pandora's brother got naked, the dog started sniffing around
his balls and pecker. This dog is big and aggressive. Pandora's brother had a reasonable fear for his nuts, so he
cleared out. Later, good and drunk and plenty high, he came
back and found Fausteen and the dog in bed together. He
told Pandora, "No wonder the dog was pissed."

So Butch doesn't care for the dog so completely as
Fausteen. Butch likes dogs and he walks it, but then he gets
tired of it, because it's such a big dog and he's got to clean

up these enormous shits. Pretty soon, Butch isn't taking the dog out much at all.

This is annoying to the homeowners. Fausteen's apartment is on the first floor—a railroad, three tiny rooms strung end to end—and when you walk in the building you can smell the dog shit. Paco complains, "Ooh, that dog smells lousy." Everybody blames Butch because he's supposed to be taking care of the dog the same way he takes care of the rent strike. Paco twitches his nose.

Pandora's more vocal.

"Why is Fausteen in jail anyway?" she wants to know. "What'd she do?"

"She's railroaded," Butch says. "The cops are always doing that sort of thing to poor people. Accusing them of something and taking them away."

"That's right!" Paco says. "What'd she do? Commit murder?"

Pandora doesn't know about that, but after thinking she remembers Fausteen tried to sell pills to her once.

This interests Paco. He never heard about Fausteen selling pills before. He wants to know how come nobody told him about it. Pandora tells him it was none of his business. "How come I didn't get any?" Paco mumbles, but he has just come back from the program so the mood doesn't last very long. Soon he's happy again and singing, "Baby, I love you."

Paco and Pandora, they have a good relationship. They love each other. According to Scarlet, of all the people in the building no one loves each other more intensely than Paco and Pandora.

It doesn't bother Scarlet that Ike and Yves, Mewie and Negrito are all gay. "Gay people can love each other," she contends, "but it's fucking hard living in this suckhole building."

The way I understand it is this: A broken-down tenement takes its toll on people. No heat, no hot water, no fun. The way the homesteaders got the building in the first place

was after the junkies came and started the fire on the fifth
floor, the landlord abandoned it. Everybody began moving
out. Then the junkies began moving in for real. Carlos
DeJesus took matters in his own hands and ran the dope
fiends out. He took his baseball bat and his flashlight, and
he stood in the hallway at night and he told them, "You
better go away, junkies, decent people live here with fami-
lies."

But then a new problem presented itself to DeJesus:
Beneficia and the gay people came. "*Señor*, we own this
building now," they said to him, "now you pay your rent to
us." According to Scarlet, DeJesus never understood this.
For eight years he'd lived in this building, he hadn't paid
rent to anyone. Not to the landlord, not to the city, not to
the junkies. Now these *maricones* come and say you pay your
rent to us. Then they run naked in the hall on their way to
sunbathe on the roof. So Señor DeJesus says, "What rent?"
and they're lucky that's all he says, because they run naked
in front of his wife and children.

Pandora said, "Okay," and agreed to pay the new own-
ers. And Fausteen too, she paid the gays for a while. Till she
went broke. Then she said, "It's coming. It's coming. The
check's in the mail." It was only DeJesus who didn't pay.
Then Butch arrived. DeJesus wanted nothing to do with
him, but Butch organized the other Spanish people and all
the white people and the students who sublet and lived in
the building, but came from outside the neighborhood.
"Don't pay gentrifiers any money!" was their slogan. "Don't
pay landlords any money. This land is our land! Rent strike."

Now that Fausteen is in jail, the corporation is seizing
the opportunity to take her to court and evict her. At the
monthly corporation meeting they put me in charge. Ike
took me to a shyster lawyer he knows on Avenue B to start
proceedings. We're evicting Butch too, but Butch says he
may be amenable to settling out of court.

Fausteen is not here to make her own deal. She's upstate at Dannemora. Butch swears he is not abandoning the rent strike, but he says he has the power to make a deal for Fausteen too. Yes, he says, he may take our cash, but he won't give up his principles.

"What are your principles, Butch?"

"My principles are . . . ," he tells Paco and Pandora, but by that time Paco is long gone. Pandora listens, however. She claims she still hasn't consented to go in on the rent strike, but admits that she hasn't paid us the rent money and it's all gone, she knows not where, and somewhere along the line Segundo, DeJesus's boy, wrote APRIL FOOLS on the hallway wall in red paint.

"Butch doesn't care about anybody but himself," Scarlet says. "He's a sly motherfucker. You think Fausteen's ever going to see that money? No way."

Scarlet says when he sees her in the hall or on the stoop, Paco says, "Yes, ma'am."

"What's he calling me ma'am for?" she wants to know.

There were rumors going around about Pandora's past. Then Dagmar says she is pushing dope out of her apartment. Pills. Probably the pills she was supposed to have bought off Fausteen.

Paco and Pandora. Paco sits on the toilet in their bathroom and those walls are so thin, Scarlet can hear him telling Pandora he loves her in the hall. "When the windows are open their voices echo in the well between the two buildings, and everybody hears," Scarlet told me one day while we're having tea. "Some people say it makes them want to vomit, but he says nice things to her, you know. How he loves her. How he can't do without her. He doesn't make any bones about it either. He knows it. She takes care of him. If it wasn't for Pandora, Paco wouldn't survive. Paco is no fool. He knows how lucky he is. He treats Pandora right. Goes to the store for her, sings to her, tells her all kinds of sweet things."

"*Mira, mira,*" Pandora says. Through the window she

catches a glimpse of Paco walking quickly but stiffly, the old-man junkie's walk, across the street. She opens the window, and a rush of cold air blasts us.

"Close that fucking window, Pandora," Scarlet orders her. "You're going to catch your death."

"*Mira, mira,*" she's hollering. "Packi! Packi!"

We could hear his voice, cheerful, but far away. "What is it, baby?"

"Paco, get a quart of milk," Pandora screams down, "and litter for them damn cats." Pandora only has one tone of voice and it is loud, baby, loud.

"Pandora," Scarlet tells her after she returns to the table. "You can't let that Butch make a fool of you."

"Like he's making a fool of you," she says.

"He's not making a fool of me," Scarlet snaps.

"No, what's he doing?"

"He ain't doing nothing."

"Scarlet," Pandora says standing at the stove, stirring her cabbage, scratching her legs. She doesn't shave her legs. She doesn't shave her chin. Good for you, Pandora. "Scarlet," she says. "I have a man who loves me. That's more than you have."

"You're one lucky woman, Pandora."

"Yes, I am."


While Pandora is in the bathroom, Scarlet whispers to me that Pandora killed her first husband. "Self-defense, so she didn't go to jail, but they put her on probation for life. If she ever kills another husband, she's going to the can for sure."

We hear the toilet flush, the door opens at the furthest end of the apartment and Pandora comes back to the table.

"Scarlet?"

"Oh hello, Pandora. Joe and me was just talking about you."

"You was? Saying only good things I hope."

"Of course. Who's got anything bad to say about you, Pandora? You're a queen, a fucking queen."

"Well, thank you, child," she says, swinging her hips like she's Mae West and living on the Bowery with Cary Grant and not Avenue E with Paco. Have you seen that movie? *She Done Him Wrong,* right? Pandora has some sexuality for a woman her age.

"Times have changed," she says, maudlin, eyeing me.

"Yes, they have."

"Times ain't what they used to be."

"No, they're not."

"It used to be people had respect for one another."

"Yes, they did."

"No more."

"No."

"Fucking shame. Excuse my English."

Scarlet tells her how we don't speak English anymore. What we speak now is called American.

"Fucking shame." Pandora turns to me. "Excuse my American."

"I am a dynamo," Scarlet says.

Scarlet claims to understand everything Pandora says, everything that was happening to her. Poor Pandora, just a victim. "Don't let that Butch make a monkey out of you, Pandora. Who is that Butch anyway? Nothing but a troublemaker."

"It was Fausteen who got him over here in the first place," Mewie told me. "She picked him up on the street, and invited him up for sex. Who knew he couldn't get it up, but wanted to rent from us?"

Pandora doesn't trust Butch after Fausteen described what had happened between them, and then Fausteen went to jail.

"There's only three kinds of people who's living over here," Pandora says. "One is poor people, one is drug atticks, and one is all these newcomers."

"What newcomers is that?"

"Newcomers is always the weird ones, these gentrifiers, Scarlet," she says. "Look at you. What kind of haircut is that?"

"Spiky mohawk. Red tips, black roots."

"How you get it to stand up like that?"

"Dippity-do."

"I'm from the reservation, you know," Pandora starts to tell Scarlet for the hundredth time. "When this country was Indian territory, you think the cowboys was all so highfalutin? No-no, they was all full of shit and crazy as loons, just like you and Mr. Joe here. My first husband was a cowboy. Nobody ever liked that he married an Injun."

"I'm one of them there newcomers," Scarlet reminds her.

"You is, this is true, but at least you ain't trying to collect my rent." Pandora looks at me hard then.

"No," Scarlet says. "I just live upstairs."

"That's right," she says. "You just live upstairs."

Later Scarlet complains to me and Annabelle, it's hard for her to remember who she is. She says Butch came to her room one night, got undressed, took out his cock and says, "Who you for? Them or us? In a case like this it's the good guys against the bad. These people come here, this corporation, try to steal your home, Scarlet, you better fucking believe you're going to fight."

# 10

## *La Baleine Bleue*

"No one knows this man, this DeJesus. He is a dark character. He is a dangerous man, Joe."

"He's nuts. *Il est fou,* eh, Yves? He's nuts."

"Yeah, Joe, nuts."

"I'll get him though."

"We all will," Yves said.

"Yeah, that's right. It's all of us against him."

"Mewie says we can't let him get away with it."

"He'll be tough in the clinches, Yves. The street man always is."

"I fought in the war in Spain, Joe. I killed Germans during the second war. I've had a hard life, Joe."

"I know you have, Yves."

"I had to eat cats."

"Cats?"

"If it were up to me, I'd kill all Mewie's cats and tell him I ate them."

"Yves . . . ?"

"I was one of the first to go to fight the Fascists in Spain. I traveled to New York and joined up. We took a boat to Paris. It didn't matter that I was born in Quebec, I am Basque. To this day I hate the Spanish."

"This *caballero*'s no Spaniard, Yves. He's no Fascist. He's Puerto Rican."

"This is where you are wrong. A Spaniard is a Spaniard. His blood is Castilian. But I understand. That's why I leave him for you. And what does it matter? When the Germans invaded France, I tell you I ran to enlist. War is war. I was not hoping for more succulent pussycats. The French variety is no better than the Spanish. You must always try to be on the right side. If he were German, then I'd fight him. I hate those cocksucker Germans. No, this man is yours, Joe. I leave him to you. You fight him. You are smart."

"Thanks, Yves, but no thanks. I don't want to fight him. Other people started this, not me. I have nothing against DeJesus. As far as I'm concerned he can live here forever. And I don't understand why he wasn't offered his apartment in the first place. Things would've been so much simpler. If he'd only been asked to join the corporation, if he'd been given shares like everybody else, there'd be no problem today."

"That's right. He's nice, Joe. I don't know why we have to fight. I don't know why we can't get along. Every time I see his little children I give them money or some candy. I feel sorry for them. They don't know, Joe."

"It's not my fight, Yves."

"No, it isn't."

"I didn't start this. Those other fucks started this. Beneficia and her little gang."

"The whole group of those pussy bumpers," Yves growled. "Beer Can, the whole group of them. They all encouraged Beneficia."

"I don't want to be anybody's gunfighter. All I want is a good place to live."

"That's all any of us want. That's the only reason we're here. You don't need to fight other people's battles, Joe. You have a wife and a child upstairs. You have a family, Joe."

He knew. For the first time I heard him speak about pussy bumpers. It took me an instant to know who they were. To him Beer Can and her group of militant women, they were the ones who were stopping everything from going forward on the block. He said when he was trying to help Beneficio and Beneficia clean the rubble out of their apartment, the pussy bumpers came around and said, "Hook up a little winch and then lower all the plaster, box by box, down to the dumpster."

"You know how long it took to do that, Joe? *Tabarnak!* I tell you. One morning I snuck into Beneficia's apartment. My God, the apartment was such a mess you couldn't step inside. I took every box of plaster, brought it up to the roof, and then you know what I did with it?" He laughed. "I threw it off. Right off the roof and into the abandoned buildings in the back, directly behind ours where the vacant lot is now. Those buildings were no good anyway, they were scheduled to come down. Let the city remove the shit. They don't care. So boom, boom, boom. I throw it all off. In a few hours it was all gone. The pussy bumpers were so mad. You know what they were mad about, Joe?" It really tickled him. He slapped his knee and began to laugh again. "The dust. Every time I threw a box, poof of dust. They hated that."

"The pussy bumpers?"

"The pussy bumpers and their leader, Beer Can. But still I have to give them their due. You know no matter what you say about pussy bumpers on this block, they're pioneers. They were the first. I'll tell you something. People thought this was a dangerous dark neighborhood. A neighborhood full of animals and junkies, unfit to live. The pussy bumpers came here. They weren't scared. They worked hard to clean up these buildings. They really did. This was always a good street, Joe. They didn't know. You know what they called this street, don't you—the Doctors' Block. Only doctors lived here."

"Lawyers and politicians too," I told him.

"Is that a fact?"

"My family came to this block in 1903," I told Yves. "I know all about it."

"Is that so?"

"My mother was born on this block."

He looked at me closely, his eyes bright, his wool toque slanted jauntily on his head, pulled down low on his brow. "I didn't know that."

"My grandfather had a cleaners right across the street there. He never let Louie Lefkowitz pass without calling him in."

"Louie who?"

" 'Where you going looking like that, Louie?' my grandfather'd say. 'A politician can't walk around with pants like that. Come inside. Sit down. Let me press your trousers before you go out.' " So the young man, destined to become the big shot New York State attorney general would come in, sit behind the drape in his underwear and wait for my grandfather to put a fresh crease in his pants. "You know how many times my mother says she seen that man in his underwear?

"I remember my grandfather," I told Yves. "I got a gold tie clip he gave me for my bar mitzvah with my initials on it."

"They met in this country, your grandfather and grand-mother?"

"On this block, Yves. They were cousins. But they had never met before she came here, and even then she was too young. She was seven years old. At first he worked in Wil-liamsburg as a presser. He carried his steam press across the bridge every day. He was scared to leave it in Brooklyn because he thought it would get stolen."

"Things don't change."

"You know what they called that bridge, Yves? The

Jewish Highway! You know why? Because so many Jews used it to get from the Lower East Side to Brooklyn."

"Is that a fact?"

"When my grandmother first came here, she worked as a maid in Harlem, but eventually she got a job downtown as a seamstress. She'd bring extra collars home every night and sew them by hand by gaslight. Then she'd lower the finished collars in a basket to my grandfather who had an apartment on the ground floor, and he'd press them. They fell in love like that. She was sixteen.

"Yves, you ever been in love?"

"Me, of course. Yes. In my younger days in Quebec, in Godbout. I was considered a fine dancer. All the girls wanted to dance with me."

"You were married once, weren't you?"

"Married? Me? What do you think, Joe?"

"You were married once, Yves. You had two little girls, didn't you?"

"Two girls?"

"*Les filles*, Yves."

"Oh, yeah, yeah, yeah, *les filles*. Two little girls. They're not so little anymore. Josette, she's married, lives in Quebec City now. The little one, Marie Odile, she followed some guy up to Sept-Iles, but when the recession hit and they closed all the pulp mills, they went up to Havre-Saint-Pierre. They opened a nice little pizza shop right on the harbor. Les Fruits de Mer pizza pie. They do very well. They really do. Little shrimps and crabs. It tastes good. You ever been up there, Joe?"

I said that I never had, hadn't even heard of it.

He sighed. "Yes, you Americans don't care so much for your French cousins to the north. To you this is a culture that does not exist."

"You ever see them, Yves, your little girls?"

"Never. Only when they need money."

"Ever see the grandchildren?"

"No." He looked at me. "You know the story, Joe,

right? We lived in Les Escoumins. A lot of Basques lived there. I chased *la baleine bleue*. Load a bunch of tourists aboard my little boat, go look for blue whale. They thought they were going to see Moby Dick, maybe. . . . One day I was coming home with a load of tourists in my little boat. My family have worked as fishermen for years on the Saguenay, on the Saint Lawrence. Still offshore a hundred yards, I would ring the bell a few times so that the little girls would know I was coming. How old were they? Three and five maybe. Not older. They would run down and meet me, Josette and Marie Odile. This day I couldn't believe it, no one came. They used to hide from me, hide right in the open where I could see them or behind a tree and they would jump out and go, 'Booo!' and I would go, 'Cou-cou!' and pretend to be scared. Oh, Joe, they would laugh. But this day they didn't come and I thought, Oh, well, they went with their mother or they're busy doing something else, playing, in the house, with the cat, something. I never thought . . . When I got to the house, everything was gone, everything. Furniture, dishes, everything. I couldn't believe it. Joe, I went into the bedroom, she had taken the bed, but one pillow was still on the floor. I took that pillow lay on the floor, and I cried. I screamed into that pillow. I went, Arghhhhhhhhhhhhhhh! loud enough to be heard in Montreal."

His eyes glistened. "I don't have to explain to you, Joe. You are a father. You understand."

I understand, Yves. If Annabelle were to run away with my kid right now—and maybe she'd do it . . . I don't know a whole lot about her. Who is she? Some French girl I met outside the Gotham burlesque. She comes over and asks me do we have *Libération,* the French newspaper? I tell her, frankly, I never heard of *Libération.* The only ones I know of is what? *Le Figaro* and *Le Monde.* Is that them?

She smiles, says thanks anyway. Then she says, "Oh very well, *Le Monde,* let me have that."

I said I heard of the French dailies, we just don't carry them.

"I thought—"

"I can order it for you," I go.

Who knows? She had immigration problems. A run-in with a bottle opener and six-foot-eight Leonardo. One day she comes to me, she says, "Zho, will you marry me?"

I look at her. I ask, "Is this a proposition?" I smile, hoping it is.

She smiles too. She's got a great smile, sexy, a come-fuck-me smile. I guess that's why she made good as a stripper. She says I'm the only American she knows, the only one she trusts.

"I'm flattered."

"Don't be. I'm not trusting you that far. This is not romance, this is politics."

Yves is saying, "What would you do if she left? If she took poor little Constance and you never saw her again?"

"I don't know. Probably blame DeJesus. He's being blamed for everything else around here."

"Don't trust women," Yves says.

# 11

## Spike and Mazie

*Newsweek* ran an article about the art scene, said that where I live you have to "step over a guy with a needle in his arm in every doorway." Maybe so, there was a guy with a needle in his arm in my doorway. Spike stepped over him.

"Is he unconscious?" Mazie said.

"Beats me," Spike said.

Spike kicked him. The guy grunted. "He's alive," Spike said.

"That's good," Mazie said, not sounding convincing.

A guy with a needle in his arm in every doorway. "Son of a bitch," he said. "Why you kicking me?"

"Hurry up, Mazie," Spike said. "Put the key in the lock."

"No, wait a minute," the junkie said, struggling to his feet. "I want to know. Why you kicking me?" He was a dirty bastard, crusted with filth. He had a year's worth of spittle caked on his chin.

"Look, man," Spike said, "I don't want no trouble."

He said, "That your girl?" looking at Mazie, weighing her.

"I don't like the way he's looking at me," Mazie said.

"That's right," Spike said, "what's the big idea looking at her like that?"

He was wearing a beret, and looked like a Yanqui Che Guevara. There were little pins and medals tacked onto the beret where he'd pulled it down over his right eye. At least one of them must have hung in his vision like a windshield wiper.

"I must have blacked out," he said. "I been sick."

"Too fucking bad," Mazie commiserated.

He nodded sadly. "I don't know what it is," he said.

"Take the needle out of your arm, you might feel a little better," she grumbled.

"What needle?" he said defensively. "I don't use no needle."

"C'mon, Spike," Mazie said. "Quit talking and let's go inside."

The junkie said, "Man, you got to let me come in and sit down. Man, I just about had it."

"Are you kidding me?" Mazie said. "Let you come in?"

The guy grabbed Spike by the jacket. "Let me in," he said. "I'm sick. I'm hungry."

Mazie hooked Spike's arm and pulled him inside. She slammed the door. "Crazy bastard," she said.

They went up the stairs. Spike had gotten used to climbing flights, no elevator, what the fuck! It's good for you, he figured. Make you strong in the heart and lungs.

When he opened the door, Mazie stopped on the landing. "You handled that just great, schmuck," she said. "What are you standing there talking with that jerk for? Didn't it dawn on you he was a junkie?"

"He said he was sick."

"I bet he was." She kissed him, soft on the lips. "Let's

take out Chinese food tonight," she said. "Maybe we ought to call the cops and have that junkie removed."

"Could you imagine if he mugged our delivery man?"

"It's happened, you know. I heard about it on Avenue C and Third Street in front of the Salvation Army. They got a guy from Hot Wok on Second Avenue."

"A Chinese guy?" Spike asked.

"Pakistani, I think."

"Oh, a Pakistani," Spike said. "Those guys are so fuckin' gentle."

"Not like you, Spike. You're so fuckin' hot-blooded and tough. He looked like a murderer," she said. "The way he looked at me. Did you see that?"

"I did. It was scary, wasn't it?"

"Were you scared, Spike?" she said.

"Nah," he said, "with all my karate, I'm tough enough. Anyway, I would've run. A guy in that condition, he could never follow."

"Where's the fucking Chinese food?" Mazie asked later.

"Did you call?" Spike said. She hadn't, naturally. "Well, neither have I. How you expect it to get here, telepathy?"

"Spike," Mazie said, "you know, do you think you could color my hair?"

"Like what?" he said.

"Like in that painting of yours. Real glossy black and that beautiful royal blue."

"Yeah, I could do that."

She wanted Spike to do it right then and there.

He said, "Why don't we wait till after we eat?"

"You got any drugs?" she asked him.

She put her hand on his crotch. "Spikey, you're so sweet."

He claimed he loved her. Always talking like a baby-doll and playing that role. What'd she see in it?

He asked her. "Sex," she said.

The bell rang, the Chinese man with the food. Spike talked to him on the intercom, told him he'd be right down and open the door. "You got any money?" he asked Mazie. She had a few crumpled bucks. Money in this neighborhood is on its last legs, after this the federal incinerator is the next and last stop.

He ran down the stairs and looked out the front window. Nobody there. Then he look down. Fuck. The goddamn junkie's sitting on the steps eating spare ribs.

Spike opened the door. "What the fuck? What you think you're doing?"

"I ain't doing nothing," he says.

"That's my food you're eating," Spike tells him.

He didn't seem to care, didn't even react. Spike said, "Where's the delivery man?" Jesus Christ! There he was lying on the front stoop.

"What'd you do to him?" Spike asked.

"He tried some of that karate shit on me. I pulled my knife, but he fell down the stairs before I could stab him."

"Is he dead?" Spike asked.

"I don't know. I haven't looked yet. I was hungry. I asked him nicely."

Spike went over. It was another Pakistani. Poor sap probably didn't even know karate, now here he was lying on the floor.

Spike put his hand to the delivery guy's throat like he'd seen on television. There was a little pulse.

"You're lucky," he said to the junkie. "He's still alive. Why don't you get out of here?"

The junkie said it was an accident.

"I didn't say it wasn't. I'm just advising you. Split."

"Man . . . I'm hungry, just let me finish first."

"I told you, I'm gonna call the cops. You want to be here when they come, all fine and good. You want to leave my Chinese food right where it is, take off, never have to deal with this again, then on your way, brother."

He didn't argue. He took the foil of ribs and struggled

to his feet. Spike saw he didn't have socks and his ankles were riddled with terrible sores. He held on to the railing tightly and hesitantly made his way down the stairs. Wisely, he chose the side without the Pakistani and didn't have to climb over the body. Spike hurried inside, banging on the door on the first landing.

Ike junior answered it. "Ike!" Spike shouted. "There's been a mugging in front of the building. Call the cops and an ambulance, man, someone's been hurt."

Ike had his alienated moments, but in time of emergency he always came through. Spike barely got back to the stoop when he heard the sirens, then police cars screeched up. A uniformed man and woman jumped out of the first. The woman took the lead, pushing Spike away, squawking, "What happened here?"

Spike said he was tempted not to tell her, but he thought better of it and filled her in. "He's been mugged. Before I called you I felt a pulse, but now I don't feel a thing."

She squeezed his neck too. She shook her head. "Nope. Dead." She licked her lips and looked at him.

"You seen it?"

Spike said he hadn't, "But . . ."

"But what?"

"But, you know, I was sort of in the proximity."

"Proximity?"

"When I come home . . . ," and he explained it to her. The male cop stood there with a smirk on his face.

"You let him go?" the woman cop said.

"I could have used my karate," Spike told her.

She sighed. "No, better that you didn't."

The ambulance came. They took the Pakistani's body away. The cops told Spike they wanted him to come to the station house the next day and make a full report.

"Don't you want me to get in the car and ride around the neighborhood? Maybe we could find the guy who did it," Spike offered.

"Nah," they said. "None of that neighborhood shit."

When Spike went upstairs, Mazie was pissed that he'd been gone so long. But she didn't give a shit about the ribs, she'd been laying off meat anyway.

# 12

## Benny and the BBs

The hand-lettered sign in front of the temple says NO JANG-ING ON THE STOOP. So Joe tells Segundo don't jang, get his ass off them stairs. The building no longer has a gate, only an old bedspring on hinges mounted to the doorframe. The caretaker throws a chain around it, one of those padlocks they shoot bullets into on tv, thinks he's invincible.

"The block's everybody's responsibility who lives here," Joe tells Mewie after Segundo slouches away toward Avenue D.

"That's my point exactly," Mewie whines.

"Benny's not here anymore," Yves says. "Everybody knows who's doing it, isn't that right, Joe?"

Segundo, oldest son of Carlos DeJesus, spotted throwing his garbage out the fifth-floor window, bouncing those paper bags off the walls. Benny and Segundo used to have a little competition going: Ecuadorian versus Puerto Rican. Who's the better soldier? There are bullet holes in Joe's windows from their little wars. Benny had been warlike with more than Segundo, but Beneficia blamed the DeJesus boy. "That's why she pulled her family out of the neighborhood," Yves says, "to protect her children." Yet others say no, she was embezzling from the corporation, and wanted out before they could catch her. "That's why she sold so cheap to you, Joe," Ike says.

Little BB holes in the glass. Sheetrock smashed in, joint compound smeared over the wound. A dull, rusted bayonet in a secret hideout full of commando magazines. The first time Joe met him, Benny was wearing full fatigues. He told Joe he was going to join up. Mewie told him, Benny's greatest ambition was to learn how to kill professionally.

"Benny had a hard time on the street," Mewie said.

"Hard on everybody," Ike grumbled, "but hardest on people he met."

Beneficia never let Benny's sister, Gloria, off the block. "She used to say, 'In this neighborhood you can't take a chance. Not with these animals.'"

So Beneficia kept Gloria in, and Benny beat her up in his war games.

Joe had never seen Benny in action, but he had seen Segundo, and Ike claimed he was only a shadow of what Benny was. "Have you ever seen Segundo crawling on his belly on the roof?"

"Yeah."

"Have you ever seen him throwing roof tiles and bricks on the cars in the vacant lot?"

"Yeah."

"See what I mean? Segundo plays at it, but it's Benny's game."

Battle fatigue had come over Benny. His mother and father were not in. His sister was locked in her room, lying on the floor and listening to Twisted Sister on her headphones, praying one of the bullets wouldn't tear through the wall and hit her. It had happened once. Hit her in the foot. Lucky she was wearing Benny's hand-me-down steel-toed combat boots and the load just bounced off. It was only a BB, but her parents had used only quarter-inch sheetrock on her walls. Ike had scavenged it for them off a construction site on East Second Street.

Why'd Benny pick on his sister so? Lying on the floor, a piece of plywood clamped to her head for protection, remembering when her hamster electrocuted himself and started a fire in the hall.

Her brother saved her then. He said, "Company G, Gomez reporting."

"I'm gonna get that Segundo," he used to say. "I'm gonna get his *toda familia.*" Segundo looked over his shoulder. There were three shadows on the wall. One was a flower, one was the cat, the other was a dude on the roof with a rifle. He went to the window and shot his gun right at the fucker.

So even though there was a fire, even though you could smell the hamster frying and it smelled like fresh meat broiling, Benny turned with his BBs and pumped them through the window. Ping, little hole in the glass, and Segundo yelps.

"Got you that time, you Puerto Rican bastard!"

The fire department came and soaked the smoldering hamster. They opened all the windows and let the air in.

"Place smells like a barbecue," Benny said, saluting.

Mewie crawled through the well window. He stood there with the firemen. Later he invited them all down to his club. Eventually the firemen said, "We'll burn the Puerto Rican out for a price." Them or somebody they knew.

"That's still operative, by the way," Mewie says.

Segundo, he's a ball buster, but it's Benny's fault Segundo is the way he is today. And if it's Benny's fault, then it's his mother's fault for being such a powermonger.

After the corporation got the building, Beneficia went around lording it over everybody. Maybe not at first, but once she got accustomed to the power.

She showed up at DeJesus's door one day, and asked about the rent. He says, "What rent?" He doesn't pay rent. He hadn't paid rent in eight years.

"It's like DeJesus's professional wrestling career, right?" Mewie says with a vicious snicker. "He walks in the ring in his regular street clothes. Tells everybody he's an urban guerrilla. Jew promoters want to put an ape head on him."

DeJesus says he's fighting the gentrifiers. He's fighting the people who come to his door and say, "Hey, you!" to his old lady, who he's not even married to, by the way, she's common-law, "from now on you pay rent to us." Like he'd been paying rent before. He hadn't paid rent in eight years. He hadn't seen the landlord in five years. All he saw were junkies and thieves. Now these people come, calling themselves homesteaders, and say they bought the building and they don't pay him any respect, they're not even civil. Certainly they don't ask him to join them in their homestead. Assholes coming to play landlord with him. Let them try to make money. Let them try to get him out.

If you don't think that that attitude went over to his son you're nuts. Let me tell you something. It was a Puerto Rican building when the corporation took over. Beneficia, Beneficio and Mewie went to the landlord, and he said, "Sure, take my building, but you have to assume my debts." No one realized the better part of that was DeJesus, not money and ten years' worth of scofflawed parking tickets.

DeJesus isn't the worst of it. His kid is—Segundo. And before that Benny. See all these little holes in the glass of the front window?

"They look like bullet holes," Joe says.

"Yes, they are bullet holes. Here, hold these. You see they're shells."

"Twenty-twos?"

"Yes, twenty-twos."

They were all over the house. Wedged in the floorboards of Benny's room. Beneficia claimed Segundo shot bullets into her house when they were away, but it wasn't Segundo at all, it was Benny. When his parents went away . . . BANG! BANG! BANG!

"Shot out the windows, did he?"

"Shot out the windows, busted down the door. In his room he threw his sister through the sheetrock."


Downwind, Joe thinks the streets are empty. It is early morning, and everything is silent except for the clanging of the cans as the sanitation men perform what they call pick-up-the-garbage.

Segundo, first son of Carlos DeJesus, comes out the door and stands on the stoop, looking up and down the street. He doesn't see Joe, he doesn't see anybody, and even if he did, he wouldn't care. He tightens his jacket at the throat.

"Hey," Joe says, "what you doing here?"

Segundo looks around because he doesn't see him, a voice, disembodied, just coming at him up from the stoop like up from the ground. Joe is under the stoop in the little alcove where the junkies squat amid their matches and Pepsi-Cola bottle tops, poor abandoned rudiments for archeologists of the future to pick up. Joe stomps, and says, "What you think you doing?"

Now Segundo sees him through the cracked stoop, now he breathes with Joe, now he smiles, and says, "Hollo," even if he doesn't look in Joe's eyes but at his haircut.

Joe stands in front of his '62 Galaxy and kicks the tires, old bald Bettys. Joe thinks the transmission case is rattling. He takes out the wrenches he bought hot on the street and crawls underneath. He doesn't have much clearance and pulls out. Then he drives the car half up on the sidewalk. Now when he crawls under he sees he might tighten those nuts, but they're stripped. He twirls them anyway, just in case. Then he gets out and says, "Shit."

Segundo's back, standing silently on the stoop. Joe puts his wrenches back under the seat. Segundo doesn't say a thing, but smiles as Joe locks up.

Joe nods and walks away.

"Don't leave you car on the sidewalk," Segundo calls after him. "They give you a ticket for that shit."

Joe turns, pulls the keys back out of his pocket. "Thanks a lot," he says.

When the car is broken into that night, who is Joe going to blame but himself? All those nice new Sears wrenches gone. Joe never will say a word, but he knows who's done this to him, but what can he do, they were long sold by the time he woke up. Segundo will get his, mother-fucker.


Joe meant to ask Segundo come upstairs to his apartment and look around sometime, explain to him all about the scaffolding over the stairway and the little wooden bunker built on top. Not that he needed any explanation. Here's where Benny gulped his K rations, here's where he drank likker out of his canteen.

Guns are healthier than shooting dope.

Like the time Joe walked over to Avenue D and they shot that little girl in the head.

"Wasn't that a shame now?" Yves bleats. "Walking home with her mother from the A&P. Poor little girl."

"You know who I thought I saw over there that time?" Ike chips in.

"Benny."

"That's right, returned from Fort Benning."

"I asked him about it," Ike says. "He was staying upstairs with Mewie. Said he was AWOL, never had a leave. See, the army has nothing on him. He lied about his age. A sixteen-year-old, anytime he wants out, he's out."

"Incredible."

"That's right."

"I asked him about cutting out," says Ike. "Benny said everything's cool. He said, 'Big deal, so one day I'm in the military, one day I'm not.' He claimed to have learned some things. God only knows what. Said he wasn't so much into killing anymore. Claimed he was still into war, but not killing. On the street, of course, he said he'd kill if he had to. But they don't want you in the military if you're not into their game. Benny told them he played one-on-one. They say, 'Fine, become part of a team.' "

But what Joe wants to know from Ike and Yves is, was there ever a winner in this war between Benny and Segundo? Did it ever stop?

"Stop? No, it never stopped."

"Benny just moved away?"

"Came back that once you saw him," Ike says. "I asked him if he'd killed that little girl. He said, who me? He talked BB guns. Said he didn't just use to shoot at Segundo DeJesus, he used to hit him. 'Every shot was true,' is how he put it. Said they were warriors, street warriors, only in the building. Claimed it kept them both occupied and out of Rikers."

Joe told Segundo one time if he don't watch out that's where he's heading—Rikers or the Tombs.

"No," Segundo says to Joe. "The only place I'm heading is after you, motherfucker."

# 13

# Chicken Delight

Five in the morning my father relieves me at the newsstand and I head home.

Before I leave, he asks how things are going.

"For the business or me?" I go.

I remember when I was a kid, my father came home before dawn with the *News* and *Mirror* and a bag of jelly doughnuts. We'd sit around the kitchen table looking at the sports pages, Mantle, Berra, Skowron, Ford, Turley, Arroyo. It was my only time with him. When I got home from school, he was gone.

"The neighborhood down there is getting to you," he says, a statement.

My father's sly. He's been watching the street a long time, and it's Broadway, bro, big-time boulevard. To put things in perspective, hey, when I was a kid—1962, first year of the Mets—me and my sister were sitting in the first row at the Polo Grounds, when Willie Mays comes over to shake our hands, and shouts, "Yak!" at my dad, short for Yakov, kisses my sister on the cheek. They're all smiles, but I only grunt.

"Jo-Jo, say hi to Mr. Mays."

My dad claims he said, "Say hey!" to Willie before Willie said "Say hey!" to him.

My dad says, "Go ahead, ask him for an autograph." Willie looks at me, looks at my father, looks at my sister. I look away.

And later, after my sister died, to cheer me up, the old man takes me backstage on the B'way to see Carol Burnett, who hugs me and kisses me on the cheek. My father knows people on the big street, and they know him, and they like him, and they do for him if they can. Still do, till this very day.

"Don't worry, Joe, we'll get you out. Whatever you're in for, we'll get you out. The prison ain't been built that can hold a Peltz."

"Dad," I says that morning at the newsstand when he asks me what's wrong, "I swear to God there's so much hate and tension going around these buildings. You know, they made me president?"

He gives me the hard stare, like he's figuring this out. "You?" he says. "Why you?"

"They think I can straighten the buildings' problems out."

"Who do?"

"They do. The corporation."

"And what does Annabelle think?" Sure, he trusts her more than he trusts me. You're a fuckup, son. Maybe not lately, but before . . . "I hope you can, Joe. I really do."

I grab a cab on Forty-seventh Street. Five o'clock in the morning, coming home from the newsstand, just the way my father used to, and the streets are black.

Nothing's ever happened to me in my neighborhood, never been attacked or mugged. I've spotted enemy troops but never been engaged. Still, I wear a knife on my leg, strapped to the calf. A steel Gerber, one-piece construction, double-bladed, only three inches long, but totally illegal.

Five o'clock in the morning, the street's quiet tonight, no one around, and still the adrenaline's pumping. Taking a cab is one way not to worry about the street. The sodium lights, usually humming, are dark. Five o'clock in the morning, I come home and I'm scared.

Like I said, nothing ever happened to me here. A couple of kids threw snowballs at me one night, laughed as I walked head down, and then, over between B and C, a junkie having a tryout running decks called, "Hey, what you looking at?" One of the boys who run that block came over, told the junkie, "Go about your own business, b," crinkled his eyes, like a wink, so I know, and I think, I'm happening, the street man knows me, dude, and maybe he's the one Annabelle told me helped her with the groceries. Maybe he's seen me walk the block pushing Constance in her stroller. You see what I'm saying? He walks home with me. I give him a cigarette. The street man knows exactly who I am!

And who you?

I'm the white folks, bro, the one who moved in over there, next block, the one where the pussy bumpers planted ornamental Japanese cherry trees every fifteen feet.

"Oh, that block!," the Seventh Street Boy says. "Whyn't ya say?"

"I'm saying it now."

"That block's the hostest with the mostest, and they keep it clean, too, man."

"Every Saturday we get out our brooms and shovels, do a block cleanup."

"You know, I used to live in this building," he says to me, standing in front of mine, leaning in for a light, "me and my girlfriend. It was a dope fiend haven then. Yeah, I had to crawl out the window more than one night running to make my escape." I cup my hands, strike the match. "You know this dude DeJesus?" he says.

* * *

The blocks break down racially on the Lower East Side. Looking east, looking west, looking for the very best. At one end there's the Puerto Ricans, and in the middle here you got the white folks, the gays, Beer Can and her pussy bumpers. All the old Jews have split, and now the avant-garde cooljerks are moving in, the front-guard jean-and-tee-shirt brigade, scouting for the hordes, all hugging each other, saying please God not me, we're just a little slice of white meat squished between two pieces of dark bread. At the other end, close to the projects, more Latinos, the Peruvians, the Ecuadorians, the Colombianos, the blacks that mix, and one building of Native Americans, no feathers, but eyes like iron. Those boys, bro, they don't ever smile at me.

Injuns on the Lower East Side. Velma from the day-care's friends with them. She tell me she goes to all their powwows, all their dances in Jersey and at the West Side Y. The Tomahawk Dance Team. The Buffalo Dance, Big Bear/Little Bear, Dance to Green Corn, twirling fire, shaking rattles, beating tom-toms, leaping through flaming hoops, rhythmic chanting, to Wakonda, the one great spirit, to Ma-ka-ee-na, Mother Earth . . .

I told Velma, when I was a kid, my best friend was half-Jewish, half-Indian, his mama an old line Commie, his father a never-was brave. We used to spend the summers up with his cousin in Binghamton on an Onondaga reservation. I still have pictures of me in costume on a horse.

Five o'clock in the morning, I come home. Not this night but another, and some savages from down the block are on my stoop, talking in low voices, smoking cigarettes. No women. Only braves.

I hate it when the brave braves are here. I get out of the cab, all their eyes on me. Like they got something on me, against me, and I guess they do, their eyes steady, black, hard. Hey, man, it's me. Remember me? The guy with the kid. The white eyes.

One slides over so I can pass. Velma has pointed him out to me, fella named Waco. Wants to be an actor but suffers from that there substance abuse. Doesn't get the part, says they're always looking for a big star. Hey, Waco! You hear Paul Newman's gonna make a movie up at the corner? Want me to put a word in for ya?

I nod an acknowledgment. No response. My keys are in my hand. I put the right one in the lock, stop, come back, pull out my wallet and show Waco and his buddies the picture I carry around, the one of me, aged sixteen, with the Onondagas, replete with plumed bustles, bow, quiver of arrows, the whole schmeer, sitting on a horse with feathers tied in its tail and mane. This impresses them, so I explain how I made the costumes myself on the reservation, at my friend's cousin's house up there in Binghamton.

"The headdress too?"

"The headdress too."

It was a full horse-hair roach and, now that I think of it, it looks remarkably like the haircut Scarlet sports—the same coloration, cut and stand-up style—but with mirrored rosettes at the temples and a porcupine beaded band.

They say, "But which is your real skin color? Are you white or are you red?" and they laugh, and I say, "I'm red in my heart, but that red wasn't my real skin color. That was brick-red Color Tone makeup." So they go, "Makeup? Aww, shit, you don't need makeup, homeboy. You a real brother, bro. You one of us!"


Not too long ago at the newsstand, I noticed the papers were all carrying front page stories about a Native American boy going to Israel. Wire service photographs showed the kid in dance bustle and headdress getting off the plane in Jerusalem. The boy was going to have his bar mitzvah at the Wailing Wall, once the site of King David's first temple, become a man. His name was Little Sun. His mom was Jewish, but his father an Oglala-Teton Sioux, a direct descendant of Crazy Horse. Mom said Little Sun would be made tribal chief of all the Sioux nations when he turned eighteen, but he tells the press he'd rather be a holy rabbi.

The next day, the wire services issued a report from Wounded Knee. The Sioux tribal council declared they'd never heard of Little Sun, and that there's no such thing as an Oglala-Teton Sioux. Besides, the council said Crazy Horse never married and never had kids.

Who is Little Sun?


Tonight the stoop's empty. I fit the key in the lock and go inside to the coolness wafting up from the basement.

They are slam-dancing in the hall again when I come in—knockabouts from Mewie's Avenue A club—for the third night this week. I'd heard tales of men running naked in the hallways. Word is they're Mewie's boys, although he vehemently denies it. He claims they're the amigos of one Howard Kumundga, tenant, second floor rear. Sad rumors abound: Those two are at war. *Howard* v. *Mewie.*

I hear the noise, the hysterical shrieks of laughter, come peeling through the well and then glimpse a group of these guys, skinheads and mohawk haircuts with homemade tattoos on the walls of their skulls. I cross the well, watch from under the stairs, sniff the stale smell left over from Dagmar's cigar. After a while I go up and tell them that people are sleeping.

And I say to the gay punks, if that's what they are, maybe they're merely disenchanted businessmen or some mortgage bankers on their weekend break, "Who are you? What are you doing here?"

Then Kumundga opens the door, comes out of his apartment and, before the bankers have the chance to answer, answers for them. "What are you talking to them for? What do you want? What's your problem, Mr. Homeowner?"

I tell him people live here, decent people trying to sleep, that he doesn't need to behave this way and had better stop poking me in the chest.

He asks what's the problem, what am I talking about? Who am I to say word one to him?

"You know me." I growl at him, brushing his hand away with an angry swipe. "We met. I'm Jo-Jo Peltz. I live right next door, and I'm the new president of the corporation." It's my responsibility to hold certain things down around here. At present his friends and I are having a conversation about proper behavior in a residential building. Do he want to sit in on the enlightenment?

"What are you talking about?"

"What are *you* talking about, Howard? Just keep it quiet, all right? You and your boys go inside, do whatever you want behind closed doors."

They look at me with eyes like saucers. Must be drugs. I say, "Why don't you boys go home, call it a night."

Kumundga says president is a sucker's job. "You seem all right, Peltz," he says. "You gonna be the sucker do the dirty work for Mewie and his string of queens?"


A few days after I moved in, I was standing on the stoop surveying the horizon from Avenue A to Avenue E, when Segundo DeJesus came up from behind and made me jump. "Blanco Maria," he said, "she looking for you."

I turned around. "Blanco Maria? Blanco Maria? I don't know no Blanco Maria."

"Oh yeah?" he said. "I must be thinking about another white guy." Then he's gone. Little Segundo, firestarter.

\* \* \*

I pick Constance up at daycare. Velma meets me at the door. "Joe," she says, "I think one of the parents is beating up their kid . . ."

Outside, we sit on the stoop across the street from my building. Velma, Constance and me. Constance climbs down the stairs, one step at a time, then begins waddling back and forth like a bowlegged sentry.

Yves says he's going to replaster the hallways. He's sick of Beneficia's pride and joy, the exposed brick. Where he comes from, he says, bare brick was worthless as an insulator, so now we're always cold. "Joe, you should have seen her work. She got one of these gas masks on make her look like a monster from outer space." He's going to nail the lathe back, put up a nice, thick, warm coat of plaster, then fill the air space with dirt and rubble. "No better insulation in the world, Joe, than earth."

Yves's overall philosophy for the buildings: Fill all sheetrock between the studs with debris. If the building ever comes down, somebody's in for a shock, but at least we'll be warm in the meantime.

Only the day before I was telling him, "Yves, you got to slow down. You got to think of yourself before you think of the building. Think of the toll the work's taking on you."

But Yves can't stop. He called me up that morning and asked me to leave a bucket of joint compound outside my door. His back's bothering him. I told him I don't want him carrying the compound over to his side of the building by himself. I told him I'll do it.

He asked me if he woke me up. I said, how can you wake me up? Constance wakes up at six, I'm home at five. I'm up with her. I don't never sleep, I don't think. Not that I can remember. I take her across the street to Velma's then try to grab a few quick ones.

He says, "Oh, Constance, what a sweet thing she is!"

"Yes, she is." I ask him again what he's doing. What's

he need the compound for? He's not doing the halls, is he?

No, he says. He's helping that ungrateful Mewie, he tells me. "Oh, Joe, that man! Why I help him?" He says disgustedly, "I don't know, Joe. You think he appreciates it? *Jamais*. It must be those cats. I can't stand the stink any-more."

Yves loves complaining about Mewie. "That man never leaves me alone, Joe. If I try to do anything around the building, he comes bother me."

Secretly, in his heart of hearts, Yves would love to finish Mewie's apartment for him, but he knows Mewie well enough to know that if Mewie knew what Yves planned, Mewie would never let Yves touch a board.

Mewie thinks he knows everything. Like the time he decided he wanted to tear down all the walls, open up his entire space, even put the bathroom right out there in the open. He got Ike to help him. They took down the load bearing walls, the stiffening walls, another classic time Mewie wouldn't listen, didn't care, he *knew*, and then he went off to his club, whistling a happy tune, and when he got back, lo and behold, the plaster ceiling was on the floor. Three cats killed. Mewie was mad, oh boy. Who does he blame? Ike! Yeah, Mewie's a beaut!

Months later, me and Mewie are smoking a joint, and Yves is on the scaffolding, hawk in hand, slapping mud on the ceiling, talking a blue streak, reminiscing about the history of the corporation. "Remember when Howard Kumundga said he was a doctor? What kind of doctor could a man like that be, Joe? We used to call him Chicken Delight," Yves says. "You know why, Joe—Chicken Delight?"

I indicate no, I didn't know why, had no idea.

Don't worry. Yves will tell me. "After he was gone, I tore out the bathroom in his apartment, and you know what I found?"

"No, what?"

He pulls his toque down over his eyes like he's some mischievous ten-year-old schoolgirl. "A pile of eggs this high. You know what he was doing? He was shoving hard-boiled eggs up his ass with his boyfriend, then shitting them behind the tub. Like this!" On the scaffolding Yves pretends to climb up on the tub and squat. "You see, Joe?"

Yeah, I got the picture. "How do you know all this, Yves?"

He indicates Mewie. "Ask his partner in crime over there, he brought him over here."

"It's not my fault. He followed me like a little lost sheep," Mewie bleats, trying to get out of it. "If I'd known what was to come . . ."

"All these prima donnas, Joe, they can't live together."

"Is that right?"

"You know what the problem was, Joe? Mewie liked his eggs soft and gooey, three minutes only, but Chicken Delight—he liked his hard, ten minutes at least. Isn't that right, Mewie?" Yves turns to him, smiling maliciously, waiting.

"I can't stand it anymore!" Mewie bellows, and stomps out of his own apartment, his big black engineer boots reverberating on the exposed pine subflooring, Boy 3 or 6 or 8 (all are identical gray tabbies with white mittens) meowing soulfully at his feet.

After Mewie's gone, Yves turns to me. "You're lucky you're not a fairy, Joe."

"Yes, I am."

"You don't have no inclination?"

"No, I don't."

"Too bad."

Chicken Delight liked to dress up as a Confederate soldier, but in leather. He wore a black leather cap and a black leather jacket, black engineer boots and, on his wrists, black leather straps studded with chrome points. He looked like one dumb-assed motherfucker, that's why I asked Mewie what's Howie's problem.

Yves says he saw him once on one of his jobs. "Man told everybody he was a doctor. I'll tell you what kind of doctor he was. I was working at a clinic on Park Avenue. I'm on the scaffolding, I look down, there's Chicken Delight following the doctors around. 'Get this, Howard, get that, Howard, clean Mrs. Berryman's bedpan, Howard.' I call down to him, say, 'Oh, Dr. Delight! Oh, Dr. Delight!' "

Kumundga was sitting on the steps while I worked, the first time I met him. I was scraping wrought iron and he came out from 312 and sat next to me on the steps in the sun.

Ike had managed to get hold of the railings from some abandoned building on Eighth Street. There were some knobs and balls and curlycues missing.

"Don't worry about them," Yves told me. "Ike got them too."

"Oh yeah?"

"Sure! In the basement."

"Ike's on top of everything."

Sitting there next to me, wearing dungarees and a white tee shirt and his little black leather cap, Kumundga told me he was a medical practitioner. His hair was slicked back, and he had these long wispy sideburns and a scraggly beard.

"Oh yeah," he said, "what you people are doing here in this building is terrific! It's really great!" He was full of all good things to say.

Who knew? To me Howard Kumundga was a good guy. How should I know he would come upstairs and attack Mewie with a wrench because he says the vibrations from Mewie's electric fan are coming through the floor?

Kumundga explained that his specialty was nutrition, that from the looks of me I suffer some kind of wheat allergy. How'm I feeling? he asked. Does stress affect me?

* * *

Paco says after what happened to Kumundga and the other renters in housing court, he's worried. I was walking in the hall and Pandora calls me in and says that Paco thinks the corporation wants to get rid of them. After all, DeJesus and them are the only tenants left in the building. They're afraid of being persecuted.

"Who's gonna persecute you?" I ask.

"I don't know," she confesses. People are ringing their bell. People they don't know. Wanting to be let in. They say they don't have nobody come visit them. So who's ringing the bell?

The problem is, they don't know how to use that new buzzer system. It's too complicated for them. See the panel of buttons, push that one to talk, that one to listen, that one to open the door. What could be simpler?

I never believed that stuff Dagmar says about them pushing dope from their apartment.

Are you kidding? Who're they pushing dope to?

Oh, there's plenty people come in and out of that apartment, despite what they say. Day and night you hear them yelling on the street: "Pandora! Paco! Open up, Paco!"

One night Pandora hobbles down, her legs bothering her, and scolds the man, "Stay away from my Paco. You the cause of all our trouble."

He's a black man standing there, well spoken but shabbily dressed. "How's that, Pandora?"

"Paco thinks we're going together."

The black man is flabbergasted. "What? How can that be? What are you talking about?"

"He thinks we're going together. So I don't want you coming around, making him jealous. You the cause of all our problems."

* * *

No one ever liked that Howard Kumundga. He wasn't a very likable guy, I see now in retrospect, no sir. He was a mean troublemaker. Maybe it's a good rule, never to trust a guy with a wispy beard and a leather hat. After our conversation on the stoop that day, I made a point of saying hello to him every time I ran into him on the street and even introduced him to my kid one day, she's asleep in her Snugli, but then he had the big fight with Mewie about the fan being too loud and then all the people in the corporation were his enemies and I was certainly one of them, me being the new president, one of the homeowners, so I was his enemy too, if I say hello or not.

Eventually we had to act against him. Ike took me over to see the Avenue B lawyer. I knew we'd have to evict him —he'd hooked up with Butch and Fausteen on the rent strike. We bought Butch out and struck that deal over there in the courts and Kumundga consented to leave. He stuck around as long as the agreement allowed, then he and Mewie got into that altercation, Dagmar complained, and Yves went up there and moved the tub and he found the hard-boiled eggs, and that's how Kumundga came to be known as Chicken Delight, as I said. Howard had a sign on the wall in his apartment. ONLY THE BRAVE TREAD HERE, it read. He had a very nice lettering, a very nice hand.

The only time I was ever in his apartment was after he left. Yves wanted to show me the pile of eggs, just starting to go rotten, smelling like sulfur. There was a sign in the bathroom too. PLEASE WASH YOUR HANDS, it said.

# 14

## Dagmar Tells All

Pandora was never as proud of Delilah as she wanted to be. "It's hard for me to say it, Joe," she said, snicking her teeth, tears in her eyes. "It really is." She was up and screaming again. "My own daughter's nothing to me. Nothing."

She asked if I knew the story of her and the cowboy, the reservation, the murder. Had I heard those stories?

I said I had heard rumors, nothing more.

"Do you believe everything people tell you?" she asked.

"That depends."

"Joe," she shouted, "Delilah's not a bad person. It's her husband, that Jew, Dagmar, who puts ideas in her head and fucks her up, turns her against her own flesh and blood. My daughter's too stupid to have ideas of her own. I swear to God I'm going to kill that man."

Pandora knows Dagmar's been coming to the corporation meetings and telling stories on her. She's worried that the corporation's going to get rid of her, kick her out of her own home. She knows her own daughter and son-in-law are making accusations in front of the whole board that Paco and Pandora are pushing pills out of their apartment.

"It's not true, Joe, I swear."

Dagmar's full of ideas, has designs on Paco and Pandora's apartment. Scheming, scheming, what for?

"Spread out, Joe, just like you. Be a big man. Be comfortable."

Dagmar loves playing many ends toward the middle, the middle being him and his big fat cigar.

Dagmar leans over, whispers to me on the stoop. "Joe, to you these buildings are like a magical kingdom. They're your beautiful kingdom, Joe. I swear to God. This is the way I see it. You've done good. Your folks must be proud. See, your apartment, Joe, it's the biggest one in the two buildings, right? Beneficia really carved out an empire for herself, and you inherited it. You're the heir apparent. The crown prince. You deserve it. A nice young rich man like you."

"I'm not rich."

"When Beneficia was here, she run the place like she was queen, Joe. That's when all the trouble started. She used to hand out little leftover crumbs to all us poor saps."

"Which poor saps are those, Dagmar?"

"You know the ones, Joe, the ones with only one apartment compared to her vast holdings. And God forbid if you were a renter. Remember, I started out renting here. I only got permission to buy in shortly before you came."

"Yeah, so, when you gonna finish paying for your apartment?"

"I'm gonna finish paying it off soon, Joe, I swear. I just got some temporary cash-flow problems."

"It ain't that much dough, Dagmar. You should do the right thing, keep people from badmouthing you."

Dagmar smiles. "Soon, Joe. My money's tied up for the moment, but it's going to break loose any day now, and then . . ."

Talking to Dagmar is tough. It takes its toll. Dagmar's

got a warm hand, a cigar locked in the corner of his mouth, as he pats me on the back. He's round in the belly, drives a big fat Cadillac car. He either has lots of money, throwing it around, or no money. When he has no money, he has plenty of excuses. Dagmar never goes too far from home, or maybe he's always too far from home. He hangs out in the back of the hallway underneath the stairs. When you ask him about it, he says the stench from Mewie's apartment wafting down the air shaft makes him sick, and all Delilah's clothes and shit lying around, looking at her face every day, that makes him sick too. But he's watching, just watching. He comes out for a smoke. Sometimes he stands in the doorway, the front door half open, leaning against the jamb, puffing on the cigar, watching people come and go on the street, and policing the people going up and down the stairs.

He says that's where he came up with Pandora pushing dope. He says it hurts him in his heart to accuse his own mother-in-law, but what can he do? He got eyes, he can see. He feels responsible, wants to make where we live a better place.

"Oh yeah?"

"You should see the characters coming in and out, up and down, all around. Hey, I don't want to be the one starts the shit my mother-in-law's pushing pills in the building. I got no choice. We all want that decent place to live you always talking about, Joe." And then he goes on to tell me how he sees these people tramping in day and night, all hours, banging on the door, stomping in the hall, it don't take a genius to know who these people are and what they want, it only takes one look at any time, at any one of them, and then you know. "You seen them, Joe. Admit it.

"They're all the people from Paco's program over there on Thirteenth Street," he says, the concern gathering in his face. With a snap of the jaw, the cigar shifts to the other side of Dagmar's mouth, the moustache bobbing on his upper lip like an arched eyebrow. He waves his finger in my face.

"Run it by me again, Dagmar."

"Now, Joe, I don't want to pressure you, but do you consider this important enough to have a special meeting? I, for one, do, and I'll tell you why. Joe, you're the president, right? You can do anything you want. People listen to you. You already busted up the rent strike, and if you're the person who deals with DeJesus, if you get him to do what you want, then no one will stand in your way, see what I'm saying? The building will be a better place to live and you'll be the king. You help me with my problems, I'll help you with yours. See? We trade, even Steven. A good deal for both of us! What do you say, Daddy?"

He sticks out his hand. Little bitty fingers like cocktail franks.

Delilah comes out to stand on the sidewalk in front of us, strike a pose, hoping for street boys to come by so she can say hello to every one of them, verify what a sexpot she is. Across the street an electric-company crew is finishing work for the day, leaving the job half done, and puts up blue sawhorse barricades that say CON ED around the hole they've dug in the sidewalk. No sooner do they leave than a group of kids from the projects comes by, dismantles the sawhorses and carts them away for a pigeon coop they're building on top of an abandoned building on Avenue D. A few minutes later another disadvantaged kid wanders over to peer into the open pit. Then he grabs a couple of old boards lying on the sidewalk in front of the temple and makes a well-crafted boardwalk, the proverbial garden path, leading right across the loosely packed dirt to the open construction pit, and he even lines it with cobblestones so it looks like a pleasant Sunday stroll through the sylvan woods. And it leads where? Right into the black hole, right into the pit, guiding you to step right up, walk right in, fall right down in his trap, deep and dark. Then he looks across the street and grins at us. C'mon, sucker!

I shake my head in wonder. "All he's missing is the punji sticks."

"That's it," Dagmar says, "that's what it's all about—neighborhood guerrilla war. We better fight and protect ourselves against these little scumbags or they'll walk all over us. Remember who was here first, Joe. We were. Me, you, yours!" Then he yells across the street, "Hey, what the fuck you think you're doing?"

The sun is on the stoop and four corporation men have now materialized. Ike, Yves, Dagmar and me with Delilah standing in front of us, flirting.

No need to tell me. Mine is the fresh blood, and I'm getting the brunt of her energy, Delilah's sex flying off in all directions. No one is amused. Maybe because Ike and Yves don't like women, and Dagmar's married to her. Ike says to her, "Don't you think you could take your routine on the road?" Dagmar laughs, he always laughs when Delilah's the butt of the jokes, but when she makes them, he never thinks they're funny.

Her long red fingernails, twisted like claws, make my skin crawl. She strokes the back of my head, runs her fingers through my hair. "You should wash your hair, Joey," she says. "You have dandruff." I tell her it's not dandruff, it's seborrheic eczema, comes from an allergy.

Delilah says the only people she knows with allergies are Jewish males. It must have something to do with their mothers always coddling them. "Is that your problem, sweet thing?" she inquires. "Your mama?"

Two Spanish kids and a black kid walk by on the sidewalk. The black kid says something under his breath, even as the Spanish kids look away.

Ike shouts after them, "Get fucked, you mothers, we got as much right here as you."

Yves calming him. "*Tabarnak! Calice!* Let's not start anything." Admitting, then, it's kids like that who scare him, that's why he keeps his apartment on the West Side, hasn't moved in over here even though he's here almost every day to work on the buildings. But he always leaves before dark.

Phil the Pisher, who lives on the street and has for fifty years, strolls by.

The Pisher, which is like a guy who leaves his waste in public places, has no regard for anybody, dropping plastic bags of rubble in every garbage can on the block, but Ike says he owns more buildings on the Lower East Side than Helmsley, Spear or Trump or any of the big real estate firms. Ike says Phil's bigger than anybody in the neighborhood, except for the city, which owns 60 percent of the abandoned buildings, but Phil's beginning to sell off. He sees his opportunity and is going to cash in. He sold a whole block of three- and four-story buildings on Avenue B after the back walls collapsed on two of them, tenants claiming in the newspapers that their buildings collapsed under dubious circumstances. PIRANHA LANDLORD JAILED, was the *Post*'s headline. But Phil walked after only twelve hours behind bars. Still, for all his holdings, he's always crying. Unless he's bellyaching about this and that, Phil the Pisher's not happy.

Yves tells me Phil was the one supposed to caretake the temple after the congregation left it.

"What happened, Phil?"

He don't know. Shakes his head, slowly, sadly. "The congregation grew old, moved away, disappeared. Most of them are over ninety years old, in nursing homes. One day, I notice the torah's gone, all the prayer books."

I look up as a pigeon swoops down, making chuck-a-luck noises. Over the door, on the lintel, is inscribed in Hebrew: The People of Hungary. BETH HAMIDRASH HAGADOL, the House of Great Study. But Phil doesn't know.

The Pisher says the neighborhood never will get any better. He's been through it too many times before, and just shakes his head. "To bring your little daughter down here, you're out of your mind! What's a matter wit you? How'd your parents bring you up? This neighborhood's always been the way it is, always been a hellhole. It's never going to change. What do you think this is?" the Pisher asks. "People have always been saying, 'Oh, sure, now the neighborhood's going to be different!' Over there by the river where all those projects are, that used to be wharves and warehouses, feed barns full of hay and rats and mice. It's where all the bums and derelicts and criminals used to hang out. Ask Ike, his own father. I remember when I was a boy, and in those days they were saying luxury housing and fancy-schmancy mansions are going in there, riverside. I'm telling ya, when I was a boy there was pirates on the East River, flying the Jolly Roger too, and I'm not talking no Captain Kidd or Bluebeard, no figment of your imagination, these were real neighborhood hard boys, cut your tongue out for a nickel."

"Hey, Phil," I say, "you know my mother's from this block. She was born here. Maybe you know her—Sarah Greenfield?"

"Never heard of her," Phil says. "She lived here, or she's just telling stories?"

"My own mother? Phil, my grandfather helped establish the temple. My family helped raise the money to buy that torah you claim just up and disappeared."

Phil's irritated. Pacing back and forth in tight little circles, he chides Dagmar for the brand of cigar he smokes. Phil taps the end of his, just a soggy butt at that point, says, "This here is a dollar cigar," pointing at the chewed-on end of his stogie. He tells us his sister just died. And since it happened his girlfriend has no use for him. He'd taken her to Florida for the funeral, and when they got back Phil gave her all his dead sister's clothes and jewelry. Now that she got the dead sister's valuables, the girlfriend doesn't want to see him anymore. But he doesn't care. From now on he isn't going to bother with girlfriends. From now on whenever he wants a woman, he'll go out and buy one, it's cheaper that way. He eyes Delilah. "Interested, darlin'?"

"Could be, what you offering?" she quips back. "I hear you already gave up all your sister's jewelry and furs."

"All this crap about women being superior to men. They only want the cash. After that, a man's never good enough."

He rubs his stubble in thought, and I wonder what he's done with the prayer books, where the torah has gone.

Delilah says, "You got it all wrong, Pisher-man."

When a couple of Puerto Rican girls pass by, he calls hello.

"Who wants an old grizzly bastard like you anyway?" Ike growls at him.

"You're right, you better off buying people to suck you off," Yves adds. "You old bastard, all you have is money."

"And what do you got, if not money?" Phil turns to face him. "All those pretty little boys must cost plenty."

"I felt so bad for those boys, Joe," Yves says, looking away, as Phil shuffles off muttering to himself. "They didn't know. There was no roof on the building. The junkies would come in the middle of the night and steal all their pipe, take apart all the work they did that day. I told them you have to sleep there. You can never leave the building alone. 'But how can we sleep here?' they said. 'How can we stay warm?' I showed them. We took a big forty-gallon oil drum. I cut out the side. That was our heat for the first year. One of us slept here every night. It was hard, Joe. They cried. There wasn't a door, a window, a roof, nothing. You could look through the brick, see the building next door. But slowly, slowly, she came around."

Dagmar is all too eager. He pulls the wet end of the cigar out of his mouth and looks at it before returning it to his mouth again. He says he knows for a fact that Mewie never really paid for his apartments, that Beneficia doctored the books and gave him the apartments.

"How do you know that?" I ask him.

"I have my ways."

"Beneficia and Fausteen were good friends," he tells me. Fausteen happened to mention it to Delilah. Dagmar's married to Delilah. So one day they're making love and she told him all about it. That's what he says.

"Dagmar!" Delilah pretends outrage, halfheartedly. "You shouldn't be telling stuff like that. That was told to me in confidence."

He seems pleased with himself. "Now I'm telling you," Dagmar says, "even though you and me ain't making love, Joe, and Delilah begged me not to tell, because I trust you and I feel it's in the best interest of all of the corporation to know the truth. People fuck the corporation, Joe, and by doing that, they fucking us, we the members, the people who live here. I'm tired of taking it in the ass."

Dagmar's always the slick operator, if only in his own opinion. Looking for the angle, Dagmar always thinks he's pulling the wool over your eyes. He thinks he's so cute. Dagmar has no humility. No, sir.

I talk it out with Spike, because Spike moved in before me and understands something of the war that waged between Beneficia and the rest of the corporation.

Surprisingly he corroborates Dagmar's story. "Look, I know it's true," Spike says. "Beneficia was no good, always stirring up problems among the gay guys. She was jealous of everyone, she'd just never admit it. Things were hard enough already, and she made them harder. Mewie was her little puppet. All the money problems we have come from her, fighting at meetings, all the problems with DeJesus, not to mention those three creeps you just finished taking care of in landlord-tenant court, Joe. Beneficia thought she knew it all, but she didn't know shit."

Mewie was Beneficia's best friend. She could always count on him to back her up, even now when she's long gone. Coming to her defense and his own, his voice strident, Mewie's saying, "Without Beneficia the buildings wouldn't be standing!" Scoffing at the accusations in emotional meetings while Dagmar pooh-poohs, puffing his cigar. Mewie says he paid the same as all the other original members of the corp, the same five hundred dollars per unit, the same as everyone else, no different, no special deal. It was already a good deal, and what's the point of stealing when you stealing from yourself, we all live here, this building is an opportunity, you're all crazy! "That," Mewie says, "is what it's all about."

The buildings were an absolute wreck when they had come. There had been a fire. The fourth and fifth floors had been entirely burnt off. The first time we had met, after answering the ad in the newspaper, sitting in her living room, Beneficia leaning toward me and Annabelle, Mewie leaning in, she saying candidly, "The first time I saw it, I didn't believe it. I said, 'Me? Live here? Never!' I didn't believe how disgusting a building could be. Who had lived here? Human animals? Drug addicts and dealers. So much trash, full of garbage. All the backyard was was discarded sinks and toilets and old appliances. The well too. Everything you can imagine, vacuums, refrigerators, stoves, hot plates, toasters, stereos. Relics of the culture. It's like people from all over the neighborhood had lugged it here as some kind of tribute, some kind of ransom." She looked at me then, very carefully. "You think you're going to be able to do this, be able to live here, follow it through?" she asked. "It takes something out of you. Something major. Every single couple who's ever lived here, straight or gay, has broken up over this building. It's only my husband and me," she said, dripping with superiority, "who've survived."

She looked at Annabelle in her high-heel shoes and imitation leopard-skin spandex pants. "Dear, I worry about you!"

Annabelle doesn't react well to this overbearing, motherly tone.

". . . and you say you're pregnant?"

Annabelle nailed her with a steady look and said, "Thanks, but I have no trouble making it if I want to."

After she and I left that first day, Annabelle turned to me as we walked west. "Something about that woman, Zho," she said, "something I don't like."

\* \* \*

But even so Annabelle is not so prepared to believe Beneficia
was stealing money from the corporation like Dagmar and
Yves and Ike charge, because there was nothing to steal, and
she thought it was ridiculous that anyone could think that
Mewie didn't pay his measly five hundred dollars for each
of his three apartments, and even if he didn't, he paid damn
close. "And what are we going to do about it at this late date
anyway?"

"That's right. What's the difference at this point?
We're all in it together. All this petty squabbling . . ."

Now the meeting coming to a close, three hours arguing back and forth. "But to steal money from the corporation? That's ridiculous. The corporation has no money,
never had any money. What did she have to gain? It don't
make sense."

"No, I agree, Zho," Annabelle says. "Beneficia was not
stealing money, she was stealing something else, something
more valuable. All the gay boys. It seems to me it was the
power. She ruled them."

Dagmar jumps up, his cigar aglow. "That's right!
That's exactly it!" he exclaims. "That's exactly what she
did! It was the power. She lorded over all those poor gay
suckers!"

# 15

# Ike and Yves: Ghetto Thieves

When I meet Ike dawn is just dawning over the East River. The sky is pink over Avenue E and the clouds is gray.

"Velvet, velvet, velvet." Ike makes his comment looking up after he unlocks the well door. "Pure velvet. Sky looks like velvet. Very nice morning, Peltz." He has two duffel bags with him and tosses one to me, then hands me a crowbar.

"Now we just hang out and wait for Yves." He scuffs his foot on the ground. "Man never been on time a day in his life. Why he don't live over here already, I will never know."

"He's scared."

"Scared! Scared of what?"

We go down through the well, careful not to fall on the rudiments of a staircase back there. All the wrought iron rotted out.

"We'll replace it eventually," Ike says. "I got another staircase just like this one from a building on Avenue B, used to belong to old Phil the Pisher. You read about that building in the newspaper? Back wall fell off it. Threw Phil in jail."

We enter the basement, where coal still remains on the floor from the old coal-burning days, careful to step over the boiler return lines. He unlocks the back door and stands there leaning on the jamb, our minuscule backyard dug to the level of our basement, like a bunker, looking out into the back lots. Nobody stirring in the early-morning air except a junkie or two on Eighth Street breaking into a parked car with a brick.

"Look at that fucker," Ike says. "Glass breaking is a soothing sound when you brought up on the street like me. Always liked that sound," Ike says. "I envy the man."

Ike tells me as a boy he used to love to go out break windows with rocks, then his crazy old man heard about it, whuped him, said, "Don't do that. I don't care if you are mine, them windows ith worth something."

"You know, Peltz, we found three or four corpses in the building when the corporation took it over."

"Murdered?"

"Dead junkies. Nobody cared. Cops don't care. Family don't care. The cops were happy we were cleaning up the mess. They said throw all the dead bodies we find in the dumpster, but we called Emergency Services. They came over. They got a nice rig, those cowboys. You should see the way they carried them bodies off. First-class. Probably the first first-class ride them corpses ever had."


By now Ike's tired of waiting. He asks me if I've had my coffee yet, then invites me into his apartment. First time into the hallowed halls for old Joe.

"Yes, sir," Ike says, standing over his stove, a surprising well-equipped kitchen all around him, copper pots, rows of spices, laminated drainboards, toaster ovens, microwave, broiler, rotisserie, juicer, grinder, apothecary jars. "The Quebecker don't know nothing. You think he knows about what goes on in this neighborhood? In any neighborhood in this whole city? No, he don't know. He thinks he knows, but he's scared of his shadow."

We take our cups of coffee back outside, Ike talking grumpily all the time. "That Yves, he should've stayed in Quebec where he belongs, that one. He don't even live here, Peltz, an apartment he's owned for how many years now? You watch, he always leaves to get back home before sunset, he only travels during the daylight. Runs home to Chelsea where he's safe. 'Fraid of his shadow. They all want something for nothing. Not that Yves does. Don't get me wrong. Yves is a hard worker. Without Yves these buildings wouldn't be standing today."

"Ees that so?"

Yves laughs to see we are startled. I spill coffee on my thigh, yelp.

"I might not be the true Quebecois, but I am the adopted son of the woods, eh? Move with stealth. So important in this life. The true *coureur des bois,* wood runner, Monsieur Joe."

Mr. Woodrunner, let me introduce Mr. Woodrobber.

My pleasure, sir.

Yves protests being given all the credit for the buildings. He humbly states, "I am not the only one. Beneficio and Beneficia worked very hard too. Give credit where credit is due. Joe begins to do a very good job." He turns to me. "Ike started the campaign against Beneficia. You want to know why? Tell him, Mr. Junior Woodrobber." Yves liked the story about Ike's father and my mother, couldn't stop laughing for a week. Old Man Woodrobber, so long ago putting his hands on everything in sight, chasing the neighborhood kids up the block, lisping after them, "You son of a bits!" his pants tied up with rope, his overcoat tied up with string.

"Was there anything under it?" I questioned my mother when she told me.

The kids tugging the Woodrobber's string to see, tearing, clawing at the rope, pathetic old Ike threatening, frantic, crying, "You better thtop it, I'll catch you. I'll thtick my ieth pick up your aeth-hole, you don't leave me alone."

"Like father like son," Yves says. "Still trying to stick things up assholes."

"Shut up." Ike don't like that kind of kidding. He shrugs. "My father taught me some things, that's for sure. I know how to survive."

I'll say.

Better than many. Better than most. Ike has vision. He's been here all these years. His roots are deep. He sees gardens back there behind our buildings, trees. Where others see only rubble, decay. Right now he's got his dogs in a muddy pen. Beneficia hated those mongrels. That's how the war between Ike and Beneficia started—over his dogs. Ike wanted to build a dog run. Before, he'd been content just to walk his dogs back there in the lots, keep them in his apartment, but take them out to do their business, run around. But the four of them, three males and a bitch, always nipping and fighting, fleas in the house, the time Mewie opened the basement door and Miguelito, the biggest male, leaped out at him.

"Tore his bicep," says Yves.

"Man's a fool," Ike snorts.

Beneficia hated the barking. Complained the dogs attracted fleas, came upstairs, infested the building. It got so bad she began wearing flea collars, one on each ankle. Rats were getting into the basement, too, eating the dogs' food.

Yves told her how to take care of it. Catch one rat and beat him good, make him squeal, beat him to death. That'll keep all the other rats away, out of the building.

"These buildings were ready to fall down in front of your eyes. That top floor," Yves says and he makes me look up the side of the building, "that top floor was burnt off.

There was nothing there. That whole back wall was crumbling. You could see the building next door through the wall. I rework all that brickwork. Waterproofed it all. Look up there when it rains sometime, all the water runs off. The other side, I didn't do that. You watch, it absorbs all the moisture when it rains. When we were first here, it was so cold we kept a fire in a big oil drum. That was another time those pussy bumpers go and call the cops."

"It was the fire department, Yves."

"Were they mad. That's when I brought back the stove. Brought it down from Quebec."

"The stove's illegal too, you know."

"Fuck them! Why is it illegal? Because Beer Can says so?"

"You can't burn wood for fuel in New York City, Yves."

"What do they know? It's perfectly all right. My family has heated their house like this for as long as they are in Quebec. The city? The city is corrupt. What do they know? Plenty of times I have the inspector here. I give him ten dollars. I show him the work I've done, and how I do it. Old world methods. He says, 'Oh, very nice.' He takes the ten dollars and I don't see him. No more violation."

Yves asks me if I ever been in Quebec.

"No."

"Ever hear of Godbout or Les Escoumins?"

"No."

"Sept-Iles? Baie-Comeau? Havre-Saint-Pierre?"

"Never. Afraid not."

"And do you know, Joe," Ike says, "that Yves is not French at all, but Basque?"

"Is that so?"

"I don't care," he says, "I still consider myself Quebecois."

Yves has a dark blue wool cap on his head. He takes it off, and rubs his hair on the top where it's thinning. Does Joe realize that the Basques hate the Spanish, that the

Quebecois hate the English, that DeJesus hates the corporation?

I hold out my hands and say, "Put it right there, sucker," and I grin. "Once more on the wrong side."

"On the wrong side for the first time."

Does Joe realize the world hates America, the land of the free, home of the brave?

"They hate America. Not Americans. There's a difference."

Yves needs a cup of coffee. He's shivering, insists we have a minute to spare before we go out. Let's go inside. Once in Ike's apartment, he asks me if I've ever been here.

"Just before, that was the first."

Yves tells me, "It's not everybody who gets to come in the old woodrobber's cave."

Ike says he's going to the kitchen to heat the brew. Yves takes me through the downstairs.

"See that clock there?"

He points to a huge face, lit, says FIRST MANUFAC-TURERS.

"You know where that's from?"

He answers before I have a chance to guess. Maybe I saw the empty clock face on the corner of Fourth and E. Yves says, "DeJesus's gym. I'll bet you never even realized it used to be a bank."

"When did you steal that, Ike?" I call into the kitchen.

"What's that?"

"The clock."

Ike's apartment, Yves explains, is all made from detail he's found or looted, confiscated, connived, or confluenced. Marble cornices, cherry newels, walnut ogees, teak tongue and groove.

"Incredible."

"Even the furniture. He's carried some of that stuff out with people still on it. That Louis Quinze divan—wasn't there some wino still asleep on that?" Yves shouts toward the kitchen.

"That wasn't a wino," Ike shouts back, "that was my father, your grandmother's playmate, the original woodrobber, Peltz."

If you don't get away from me, I'll get my ieth pick and thtick it up your aeth-hole, sucker.

Poor guy. Eyes burning. My mother says he had the shiest smile, his eyes sparkled, like a light was shining in them, anytime he saw what he considered to be a pretty girl. Needless to say, Ike the Woodrobber's taste in a Miss America did not require accepted beauty. He liked the ragpicker's daughter.

"You think that was Ike's mother, Mom?"

I asked him. He said, "Could be. They found me in a bundle of rags. Who knows?"


This morning is cold, with a sharp bite off the river, even though it's early in the fall. Ike says, "You got to go out this early. We should've started earlier, actually. Stupid to waste our time dawdling over coffee and then wind up in trouble with the cops."

His dogs are locked up in a kennel he's made out in the back out of pilfered cyclone fence and scavenged steam pipes. The dogs stand up, stretch when we come out, see Ike. There's about six dogs in there. A stray goes by or hangs around looking forlorn, Ike can't stop himself from picking it up. Him and Mewie between them got a lock on the neighborhood, dogs and cats respectively. But really, truthfully, it's never enough. There's always litters of kittens around, although one thing I'll say for Ike, he always get his dogs neutered. He says he could think of some ethnic people he'd like to do the same to.

"What ethnicity is that, Ike?"

And he says, "You might fill the bill—Joe the Jew,"

and only half don't mean it, even though he's Jewish himself, says he's thinking about joining up with Jews for Jesus,
see their ads in the back of the *Village Voice* or sometimes
on lampposts. His old age beckons, he says.

"Is that good or is that bad, Ike?"

He says to me, "You got a nice place where you live up
there, Joe. You like it? That Beneficio and Beneficia, they
never appreciated what they got. They had this attitude
where they were real-life prima donnas. But they treat you
right, Joe, ain't that the truth!"

We tramping through the vacant lot, Ike, Yves, and
me, Jo-Jo from Kokomo. Stumbling over bricks and broken
bottles, duffel bags slung over shoulders, hammers and pry
bars clanging together. Yves-style watch caps pulled low on
our brows.

"Shhhhhh!" Ike says when his dogs begin to yip and
howl, wanting to come along. The streets are empty now,
silent. Vacant hulks of buildings watch us with empty eyes.

Ike leads the way, never hits the street, always slipping
up alleys between buildings and across trashed-out lots.
Then we're standing in front of an abandoned building on
Third Street. Ike says this is the building with the flooring.
We all look at it. Cornice hanging down like some terrible
torn sword, window frames splintered and flapping malevo-
lently: Don't come inside me, if you know what's good for
you! Ike nods with his chin. "You go, Joe," and I step
forward, shiver-shiver, shake-shake, move stealthily to the
door—"Cut the comedy," Ike growls behind me—and peek
in. Sure enough, beyond the hallways I can see there's flooring on the floors.

"It's there!" I call. Sergeant Preston reporting on his
scouting activities, sir!

"Oak," assures Ike's raspy voice behind me, prodding
me further.

"Goo' boy, Joe."

"See, he knows," Yves says.

I enter and edge forward through the torn gape of a

doorway. The oak flooring is a little beat, and there are thousands upon thousands of foil wrappers on the floor. This is a coke house. No question. Been in a few in my day. Lotta guys come in here, shoot up their speedball, but I don't have time to dwell on it, or how long ago it might've been, because from behind comes a ratchety snicker and from in front a *grrrrrrrr* and woof-woof and before you can show me the way to go home, a pack of dogs is on me, tearing down the stairs from the fifth floor where they must've been sleeping, sharp brown teeth bared, saliva flying, and I have to run, hup-two-three and out!

I sprint down the scrungy hall, now smelling dog in my nose, no time to peek in the rooms, coke or no coke, fly through the hole punched in the cinder-block doorway, and outside to safety. Ike is standing there hands on hips, laughing with Yves, bent at the waist. Very funny. Get a good laugh, you guys. The dogs come outside, stand in the doorless doorway growling, showing their teeth and salivating.

"They look like we're their next meal," I says.

"What you mean *we?*"

"Just you, Joe."

Damn skinny dogs, bro. Hungry. Got the mange. They live here. It's their building. No one else's . . . Their building? I never heard of no dogs owning a building. Hard landlords, don't pay no taxes, or put up with human trespassers neither.

"They're homesteaders just like the rest of us," Ike says. "Stake out their claim, and fight for what they got."

"Nice of you to tell me," I scold Ike. "I almost got my tail chewed off."

"You got to be smarter than them. That's the lesson, Peltz. Don't be scared, be smart! You got to always be smarter than your competition."

And with that, Ike pulls a brown paper bag out of his pocket with a couple of bones and some pieces of meat. "Yeah, these are nice dogs." He says the butcher saved him some ends and pieces of fat and joint bones. "Here, boys," he calls, "you stupid bastards," and throws the bones, and we politely waltz inside.

"Impressive, Ike. You know what you're doing," I tell him.

"Born and bred on these streets, kiddo."

Once inside I say, "Look at this place." The place gives me the heebie-jeebies. Look at the shooting gallery, the dirty pillows, the torn beanbag chairs, the stained mattresses, itty-bitty stubs of candles, dirty cottons, bloody towels.

"Dogs don't stop the junkies."

"It's a Mexican standoff in this neighborhood. Some of these fucking crazy junkies, they get the dogs high too. But even after a payoff, it's always the dogs' building. Remember that. The dogs—they're in control!"

"Like Mewie's cats," Yves says. "That cocksucker has so many cats he doesn't know what to do with them. They own him."

"Let's get the floor," Ike says, setting to work. The first thing he does is shove his pry bar under one rotted piece and tear it the fuck up so's he can get to the other slats. Then he starts prying the tongue and grooves up with the crowbar.

Yves starts at the opposite end of the floor. I watch from off to the side, unobtrusive, out of the way, watching to learn, shifting my weight.

"Well—?" Ike says, noticing an absence of movement on Big Joe's part.

"I'm just watching how you guys do it."

"Joe don't know," Yves says. "That's all right, Joe. You load the duffel bags."

The floor creaks like some battered old battleship abandoned over the navy yard when they yank up the planks.

Ike shows us the door moldings, holds up a piece triumphantly. "Joe, look at this." He shows me how many coats of paint been put on the molding around the doorframe. Paint a quarter inch thick with rings like a tree's, but of different colors, the colors of landlords over how many years?

"See the red? You know what that's called? Landlord red. All the landlords painted with it, full of lead."

"Building's a hundred years old if it's a day."

"See the detail!"

"I got a lot of molding out of here," Ike says, "and pieces of marble, two toilets, a sink with brass fixtures. This was a good building, but you can see, not much left at this point."

"After we take out the floors, it will be that much less."

"We'll leave the underflooring, though, ain't that right? No reason to destroy the whole place."

"No way, I need that. The place is already destroyed. We gonna leave that big drop into the basement. Don't worry, the junkies won't mind a bit. They hit bottom, they just bounce."

"Reagan doesn't care, he's trying to get rid of them all anyway. You hear, country's in the middle of a drug crisis?"

Ike, banging away, tells me to finish filling the duffels the rest of the way with floorboards and start carrying them over to our building.

A woman's voice screams out then from next door. "Who's that?"

Her voice freezes us. We go silent, holding our breath.

"What are you doing in there?"

"It's all right," Ike calls to her through the wall.

"No, it's not," she calls back. "It's not all right! What are you doing in there?"

Ike mutters for us to hurry up. He and Yves will take double loads back to the building, he tells me, while I finish up with the floor and start on the staircase railing, remove the newel post and the balustrades. He shows me what he wants me to do and how to do it his way.

"But do we have enough flooring for me?" I ask him. I want to put a new floor in Constance's room upstairs. That's the whole purpose of this little early-morning adventure. I don't think I'm gonna make a habit out of it.

"C'mon, Peltz," Ike badgers, "it's not so bad."

We've pulled up a lot of floorboards, but is it enough for her new room? I try to explain my skepticism, but he barely listens. He simply says don't worry, he'll lend me the rest, any flooring or pieces that's missing, just get the bannister for his stairs, and dismisses me.

"Okay, Peltz," he says, "now do what I say. Me and Yves will be right back, and we'll finish up. Okay?"

I watch them from the window.

They cross the street, tramp back through the vacant lot to the back of a tenement across the way and disappear. I return to the front of the building and begin to work on the newel post. I put the pry bar between it and the rail and it makes a terrible squeak. I pull harder, move the bar a couple of other locations, it's beginning to come, but crying horribly all the way, must be a terrible exorcism, screaming in agony, what a death, only to be reborn, Ike's interior stairwell coming right up, don'tcha know?

The lady next door scream, "Now you done it!"

I say, "Fuck you, lady," and take a nice leisurely stroll through the building, a breather, see what I can see, relax. I find room after room with old cookers and coke wrappers on the floor, and search some for any excess dope. (I tell myself I won't use it, I just wanna see.) From the top floor I look out on the bleak landscape, the Lower East Side. The dogs growl at me, but I go, "Nice boys," and give them pieces of meat from the brown paper sack Ike thoughtfully left with me for exactly such an occasion. Across the street I hear a car pull up. I slide to the window and carefully peek out. Two cops sit in a marked blue-and-white patrol car surveying the building. They sit there, not really doing anything, looking my way occasionally, giving the building the once-over.

A wave of fear runs through me. I wonder if the lady next door has called them, or if they're just doing routine. I pray they won't come in. Feel like John Garfield, another nice Lower East Side boy. They made me a criminal too, John. My crime? Murder in the first degree. Premeditated —a hanging offense. But not this time, this time only looting a building. Not that it really matters, not that anybody cares. When I'm through this building coming down.

Hey, the city wants to get rid of all these old piece-of-shit tenements like the one I'm standing in, pressed against the wall, a zillion coke wrappers at my feet, a pack of wild dogs sniffing my ankles, some itchy-fingered cops breathing down my neck. This house is doomed. A big green fluorescent cross painted on the front by the city. You know what that connotes, don't you? That connotes ultimate demise, bro, there goes another one. On the grand scale, what is looting a condemned building? What does it amount to? A hill of beans? A bucket of *frijoles?* Nothing. *Nada. Rien.* Zero. Zed. *Bupkis.*

So, why's the cops after my ass?

I wonder, maybe I should hide in the closet. You open the door, you see me there. Or when the cops come in, maybe they wouldn't find me, maybe they wouldn't see me. Or maybe I should go downstairs with my hands up. Surrender. Coming out of the building hands in the air, reaching for the sky, stretch, show them my open palms, nothing in them. The cops watching me, their fingers on the triggers, gently squeezing. Duck, Joe, duck! The dogs bark and so do the cops' service revolvers. Annabelle and Constance, poor things, are left to weep at my grave.

"We seen him, oh yeah," the cops say, "but we didn't expect him. An unsavory character like him. Weird haircut, weird skin, weird nose. We saw his hands raised, yeah, but we thought there might be an Uzi in 'em, somehow concealed. He leveled it, we fired. Usually it's a black guy, walks out all innocent, we blow him to kingdom come, but it could just as easily be a white guy. We're sorry. What a error! What a mistake! What a accident!"

No matter. Circumstances like this notwithstanding,

cops, they're human too, bro. After a few more minutes, looking, taking notes in their leather note pads, the police vehicle rolls on. Bye-bye.

I breathe a sigh of relief. Quietly, I sit and wait. When Ike and Yves come back, they find me cowering in the corner. "Why you not working?" I tell them about the cops, maybe we should split. What do they think? They assure me everything's okay. "Take it easy," they say. "Everything's under control."

Ike pulls up the last of the newels, the last bits of railing, the last cranky posts. Without a sound. And we kiss that building goodbye.

As a result of deft work, you can see through the joists clear down into the basement. Only a beam plankway left.

"Dollars to doughnuts some crackhead falls down there," Ike says. "Wish I could be here to see it." Arms flailing, dogs howling . . . then snapping jaws, tearing teeth. No, not really. Just canine wuffing.

We sling the duffels on our shoulders, grunt with the load, steal across the lots, still barely a soul alive on the streets, a couple of drug dealers just beginning to come out on Eighth Street to catch the early-morning trade. Ike nudges me and points. "Nubia, DeJesus's oldest kid."

We cross into the vacant lot behind our building when a shot rings out, the bullet stinging the ground between my feet. "Down!" Yves yells as a little puff of smoke rises up and I taste alkali dust.

I hit the dirt, scrambling for cover along the fence, near the perimeter of the dog compound, crawling, crawling. Charlie Company, like my father showed me, just a boy— "Head down, Jo-Jo, Nazis ahead!"

Safety. I imagine I felt the wind of the bullet, the friction, the heat, the impact as the lead slammed the ground. My feet in my sneaks are hot. I survey the roof from my hidey-hole, a bunker of bricks, beer cans and bottles, another slug slams in, who knows from where, no cover here, but no one above us, the red line of brick and camelbacks

etched against the blue morning sky. Nothing moving. All
quiet. Dawn still dawning somewhere. Ike whispers, "You
see anyone?" We wait fifteen minutes. Nothing more. Everything still. We make a break.

When we get home, safe and sound inside, I run upstairs two, three steps at a time. Annabelle's still in bed, eyes
closed, mouth open. The baby's in her room, asleep too. I
shake Annabelle, tell her what happened, how I survived
some scumbag firing shots at us. Creeping on our bellies
across the lost American urban wilderness. Still sleepy, she
doesn't understand what I'm talking about, I make only a
dull impression on her, on her dulled sleepy state.

"Someone shooting! Someone shooting!"

She sits up astonished. "Oh, Zho! Are you all right?"
She takes me in her arms, wants me to know that she loves
me. "I love you, Zho."

"I love you, too," I say, and smile. A shiver runs
through my adrenalized bones. Then I say it in her language.
*"Je t'aime."* Maybe we don't kiss. Maybe we hug real tight.

She says she tastes the tenement dust on me, the dirt,
the old and acid, the same dust I tasted downstairs. She says
she tastes New York. America.

She says, "Zho, when I press you hard against me I feel
a new sharp strength in your body. I know you can do it. I
know you can do anything."

I tell her I know I can too. Then the baby starts crying
and I go to her.

# 16

# Joe and Annabelle in Love

The way I figure it, correct me if I'm wrong, I have certain responsibilities to myself. To others as well, my kid, of course, my wife, my parents, to the other people who live here in the building, but primarily to myself. That's the reason why—when they came to me in the first place, Yves as the spokesman—I said okay to being the president, taking responsibility for where I live, how I handle my life.

"Not to mention, it was . . ."

Annabelle's money that bought this apartment in the first place, not mine. I didn't have two dimes to rub together. I was here during the day, getting sucked into the daily hysteria, the gossip at the clothesline, watching the building going nowhere fast. I had to participate, had to put up or shut up. Wanted to.

"You handle it, Zho. You can straighten it out. You are the only one!"

I can't! I can't handle anything. Please! Leave me alone.

The very first time I met DeJesus it was in the hall in 312, helping Mewie replace beams under his bathroom where his were rotted over the years by a leak. We'd torn up the floor, cut out the rotted beams, were about to strap in new ones when DeJesus came trudging dejectedly up the stairs from his construction job. A solid muscular man, tired, coated with dust. It's the first time I'd laid eyes on him, although I'd heard all kinds of stories.

He stops at the landing, and watches us work for a few moments. Then he reminds Mewie that he had offered to get the corporation materials off the building site where he's working, city housing going up on Ninth Street. He could get us drywall, sheetrock screws, joint compound, cement, whatever we needed, just say the word, nobody cares, everything just lying around in excess, typical city sloth.

"We don't need nothing from the likes of you," Mewie says.

DeJesus glares at him.

Mewie glares back. "Nothing," he repeats for emphasis, just so the man knows, really knows, but he already does.

"Hey, *hombre,*" I interject, Mr. Nice Guy playing politician, *muy simpático,* trying to ease our corporate conscience, or at least mine, don't want to have to watch my back on the street as Mewie so readily seems to relish. "That's super of you to offer. We'll let you know, okay?"

Intervention can be heartwarming, isn't that so? Into the belly of the beast rode the six hundred.

After DeJesus slips into his apartment, Mewie says, "The nerve of the man." I say, "Well, like I said, it was nice of him to offer."

Mewie says DeJesus didn't mean it. No way. It was his game. Some kind of sick trap. A setup, pure and simple. The corporation receives stolen goods from the site, ostensibly from DeJesus, in good faith, and the next thing we know someone with a Spanish accent drops a dime and the city's down on us like a ton of bricks.

Or DeJesus thinks, oh, because I got them all that building materials, I don't never have to pay no rent.

"One don't preclude the other, Mewie."

"No, I guess it doesn't."

"He'll never pay his rent."

"You know it, and I know it, but does he know it?"

"Of course he knows it. Better than we do."

The man's inflexible. No matter how we try to manipulate him, he does what he wants. What's the matter with a man like that?

I asked Annabelle was she coming to the special election meeting with me—Ike's stepping down from the presidency—to cast her routine vote for the man in her life, the new *el presidente*, namely me. She says she wouldn't miss it. Technically I don't own a share in the corporation, can't vote for myself. Is it morally correct to do so anyway? Is there a voting booth? Who will know if I put a check by my name on the chit? Is there even an opponent? Who am I running against anyway? Can you pass that ballot over to me, please?

Annabelle paid the money, the corporation stock's issued in her name, but that didn't make her a player. She was never into the action. The daily talk. Sure, she wanted the buildings to improve, to come together, but she never thought the meetings were worth the aggravation, accomplished anything, just a bother, constant bickering and fighting.

"This is democracy? American democracy in action, you can have it, Zho-Zho," she says to me. "Democracy, it's worthless with this bunch of jerks we got living here."

*Liberté, egalité, fraternité,* that's the real democracy for my French girl.

"Not mine, *mon amour. C'est la tienne.* It's yours.

French democracy is modeled after American democracy."

Ha! These French women, always joking, always cynical, ironic, sarcastic. But sexy.

I'll tell you one thing, if we'd listened to Annabelle in the beginning, we would've been in a much better situation today.

You mean you yourself would've been.

I'm not arguing. Nobody else but, man. I'm the one who's taking the lumps, right? I'm the one they got under lock and key. . . .

And what did she want to do?

Stop the fighting. Treat DeJesus like a human being. Protect her investment, her place to live.

"Zho-Zho," she says, "you know sometimes life is difficult in America. I find it hard at every turn. Nothing is as I thought it would be."

"Sure, join the club. Life is chock-full of surprises, right?"

"I am in a state. I cannot think clearly."

"Your head's a mess, but it keeps your blood boiling, doesn't it?"

She laughs. "Yes, it does," she admits. "And this I like. This hot blood."

She wanted to know, however, how come my blood was so frigging cold. She said it's as she suspected, we are not the perfect match.

I said I thought we were—the perfect match. What's happened to prove it different?

She doubled over in laughter. The baby began to cry. Annabelle threw down the dish towel and screamed, "Not again, I can't stand it any longer!" I said calm down and went for the kid.

Yves asked her one day why we decided to have a kid, if she was so adamantly against it, if she thinks she's such a terrible mother. She gets pissed, asks him why he hates women. She said Immigration, she wanted to stay in the country, and she didn't trust just being married. She said a girl at the Gotham had paid some two-bit American guy to marry her, but when they went down to Immigration, the officer didn't believe it was love for real, even though they both knew what color sheets they slept on and what they had for breakfast. Kicked her out of the country. Annabelle wasn't about to let that happen to her. She said it was more convincing with a kid.

Stop!

Annabelle, you want us to believe you are really a hard-hearted person, don't you?

"Hard-hearted? No! Zho, I think with you. You are difficult to deal with. I make my own way. I always have. I am what I have to be to survive. You forget this is not my country. This is your country. There are many things I don't understand. France is very different from the States."

"Hey, listen, I'm not holding my breath, waiting for you to get all dependent on me."

"That's good, because I won't."

"I wouldn't expect it of you."

"But I would of you, Zho. You are becoming dependent on me. You confuse me with someone. You expect something from me, but I'm not giving it, and it drives you crazy. I am not an American. You forget I am not your sister, nor am I your mother, and because that is exactly who and what you are looking for, it makes you out of your mind."

"I'm under control."

"You're not, Zho. And this so-called corporation, none of you people are under control. Yves is right. A bunch of fools at their petty war, after their petty power. They make it more complicated than sex, more of a driving force. Poor pathetic creatures."

She says it's like when she was a little girl in France. At her school all the girls are together. There are no boys. The girls don't even see a boy all day. It's unnatural. And all of them together, a frustrated pack of jealous, confused little animals, competing with one another. And there was one little girl who all the other little girls decided was a witch, and they picked on her and wouldn't let up, and all the other little girls teased that one little girl until she was hated, genuinely hated, by every other little girl in that school.

"Yeah, tough on her."

"Of course, tough on her, very tough." A little girl in that position going home crying every day, in the morning never wanting to get up, never wanting to eat her breakfast, never wanting to go out of the house, her parents not understanding, yelling at her, accusing her, saying what's the matter with you, that little girl will either crumble, fight back or run away.

"I ran away, Zho, but Señor DeJesus, I suspect he will stay and fight." Her voice trailed.

I said, "Annabelle, *je t'aime.*"

She said, "Sure."

So maybe I don't want to be the president. I don't have to be. No one's forcing me. I tell her I won't.

"No, you must. The power of the presidency could work for us. You could get things together. You are the only one I trust to do it, Zho."

"You want me to be president?"

"Yes, I want you to be president."

Why not, right? Give me something to do. Who else do you know who can sit in judgment, think fairly, is a direct descendant of wise King Solomon? Perhaps she's right—I am the only one.

"Just like your friend Dagmar says, Zho, one day you be king."

Yes—King Joe.

"King Zho. Long live King Zho!" She grins.

Halt! Who goes there? The drawbridge comes down. The moat is traversed.

Did I tell you what Annabelle's family calls me?
*Zho-Zho le sauvage Commanche.*

That's right.

You say it's because of my wild hair, my lack of table manners, my untamed *esprit*. But it ain't necessarily so. No, bro, it could be something even more perverse than that.

I'm second-generation American, and Annabelle is amazed how I'm imbued with what? The American dream? The American spirit? She asks me, "Do they put it in the drinking water?

"What is that?"

"What's what?"

"The American dream. The American spirit."

"It's something we Americans stand for, Annabelle. If you were American, you'd know. . . ."

Annabelle's parents come to visit. I can see her father's not thrilled with me. I say, "Why don't you come out with me, Jean-Jacques, we'll have some lunch." I take him down to where Spike and Scarlet used to work, Goodman's on Delancey. We have Roumanian pastrami sandwiches, well-done pickles, Dr. Brown's cream sodas. When we get out he's holding his gut, but he gotta admit the food's good.

"Okay, keep going. . . ."

Annabelle's mom takes one look at DeJesus (we pass on the street and I grunt) and says who's that?

Annabelle takes her mother aside, says, "You remember Scarlet, the girl I introduced you to next door? She's having an affair with him." Annabelle's mom looks more closely, broad retreating back. "He's attractive in his way," she says.

"A troublemaker," I tell her.

"I can see that," she says. "The way he—how you say?—carries himself." She's talking about the street-man walk. She wants to know his nationality, where's he from? She wants to know this question of everyone. "He's no American," I tell her. "Not a real American."

"Man's more *sauvage* than me, Mama," I kid her. But she says, "No, Zho-Zho, you are pure cannibal."

"Gee, thanks."

Annabelle's mother and father have come to America to view their first and only grandchild.

*"Bonjour, madame. Bonjour, monsieur,"* I say, first thing out of my mouth, every morning, even before my coffee. They sit in the kitchen staring out the window at the rubble and decayed buildings. *"Bonjour, madame. Bonjour, monsieur,"* and not a word out of them, only silence and stares.

Annabelle's mother asks her didn't I learn *le français* in *l'école?*

He didn't go to *l'école*, Annabelle tells her. He quit when he was fourteen years old.

But why?

Ask him.

"Zho-Zho, why you quit school, sweet thing?"

No answer—I have no ambition. None. Nothing.

Or better that she should understand? "I just felt like it, *Maman.*" Drugs. Boredom. What you want me to say? My sister died. The bottom fell out of my life. I couldn't go back.

"What's the diff?" could be what I say.

My father was on the street when he was four selling light bulbs on the corner to feed his brothers and sisters, gave his money to his old man so he could get over, the old man could never make money his ownself, didn't have the touch, sat at the pinochle table all day long, losing, losing, losing, so I'm an incredible step in the right direction already, why should I push it? Besides, my family needed me to work. The newsstand had fallen on hard times and we didn't know where our next dime was coming from. We got kicked off the standpipe and had to find a new place to set up. It was me who worked out the details so we got the kiosk outside the Gotham. Me and nobody else! And anyway, I could get back into education anytime I want to, lot of good it'd do me. Right now, sitting in the penitentiary, sign up for a mail-order course in criminal justice or brain surgery. . . .

Annabelle's family thinks maybe I'm unworthy of their daughter. They have Annabelle's daily photographs spread out in front of them. The floor is dusty and dirty from crumbly mortar and construction dust. The grit disgusts Annabelle's mother. *"Pauvre petite* Constance, forced to crawl on such a floor!"* She clears a space, arranges the photos in chronological order. She's outraged and sad that Annabelle has abandoned the day-after-day photographic ritual, and hurt that we have not begun one with Constance. We hardly have a shot of the baby. I tell her our plan: When Constance is old enough, we hope to tell her she's adopted. Poor minuscule pile of photos. One, the second day in the hospital, a few more at home. Me holding her, bare backed, Annabelle in the tub, the baby floating face down on her still-loose stomach.

Annabelle's mother examines the last of the daily snapshots. She shuffles through, finds the day before the scar, the day of the attack, the day after. She stares. Her father looks down, looks away.

Must make him sick see his daughter defaced like that, although the scar can barely be seen now, is barely visible. Annabelle's lucky, really, her skin doesn't take on that heavy scar tissue.

Her mother shuffles the last of the photographs, replaces the pack, looks to me, asks if I ever thought of making something better of myself. Return to school, complete my education.

She is amazed when Annabelle tells her I once wanted to be a doctor.

I say, "I don't have to be doctor anymore. One day I'll be king."

"King of what?" She looks at her daughter. She doesn't understand and why should she?

Annabelle explains the corporation, the way we live here. *"C'est fou,"* she tells her.

*"C'est incroyable."*

"The problem is," I explain, "there's one family who

lives here, you saw the guy, DeJesus, the Puerto Rican, he doesn't cooperate. He's the only one keeping the building from coming together. If we try to improve something, do something better for ourselves, he'll go out of his way to ruin it. The family won't clean up after themselves, instead they make more of a mess, throw their garbage out the window, scribble graffiti in the hall, their teenage son wrote APRIL FOOLS in letters six feet high on the wall by the second-floor landing, looks like blood. They broke the front door, glued their key in the lock, constantly overflow their washing machine so water drips down for hours. But the worst thing is, they never pay their rent."

"Never pay their rent? *Je ne comprends pas*. How are they permitted to live here?" Jean-Jacques says. He's always asking the pertinent question.

Well?

"*Papa*, it's not that simple," Annabelle tells him, "There's racial overtones here. You don't understand this country. Because this man is Puerto Rican, he was never given the opportunity to become part of the tenant group that took over this building. To him one landlord is the same as another."

"That's not entirely true, Negrito's Puerto Rican."

"He's the only one, and a lot more docile than Carlos DeJesus."

"Docile, gimmme a break."

"But you know what I'm saying, Zho."

"Do I? Do I know?"

"I'm not attacking you, Zho. Don't get so defensive! This is just the way it is here. You must recognize this."

"Must I, Annabelle?"

I gotta go outside. I got to get some help somewhere else. . . .

Why wasn't the DeJesus problem handled by Beneficio when he was here? They spoke the same language. They were from the same culture. You would think they'd have had some kind of connection.

"But they didn't. *Tabarnak!* You know that, Joe."

"Oh, it's you, Yves. I'm glad you could come visit. How you doing?"

"All right, Joe, my throat's been bothering me. But I'll tell you what the trouble was between Beneficio and DeJesus, they never liked each other. They competed. It was that Latin machismo crap. Spanish blood, all that. Beneficio, because he was educated, thought he was better than DeJesus, and DeJesus hated that attitude, and although Carlos acted polite with him, he couldn't stand him, and finally it erupted, and they had words in the hall, and Beneficio became scared. Afraid of the violence."

"What was the nature of the words? What was said?"

"We don't know," Yves admits. "Delilah overheard them, but everything was said in Spanish and she didn't understand so well. She just said DeJesus was very mad, and Beneficio looked terrified. And that was it. I don't think Beneficio spoke another word to DeJesus. After that he let his wife deal with him."


"There's no rationale how we live here," Annabelle says. "We just accept what is. I've invested my money, I'm in for the ride."

"You pay how much for this apartment?" Annabelle's father asks.

Annabelle tells him the price. Annabelle's mother's eyes widen, but where'd she get the money? She knew Annabelle's maternal grandfather gave her some dough before he died to buy an apartment in Paree, which she did with her boyfriend, and when they broke up, and she split, well there you are, the boyfriend bought her out, and at the time the franc was strong and the dollar weak, pre-Reagan, but that wouldn't be riches to overflowing in the New York real estate market. "How much does an apartment like this cost?"

"*Ça a suffi,*" Annabelle says. It was enough. She doesn't tell them about Leonardo and when they ask about the scar on her face, she says she went through a plate-glass window by mistake, right into a bank. "There was some insurance money. We used that."

"Le Commanche had no money, of course?"

"Of course."

"A man of his education . . ."

"Listen, *monsieur* . . ."

"Zho, he's not saying anything against you. He's always been a sour, bitter little man. He only tries to gain an advantage on you."

"I hate when they're here."

But now with Constance! Their only grandchild. We can't keep them away.

"They confuse Constance with their own baby. The baby you never were."

"Perhaps that's true. They do confuse me with Constance."

"It is true, Annabelle. You know it. They're sick."


That night Annabelle comes to bed after staying up talking with her mother at the kitchen table. Her body is ice-cold as she slips under the covers. I move away from her as she tries to snuggle up to me. She tells me she has told her mother about my sister.

"What did you tell her?"

"That she was a doctor, killed in Vietnam, and that it affected you deeply."

"It didn't affect me."

"Zho? It affects you today, and you know it."

"Annabelle," I say, "it didn't affect me. Anyway, what's the difference? The French started Vietnam, we were just suckers enough to join in. If I'm going to start passing blame, I blame you! *Les français!"*

"Zho, don't fool yourself!"

"Fool myself!" I scream, indignation clouding my voice. I sit up in bed shaking violently or I lie, my mind a blank, a shield like a sheet of three-quarter inch plywood protecting my mind from any thought, any emotion, any intrusion.

"Zho?"

—from any thought, any emotion, any intrusion.

"Zho?"

The baby waking up, crying in the other room.

—from any thought, any emotion, any intrusion.

"The baby's up."

No response.

—from any thought, any emotion, any intrusion.

A red veil comes over me, descends on my mind.

"Zho."

—from any thought, any emotion, any intrusion.

"Zho."

No response. Nothing.

"Zho?"

I am wood.

"Zho?

Wood. Impenetrable. There will be no response.

Zho?

Not now. Not ever.

Zho?

She gets up. Goes to the kid.

Not now. Not ever. No response. My eyes are pinned to the ceiling. In mind there is nothing. Protecting my mind—

—from any thought, any emotion, any intrusion.

# 17

# The Loves of Scarlet's Life

Scarlet is sitting at the kitchen table when she hears him on the stairs. She's had this conversation with Pandora, she can tell every person in the building from their footsteps on the stairs. Big deal. She says she knew it was Carlos.

She pokes her head into the hallway, says, "Come in a minute."

He says, "What do I want to do that for?" and Scarlet doesn't have an answer.

She goes back to the kitchen table and drinks her tea. Now someone else is pounding up the stairs. This one is easy for her too—Segundo.

The door's half open into the hall, he peeks in.

She tells him his *papi* has just been by. Don't seem to excite him much. He asks if the old man has just stopped by or come in.

"Why?"

"Just wondering," Segundo says nonchalantly, giving her the once-over.

"You're such a bullshit artist, Segundo," she tells him.

She says he didn't know nothing. He played that hep, down cat, oh yeah, Forty-deuce and "Poison" on the corner, but what did he know? She tells him now that Benny's gone, he is just a mild dude. He looks at her for a second after she says that, then he decides she's just being funny and laughs, hard, too hard, loud and shrill. "Oh yeah, Scarlet, you know it all. You so tough."

She tells him she wasn't trying to pull any power thing on him or his family. He has suspicions of her, and he says his mama has suspicions of her too. "Only *Papi* got the big hard-on for you, Scarlet."

The big hard-on.

She likes that. "Well, I got a pretty moist big one for him too," she tells him—Segundo—fifteen-year-old hard-ass kid. He says, "Well, maybe we can get something going together, Scarlet," and she tells him, "Maybe we can."

He stands in the hall now, inspecting her, saying, "Benny, you know, he never carried no real weight around here. I'm the man."

The picture she had in her head was something completely different. She says she dreamt about this cute little Puerto Rican boy next door, and he was smooth skinned and brown, supple, animal tempered, with a knife. He turned out all those things, although he didn't have a knife, it was a razor, and he had a personality problem.

She tells him his father wouldn't pull his knife on her. "Ha!"

He has nerve. She likes that about him. He would die if he knew Mewie calls him Little Pecker behind his back. Pecker *Pequeño*.

She tells him invite his mama down, they'd have a heart-to-heart talk about Scarlet sleeping with her son.

"My mother doesn't give a shit about you," he sneers.

"She even says she likes you. She thinks you're crazy, but she don't consider you a threat."

"I like your father best," she tells him, "when he's coming hot and dusty from the construction site."

"From the construction site? That's a laugh. He don't work. That a load of crap. He uses that shit to get over on the welfare, so they don't kick him off the roles. He slaps that red dirt on like it's aftershave."

"Another possibility," Scarlet says, "rather than waiting all night for Carl to come visit me when he feels like it, rather than go out looking for a man, or even go up a flight and bring Butch down for an evening's entertainment, although it ain't much of an evening or very entertaining, rather than go get Mazie, ask her if she wants to come sit with me, I could come get you, Annabelle, we could drink tea together while Joe here's at work."

"What's the matter with you, Scarlet? You don't seem like yourself," I say.

"Oh, tired, just tired."

"You look more than just tired, girl."

"Sometimes I think I just want the city to myself," she says. "I don't want anybody else to live here. I want to live by myself now. I'm sick of everybody else, always coming around, always wanting something, always on my case. I'm sick of them males. I've had it with them, all of them. If any of them human dogs come around here, I'm gonna tell them no more, I don't want no more, Scarlet B's finished, used up."

There's no solace. I'll say that for it. A neighborhood like this, the building so quiet. I can't imagine shooting guns back and forth across the well.

"Oh, Segundo'll tell you, it was all in fun."

"But what about Mewie?" I ask.

"What about him?" Scarlet demands. "The man's hysterical. Has been from the first day I met him. Bigmouth troublemaker."

"That *maricón?*" Segundo says. "Who cares about him?"

"You don't give a shit for anyone, do you, Segundo?"

APRIL FOOLS! What do you think? He write it in letters the color of blood, six feet high.

But Scarlet warns him, he better watch out for me. Thanks, Scarl, appreciate it.

Reaching for the pepper, Scarlet says to him, "So, Butch, what more do you want to ask me?"

He leans over, tells her he's working on an assignment for grad school. Butch is getting a Ph.D. in social work, our building his project. Isn't that interesting! Isn't that sweet! She offers him something to eat, some leftover chicken wings from the Chinese take-out on Avenue D. She asks him if he got that in his sociological report, a Chinese restaurant with chefs cooking behind bulletproof glass?

Butch sits there with his mouth open. He doesn't know what to say. He stands up. He says, "Are you having an affair with DeJesus?"

"An affair, for Pete's sake!" Scarlet chuckles acidly.

"And another thing I have on my mind right now, Joe, if you don't mind me mentioning it, is the day Segundo came in here off the street with his buddies, Espina from Third Street, that bunch."

I nod okay, go on, she says, "Segundo put his hands up like it's not his fault, like he surrendered to them, this gang of street hoodlums, they're making him do it. He told me he didn't have anything to do with them. Third Street at

Avenue C, that end is all Peruvian. Pacific Coast fishermen trying to put together a little stake to go back to Lima, buy a boat."

"Yeah, so? What'd they want from you?"

"Joe, you don't mind if I'm straight with you, do you? You probably prefer it. When Segundo came into the picture, I was already washed up with his old man. And if you think him being fifteen years old was a problem, it wasn't.

"I liked him that way, young, a punk. He was so slight, slighter than me, and he wore that felt slouch hat, and a black vinyl jacket. Says he's working out with his old man. Can't prove it by me. Skinny little twerp.

"Make me laugh. 'What's it like to make love to Butch?' he asks me. He says, 'You like the macho man or the wimp?' "

Segundo, she claim she can't expect him to understand her. She expect him to be full of himself, exuberant. "I want him to come after me and really do a job," she say. "It's interesting to see how he perceives his father."

"Watch this, Joe," Scarlet whispers to me, turning to him with an evil grin. "Segundo, your old man?"

"*Señorita*, you ask me of my father. What's he like? You ask me, I'll tell you. On the street Carlos DeJesus is someone. They know him from the gym. They see him on tv. On Fourth Street no one mess with him. They respect what he is. But in his own building, in his own home, his home for eight years, the white people treat him like a cockroach."

"Go on, Segundo."

"One time we were standing there, my brother Fidelito and me. We was on Fourth Street, and the man comes up to us and he says what you doing hanging on this corner? I says it's my business where I hang. No it's not, he's telling me. No, it's not. You on the street, little man. On the street your ass belongs to me, to the poh-leese. I says why shake me and bake me, and he almost whupped me on the coconut. My old man comes out, and that's that. He says who you messing with here, *hombre*, a five-year-old and a twelve-year-old? The cops pulled out without saying another word. They all know him. They all respect him for who he is."

"See?"

"They all know him."

"Carlos DeJesus!"

"My boy Segundo call him *Papi*," Scarlet says, and Segundo nod.


DeJesus comes into her apartment hollering her name. When she tells him to quiet down, he asks why, he's happy. Then he takes her in his arms and kisses her.

"He's not a bad kisser. Very passionate, and he don't smack down my lips. Segundo kisses like a cat in high-tops, on the run, very tentative. But his old man's the real thing, a romantic.

"Butch downstairs, now he's a good kisser. 'But Butchie,' I used to tell him, 'lips that spout all that mushy bullshit politics will never touch mine.' A fuck every now or then, but romance is too much of a hassle with an asshole like that. Now what you think Butch makes of that, Joe? What would you make of it, big boy?

"I got all these men in love with me," Scarlet says. "What do I do?

"Joe, the city's packed with them. All these men on the make, and me, just a working stiff. Now who do I love?

"Who else you want to know about? Spike across the hall? He's a cute customer now. All that green hair and matching green money. And you buy his rap? Now that's a liberal, middle-class boy, from the 'burbs, ain't it! Wild looks, but so fucking conservative.

"He's never made an overture to me, so to speak, you know what I'm saying, Joe, and you know how long we know each other for . . . ?

"And your guy, Joe here, Annabelle? What do you think he's like when you're not around?"

The girls looking at me, barely suppressing the giggles between themselves.

"Joe walks around like he's got the weight of the world on his shoulders," Scarlet says. "You ought to give the dude a massage, girl. What's the matter with you, Joe? Tension between your shoulders, in your neck, got you down, ought to take an Excedrin."

"What do you think about the gay guys, Scarlet?"

"They're okay. Ike and Yves are about as unlikely a couple as you get, not exactly what I would call a marriage made in heaven, but still . . . and poor Mewie, he's just crying his eyes out."

"Mewie loves them, does he?"

"Nope. Mewie's incapable of human love, just a gossip, can't stand anyone else being happy. It tears his heart out."

"Not like you, Scarlet?"

"Not like me. I like to see the world all smiles."

DeJesus sits there and looks at her not saying anything, a silent man, broad, heavily muscled from the gym. What everybody says about him is true: Che, Che Guevara, is who he looks like. Gray speckled through his beard, his eyes creased from too much looking, too much squinting, too much distrust, too much being the player.

"Player?"

"Loisaida player is what he calls himself."

"Loisaida?"

"If I didn't know Che was dead in Bolivia," Scarlet says, "I'd say, hey, man, I just fucked him."

He sits, now he gets up, he looks in her cupboard. "What you got in there?" he says. "All I see is potato chips."

"What do you want?" she says.

"You got wheat germ, some whole-grain cereal, any health food?"

She give him the puzzled look she so good at. "Say what, Señor Muscle Man? *Frijoles es frijoles.*"

Scarlet claims that Carlos had a plan. "We were together and he used to say, 'If I have to, I'll burn her out. Don't worry. *No te preocupes.* Nothing'll happen. I'll pick my spot. I'll wait till no one's home. Social Services will take care of her, put her and the kids in a welfare hotel, buy them new clothes, increase their monthly money, they'll be better off without me. Then you and me we get a apartment together, Scarlet, or go to Puerto Rico.'

"I told him he's out of his mind, he didn't want to live with me. I'd be too much for him. I don't subscribe to that bullshit macho mentality he goes around with. I don't roll around the floor after he kicked me waiting for my belly to be rubbed like his precious little *gatito.*

"He says that's all right, he'll change.

"Fat chance," she answered. "Don't change anyway. I don't want you to change. You're perfectly suited for my purposes.

"See, I made no bones about it," she says, "what I wanted from him.

"Carmencita was his second wife. His oldest girl, Nubia, was from the first marriage. I asked him once if he had any control over her. After all, it was a little bit weird that here is this big neighborhood antidope kingpin, and his only daughter is out there on Avenue D selling *tres* bags.

"He said something then, I don't remember it exactly, but he made some little comment about life, with this crazy little glint in his eye like he just learned the words, and in truth he didn't have that big a command of the English language, but I remember it because it was like the lyrics of a rock-and-roll song, something like, 'Life is cruel, boo-boo-bee-do!' You hear me, Joe? Something like that. 'Life is full

of suprises, do-woppie-do.' Something strange. Tra-la-la!"
"So what'd you say?"
"I agreed. I said, 'Carmencita don't deserve it, and you wouldn't be happy with me.' "

Carlos's gym is in an abandoned building on Fourth Street, on the Avenue E end, a block away from where Segundo says Espina and the Peruvians hang. Still, it was a heavy block until the gym moved into the building. The building had been a bank, then a nursing home, then community groups took it over, then squatters. The junkies were next to arrive, then DeJesus. He had a name on the street, and he got together a few other guys, his cousin Shorty, their friends Dynamite and Bucky—two brothers, I'm talking same mother and father now, not brothers in common cause, though they were that too. DeJesus went down there with his troops and told the junkies what was happening. He said, "*Mira*, look, this is the perfect place for me and my crew. We're gonna bring in the equipment, put a ring in, some weight bars, set up benches, squat racks." What could the junkies say? It was summertime. DeJesus is standing in front of them. He's small, 5'8", but 260 pounds if he's an ounce (" . . . and take my word for it," Scarlet says, "he's been lying on top of me. I know how much he weighs, brother!"). The neighborhood kids see him on tv. The neighborhood big boys too. Saturday morning one of the car jockeys brings a tv down to the sidewalk and everybody gathers round to watch *Wrestle Mania*. "Hey, saw you mix it up with the Hulk, good-buddy. Got your ass whipped." He asked them, you ever see a Puerto Rican beat a blond white man like Hulk Hogan on tv or at Madison Square Garden? No way! Said in a street fight he could whip Hulk's white ass any day of the week. "Coulee to the sidewalk, nigger. Hulk Hogan's a sissy man. Beats up on reporters and newscasters, but me, Young Che, I smack around the biggest and the baddest, and I don't never back down. Dig?"

Yo, man! It's Latin Rambo.

They believed him. They all believed him.

"I saw him do it to Espina over there from Third Street," Scarlet says. "The time he come in with his gang, held a gun to my head, then laughed, *har-har-har,* said it wasn't loaded.

"I pulled the little gun Carlos gave me out of my garter, shocked the shit out of him. Took him by the hair, told his friends keep still, then I sent Segundo after Carl, because it was Segundo who brought Espina to my place in the first place, said he had some business.

"Carlos come back, his eyes red, the pupils tiny, black. Wanted to know what Espina thought he was doing.

"Espina says his gun's not loaded. Then he says he forgot, the gun is loaded.

" 'Make up your mind,' Carlos says.

" 'I got it made up,' Espina says. 'It's loaded.' "


"Carl, honey," Scarlet says demurely, "you know that time when Espina shot you, over at my place, did he really shoot you, baby, did he actually hit you or did the bullets just miss?"

"No, he hit me," Carlos insists. "Hit me good. Remember the way I go back against the wall?"

"I remember this incredible bang of bullets going off in my front room," Scarlet says abstractly. "That's the power of a six-gun for you."

But Carlos says the dude didn't hurt him.

He takes out a little tin box. The bullet had hit it, tore a jagged slit in the metal, but hadn't gone through. Carlos points out the hole, rattles what's inside.

"What do you keep in there?" Scarlet asks.

He flips the lid and she half expects to see the bullet lying inside, a little piece of lead in its tin coffin, but there's only some pills inside.

"What's that?"

"Steroids," he says, "but I don't take them."

"Those guys there, that Espina," Scarlet says, "they were after me. Yeah, I remember them. Third Street."


"There were other times, you know," Scarlet tells me. "Times to dance, that street dance, they dance down here. Go out on a hot Saturday night in August. Me wearing a white cotton dress, or black torn dungarees and painted-up tee shirt. How do I get my tee shirts? Go in to Spike, say Spike, 'Wipe your brushes on me, honey.' "

Smear that magenta on me, homeboy. On me. On me. On me.

"I go out dressed like that and Carlos is sitting on the wall in front of the Pentecostal church on Avenue E and Sixth Street drinking beer with his buddy Rigoberto, the church sexton.

"They both look at me appreciatively as I walk by.

" '*Ella no está flaca,*' Carl's buddy says.

" '*No,*' Carlos agrees. '*No, ella está gorda, muy gorda, bellísima.*'

"Yeah. Not skinny. Fat. They got me.

"The street's like a sex gauntlet for me, guys cupping their balls saying, 'Hey, woman, I'm the one, deliver you from you pain and suffering, from you worries and woe.'

" 'Thanks, lover,' I says. 'I been looking to get rid of them things anyway. Whattayousay? Worries and woe, no mo'!' " She grins. "Intriguing fucking idea, wouldn't you say, Annabelle? I'm like Pandora, Joe. I been here too long. Too long in the neighborhood. I heard all the lines, I seen all the techniques, I know the street. Changing neighborhood? Same old shit. The money's here today, I'll have to admit that. One day Carlos asks me, 'Don't you want some?'

"I said, 'No, *pesos* don't interest me.'

"But that's a lie. I do want some. I do want *pesos*. Shit, look at Spike. You know, me and him used to work together, Joe. That's right. At Goodman's Delancey Street deli. We both worked the floor. That's how we know each other. His old man and my old man been working together for twenty-six years. Now look at him, making money hand over fist, and he acts like he's God's gift to the world."

She says she asked Carlos if he knew Spike.

"*Quién?*"

"Spike! Guy with green hair. Lives in the other building, couple floor below yours. You know him? He's an artist. Thinks he's Picasso."

"Who?"

"El Greco!"

"Who?"

"You seen him? Green hair! Couldn't miss him."

"Oh yeah, yeah. *El Pintor.*"

"Such a brilliant conversationalist. I says, 'Carlos, you know the guy, don't you?'

"Finally he admits he knows the guy. Thrilling. I don't know what the macho thing was, pretending not to know who I'm talking about. But in Carlos's mind, knowledge diminishes power in some way. You understand that, Joe?"

"Spike's your friend," Scarlet told Carlos. "He's the friend of the poor."

"And then I asked him about you, Joe. Does he know you? A guy with a baby strapped to his chest all the time like some sort of weird gold chain. I told him the landlord was changing, and, Joe, I told him you were the latest and the greatest, the best of the new breed."

"I don't want him to know me," I says. "I don't want him to know who I am."

"Carlos's children with Carmencita are just the two little boys," Scarlet tells me. "Fidelito and William Guillermo Morales DeJesus. Fidelito for Castro, of course, and little Willie for the Puerto Rican revolutionary hero who blew his own hands off. The older ones, Nubia and Segundo, are from the first marriage. Except I hear Carlos and his first wife were never married, just common-law. A Spanish girl, they split up, then she died. Overdose. In a shooting gallery on Second Street. He went over to see the body when he heard on the street. The kids were there. Sitting hard eyed. He said, 'You see this happen?' They said they had. Welfare wanted to take them that night, put them in a foster home. He fought them, but Social Services seized the kids, then he got them back. They'd been in Long Island City. They said the people who took care of them were nice. 'You know what, *Papi?*' Segundo said. 'They had two beds for us to sleep in. One each.'

"He took them home. Carmencita was living down on the third floor with her father and his lady friend. Her old man was named Huaquero and he had the social club, down on the Avenue D corner where the smoke shop is now. Carmencita came up every day and helped with the kids, cooked dinner, looked after Carlos. Soon she was pregnant. Her father didn't say anything. He was friends with DeJesus, but he had to go back to P.R. to straighten out some business. He was satisfied that DeJesus kept half an eye on her. Carmencita's father's old grandmother had died and all the cousins were fighting over her farm, how it should be divided or who should have it, all the land, the whole thing. While he was away and Carmencita was upstairs, they broke into Huaquero's apartment and tore up the floorboards looking for his stash.

"Huaquero never came back so I don't know if it was there. Maybe it was. He never came back.

"I got my apartment pretty much the same way," Scarlet says. "The old lady who lived here, God bless her soul, lived in this building for more than sixty years. Three years ago she was going to the A&P on Sixth Street and Avenue D one morning, a Sunday I heard it was, before most of the people were out for church, just eight o'clock, somebody pulls her into the entranceway of where the Chinese restaurant and the check-cashing place are and raped her, eighty-one years old. And since she didn't have enough money, they punched her in the face."

"They ever get them dudes, Scarlet?"

"No, never. They wound up killing her. Crushed her cheek and jaw so bad she couldn't eat. She died about a week later. Then Spike told me the apartment was vacant, and I moved in."

"Benny's a tough one, now ain't he, Scarlet? I never knew him, but I suspect that if I had, I never would've gotten along with him. I know he was the one fucking with the guns."

"He led Segundo around by the nose."

"That's what I hear."

"On the street, Benny was cool for his age. He had a lot of insight into the world. But he's a dope."

I'm sitting here thinking while Scarlet's going on about all the men in her life. All the men in this building she's involved with, how different they are from all the others she must have known. "I was straight once, Joe. I really was. Looking for something—just, calm."

This world, it's a big enough world. It's a world. Then there's another world, a world outside our world, for tv and movie personalities, politicians and sports heroes.

One of the trickiest things was to identify the voices, who was talking, what were they thinking?

Scarlet says she relied on the hall so much, the comings and goings, "That's why I liked the front apartment. I'd never leave the front, looking through that big picture kind of window, double window, leaning on the sill and seeing the street right out there, only sometimes I wished I didn't have to see them looking back up at me, and I wonder if I would see them when they came for me. Espina and the Third Street Boys, for example, them or somebody else. Come kill Scarlet for fifty bucks.

"Living so close to the street, I like that, seeing the dog shit, that fat man from next door bending down to pick it up and wrap it in newspaper, Pandora cornering the mailman, screaming at him in that incredibly powerful voice of hers, 'What you got for me today? Is my welfare check here?' The guy in his uniform and post-office-issued safari hat overwhelmed by her at first, but then getting to like her, and going in, I could hear them in the hall, climbing the stairs for soup and cabbage, but then he got busted off the route because people were complaining their mail was late. I don't imagine it was only Pandora he stopped at, he was a good-looking, coffee-colored Latin guy, can't tell me the mail couldn't have been on time if he wanted it to be, no, but I don't think anything was happening upstairs. Paco was in and out, it was only the mornings he was at the program. In the afternoons him and his buddies were up and down the stairs, talking loud and laughing, Paco singing that old neighborhood hit of his, 'Baby, I love you.' "

" 'Scarlet,' Segundo said. 'You're a beautiful woman.'
"I laughed in his face. Who'd he think he was? He looks fifteen, he acts fifteen, he is fifteen. He was coming into my place with his street friends, and just because I was fucking his old man he thought he could say whatever he wanted. He called me *puta*, but actually the only *puta* around was him."

"Butch says: 'Scarlet, what's the use of us always fighting? You're on one side, I'm on the other. Why can't we just leave it that way?'

" 'I don't know, Butch, why can't we?'

" 'It's over.'

"Butchie-boy don't live here no more. He knows it and I know it, and we both know he sold out, 'So don't be spouting all this bullshit to me, all right, Butch?' I tell him.

" 'Butch—get your ass out of here,' always simpering around the door, little wimp, Segundo's right, little wimpy weasel.

"He's gone now, though, isn't he? Butch gone, Fausteen's gone, all gone. So what's he doing knocking at my door, Butch coming to visit, saying, hey, Scarlet, how they hanging? Very funny man, Butch. Hey, Butch, what brings you back to the old neighborhood? Need some footnotes for your thesis? I heard you were living in suburbia or at least the West Side.

"His voice gets real earnest, you know. He says, 'Scarlet, it's not over yet. They're planning something for DeJesus.'

"I say, 'You don't say! What are they planning for DeJesus that's different from what they planned for everybody else? You sold out, Butch. Money talks, everybody walks. You and the corporation, you guys are all the same, and don't be pretending different.'

" 'I'm telling you, Scarlet,' he whines. 'The word's on the street. I have my sources. Joe Peltz and the corporation, they're up to something.'

" 'Up to what? Who do you think *they* are?' I tell him, Joe, the corporation's just regular people. Some good eggs, some bad eggs. I tell him you're aboveboard. People work hard, they're entitled to a decent place to live. I want it too. Carl understands that. You think he wants to live in a shit hole himself his whole life? The game he plays is his choice. 'You seem to be the only one who don't realize that, Butchie-dear.'

"He talks to me like I'm a child. I hate that. 'They're rent gougers, Scarlet,' he says. 'Gentrifiers. Little money-grubbing landlords. They don't belong here. What are you going to do about it?' "

Scarlet laughs to herself, recalling the scene, the veins standing out on Butch's forehead. "You know what I tell him, Joe?"

"No. What?" (I can imagine.)

"I don't say a word, don't tell him anything, just kick him right the fuck out the door! All he wants is to get laid."

# 18

## Joe Pays a Visit

It is six o'clock, late afternoon or evening, you make the choice, in Mewie's apartment and the window is open, so he hears Scarlet's voice.

"Mewie!"

He looks out the window and she's standing there five flights below on the sidewalk, underneath the linden tree. The garbage cans are still stacked at the curb from the garbagemen's rounds that morning.

"I'm locked out," she shouts up. "Throw down the key," and he answers that he will, but first she should put the garbage cans back where they belong against the building. Then he gets his extra front door key from the nail by the sink and picks a dirty sock off the floor. He puts the key in the sock, knots it, looks out the window and tosses it down to Scarlet. "Here it comes!" he shouts as he watches it drop, watches her circle, the futile lunge, the sock bouncing off the sidewalk.

"Nice snare."

The cats are rubbing up against his ankles and calves. Boy 1 and 9 are particularly affectionate. Two calicos with nerve-wracking voices.

The door is open and he can hear Scarlet coming up, but first she stops on the first floor to have a word with Delilah. Then he hears Delilah shouting to Pandora, "Maaa!" Then Pandora answering, "Yeah?"

"Here she is!"

Now Scarlet's stopped and saying something to Pandora. Paco singing, "Baby, I love you," followed by, "How you, ma'am?"

Mewie looks down the stairwell at the three faces that look up when he shouts, "Will you leave her alone already and let her come up?"

"Nobody's bothering her!" Delilah calls up.

"You bother everybody, Delilah."

"And what's eating you? Your boyfriend didn't make it home last night?"

"Petty, petty."

"Watch out! You still got lots of enemies here," she shouts up. "Just because Howie and Butch are gone doesn't mean you can get away with persecuting us tenants."

Mewie retreats to the sanctity of his apartment. He has two apartments converted into one huge, open space. Everything raw, like it's never been touched, only made worse, old, rotten wood, bare beamed ceiling, plywood roof showing underneath. Splintered, sloping, uneven, battered floor. Although he's lived here for four years, Mewie can't seem to get it together. What else is new? Brick walls with holes worn through the mortar, open to the weather, plastic stapled into the windows, the old frames rotted and falling apart, the floorboards mismatched, uneven, splintered and rotting. He says as soon as DeJesus is gone, he'll finish his apartment, but until then, it's not worth it. He has done one thing. Made a lavish bathroom with blue tile he ordered directly from Morocco, and gold fixtures for the sink, shower, Jacuzzi and even the drain and toilet flush.

Scarlet falls in, sighs, drops into a chair and says, "Got a joint?" Immediately a cat jumps into her lap.

"Who's this?" she asks as Mewie goes off to find his marijuana.

He looks back over his shoulder. "Boy 2," he tells her. "I think she has homophobic tendencies. She won't associate with any of the other girls and, as a result, she makes them all so glum. She won't even accept them cleaning her or licking her balls."

"The only male ever been in this apartment could ever say that, feline or human."

"Isn't that the truth."

Presently he has eleven cats living in the apartment with him. All male. Mewie wouldn't have it any other way. All strutting their stuff. All street cats at one time or another. He has another dozen or so that he feeds on the sidewalk, lowering a few pie tins full of dried food out his window three times a day. But he won't bring a she-cat inside. "Let them suffer down there," he says, pointing to the vacant lot. Right now he sits down, begins rolling the joint, and starts complaining about some subhumans from the corner who like to bring their dog to the lot and hunt the cats when they come to eat.

"Pit bull. You know that breed?" he says.

Scarlet knows. One had attacked her one day when she was walking west on Seventh toward Avenue B. One of those black-and-white ones, a jaw on legs. "I see them hanging by their teeth off old automobile tires suspended on chains. I understand it's suppose to be training for the dog-fights."

She had had a leather mailbag and this pit bull had suddenly lunged, not at her but at the bag, grabbed hold and wouldn't let loose. She pulled, but the more she pulled the more the dog bit down, thinking it was a game, and wouldn't let loose, "Not never," the animal's master had said. And the guy, one of the coke dealers from the red building over there between B and C, finally enticed the dog to let go and he apologized profusely, embarrassed, and played up to Scarlet in a polite, sort of sweet way. His dog was sharp, razor sharp, he told her. "A fighting dog who's never lost." Seemed to Scarlet if a dog like that lost, he only lost once. The coke dealer said that was right.

A few weeks later, Annabelle clipped an article from the newspaper about how one of those pit bulls had killed a baby only a block away. The wife had begged the husband to get rid of it, and he had, he'd given the dog to a friend, but then the dog had attacked the friend's baby, not bad, and he'd returned it. The wife said no, but the dog stayed and before long was left alone with the original owner's child for a few minutes. When the husband's brother came in, the baby was clamped in the dog's jaws, and the dog was shaking its head and growling.

"I don't like those dogs," Scarlet says. "I don't understand how anyone can have one. They're so ugly."

"Hunting my cats," Mewie says. "I'll drop a brick on their fucking heads if I see them."

"Have you seen them?" Scarlet asks.

Mewie hadn't, but Olga the Catlady from up the block had told him because they were hunting her cats too, and she warned him, her partner in felinity. It was tough out there on the street for a kitty.

Scarlet took the joint, and relaxed in the silver lamé director's chair that Mewie had gotten from the club. "Such a nice club," Mewie says, even though they'd fired him. "So trendy." Scarlet used to hang there with him. Her fag-hag period. Now Mewie's buying and selling on the street outside the club, on the corner of Seventh and A. There are rumors that the club's closing for good—the mayor's closing down homosexual haunts, AIDS terror rampant—and the owner wants to put a performance bar in, all the rage, Mewie hoping for his job back.

Scarlet breathes into the joint and a puff of smoke

comes loose, and Mewie admonishes her, "Don't do that," he doesn't have enough for her to be puffing away like that, and she says, "Sorry, just thinking.

"You know, Mewie," she says, "We all better get our shit together here, because I don't think things are going to stay this way for such a long time. Neighborhood's changing, things are changing," and he says, "What are you talking about?" and she says, "I don't know. Maybe Butch is getting to me."

Today Joe saw brand new graffiti on the street—FUCK ALL GENTRIFIERS, PUNKS, NEW WAVE, FAGS AND YUPPIES!

Scarlet really only comes over here to gossip with Mewie, to chat, to talk about their boyfriends, one and all, giggle and smoke, but once again the odor of the cats is getting to her. So Mewie puts a fan at the window to air out the room, and Scarlet warns him it isn't going to work, the stink's in the floorboards, in the wood. She says, "Don't your neighbors complain?" and he says, "Who are my neighbors? DeJesus?"

As if that answered it, and obviously in Mewie's mind it did, because he kept his door open so he could see into the hall and could see when DeJesus came and went, like everyone else in the buildings, everybody minding everybody else's business but their own, looking down the halls, seeing who was coming in and going out, and no one had any secrets from anyone else, yet everyone did.

"I don't see Spike," Mewie says. "You see him? You see him or Joe?"

"Hey, Mewie," Scarlet says, "don't get me involved, building politics aren't my problem."

"No, they aren't," Mewie agrees. His problems with DeJesus were different than hers.

"Your problems with *everybody* are different than mine," she says. "What about the time you and your good friend Howard K had a fight about your cats smelling up the whole building? What'd he do that time, beat your door in with a wrench?"

"I swore out a warrant for his arrest."

"I know you did, dear."

"It worked. If only we could figure out a way to deal with DeJesus now, it would be the most perfect building!"

"You ever notice how everybody wants to fight you, Mewie?" Scarlet comments.

"Oh, familiarity breeds contempt. But it'll pass, I know it will."

"I like our neighbors," Scarlet says. "All our neighbors."

"Some are slimier than others, with the exception of you, of course. You're just the most perfect creature, Scarlet."

"Mewie," she says, "don't get me started again."

"Okay, I said it! I like everybody. We're all friends."

"Even you and Carlos?"

"Bosom buddies. You know what he did now? I mean, aside from calling me *maricón* and spitting at me when he sees me, and starting fires in front of my door with my trash?"

"Don't tell me."

"Well, it wasn't him, in case I'd betray a little soft spot. Oh no, it wasn't him, it was his son, you know, little eensy-beensy, teensy-weensy Pecker *Pequeño!* Sweet Segundo. If it weren't only the good who died young!"

"Oh my. So bitter, Mewie!" Scarlet leans back to get a good look. "You can't be doing yourself any good."

"Stole my pot! I was standing right there when he did it. Beneficia left her refrigerator for me with Joe, so I finally made arrangements with Paco to have him and a couple of his friends move the refrigerator from 310 over here. They carried it all the way over the roof, but for some reason they did it when I wasn't home so they couldn't get it inside, and they left it in the hall, and I couldn't get in or out of my apartment, so Spike was just coming home and I got him to come over here and give me a hand and while we were moving the refrigerator I put the pot in a bag of groceries and left it on the step. We carried the fridge inside, but when I went back for it, the bag was gone."

"The marijuana and the groceries?"

"Nope, just the pot. And a package of potato chips."

"And you think it was Segundo who took it?"

"Wouldn't you?"

"I don't know. *I* like potato chips, and *I* like pot!"

Scarlet looks at him. Mewie, perfectly tailored: black leather motorcycle boots, torn dungarees, white tee shirt with a frayed neckline and holes under the arms. Leather wristlets, leather belt, and a leather dog collar around his neck.

"We were here first," he says.

"Who was?"

"Oh, they might have lived here, but they didn't buy and they didn't give a shit about where they lived, or about the building. As a matter of fact, they took everything out on the building, all their animosity, all their aggression, all their aggravation. They trashed their home, the very place they lived, and now they've stolen my pot." End of argument for Mewie.

"C'mon, Mewie," Scarlet says, "you can afford it."

"That's not the point, and anyway, no, I can't, now that I'm not working."


The light came on across the well, and they could see Joe coming home to his apartment. He turned and peered through the window into Mewie's apartment, and when he saw Mewie and Scarlet smoking and chatting and looking out the window at him, he called out, "Hey, what are you two doing?" Then when they said, "Smoking and gossiping," Joe said, "Okay if I come over?"

Joe slid his window wide open and climbed from one sill to the other. Mewie was expert at this move, but Joe had never done it before, and said all he wanted out of life at this point was to live dangerously and, "Mewie, why don't you pass that joint over here to me?"

And here they sit at the little table that looked out over the drug traffic on Eighth Street, Joe says, "That's some serious stuff," as they watch the runners chasing cars and taxis down the street, as they cruise, Jersey plates, looking for coke and dope, "C & D" reverberating in the crisp late-fall air. And Mewie points her out, watching her scurry as the lookout on the corner shouts, *"Bajando!"*

Now Joe watching DeJesus's daughter, Joe saying, "Nubia's not so bad looking."

"Better looking than her father," Mewie says.

"Why she wear that cap?"

"She thinks she looks good."

"Tough little girl," Scarlet says. "Ever see Carl in his straw Chinese coolie hat? I gave it to him."

"I wish she wouldn't come around here anymore."

"Oh, you like her, Mewie!" Scarlet teases.

"Like hell I do."

He does. He often said she was his favorite, but then Scarlet put her finger on it, said the only reason Mewie liked Nubia was because she had a whole bunch of queens for friends.

Joe almost barfs, or is that his laugh? "Queens?"

"Not the dealers, dummy, the little faggots that come calling for her. You never heard them: *Nubia! Nubia!* From the street? So shrill, likely to wake the dead?"

"Oh, yeah."

"Hey, you know who I heard from?" Mewie blurts out, suddenly really excited.

"Who?"

"Benny! Yaa mon, Benny."

"Benny?" she repeats his name, unimpressed.

"Guy's been in Ecuador. He wrote, says he joined the army."

"What else is new?"

"Do you believe it? He says he's going to come back for a visit. He wants to spend Christmas here."

"What'd you say?"

"What do you think I said? I said, Sure! Of course! I can't wait! Come!"

# 19

## Fire

The fire began when a person unknown cut a hole in the roof, poured gasoline into DeJesus's kitchen and lit it. The flames started on the wall near the fuse box, then spread from the kitchen, through the hall, the living room, the bedroom. No one was home at the time.

Mewie Cotton, from across the hall, had been out all night. He should've woken up at eleven to go to work. Now it was twelve and he heard a crash like sheetrock falling. He'd been in a deep sleep and leaped out of bed. Construction accident was his first thought, but when he went into the hall and saw smoke rushing from underneath DeJesus's apartment door, he stood there for a moment till it dawned on him. Then he thought, Do I let it burn?

Carmencita pulls her children to their feet as the bus stops ten feet from the curb on Avenue D. The poor little one looks sick despite what the Medicaid doctor had said. Carmencita lifts him into her arms, kisses his forehead and carries him off the bus, wading through the slush that borders the sidewalk like a moat.

In front of the bodega stands Nubia in her watch cap and wool shirt. Carmencita cannot believe she isn't cold, dressed like this in such freezing weather. Nubia is lined up with the other drug peddlers, and she rushes for the junkies who push off the bus in front of her stepmother and half brothers.

Little Fidelito spots her. "*Mira!* Nubia!" he cries excitedly, letting go of his mother's hand and running toward his half sister.

Carmencita spits on the sidewalk.

"You're getting yours!" Nubia says in her vicious way. "You got a real surprise coming, bitch." Then she laughs, returning to her street business.

And what do I care? thinks Carmencita, conveniently blaming Nubia for all that has happened between her and Carlos, even though she knows this isn't the case.

She has lost him. She needs no one to tell her that he's trying to rid himself of her. "Little instigator, Nubia!" She spits a second time, clutches the baby to her bosom and regains Fidelito's hand.

She walks to the corner wondering what surprise Nubia could promise her—has Carlos finally left them? Things will be no better, no worse, without him. Life will continue. Where would he go? He would *have* to stay close. Surely he would not return to Puerto Rico. Leave the city? That was only a threat, muttered when he was frustrated or upset.

All Carmencita's senses are aroused. If something were to happen she wanted to be prepared. She could not fight him physically, but she would make her feelings known.

She hears a buzzing and, when she turns the corner onto her block, she sees the street blocked with fire trucks, people milling around and talking.

From the corner it appears to be her building. Pulling

Fidelito along, she hurries forward. Sure enough, now she can see clearly, it *is* her building. The fire fighters are standing, chatting. The gleaming red trucks are standing idle.

"Is it over?" she cries in Spanish. "What has burned?"

"Lady," a fire fighter pleads. *"Señora."*

"It's yours!" a voice in the crowd shouts.

Carmencita turns, startled. She sees Rigoberto from the church. The man who stands in front of the liquor store with a microphone and tells all the junkies to come home to God. *"Es tuyo,"* he says.

"It's mine?" She turns and heads for the building, one hand clutching the sick little one, one covering her mouth. She sobs even before she sees it.

The cop at the police line lets her pass without a word and she runs up the concrete steps of the tenement. The front door is broken and cannot be locked. She pushes through the door and water drips at the end of the hall, down from the landings above, a great deal of water, and she can smell something burnt.

Fidelito and the baby are crying. Carmencita is crying. Down the steps comes Pandora, the lady on the second floor.

"Oh, I'm so sorry," shrieks Pandora.

Paco is trailing after her. He starts chattering at her in Spanish-English gibberish.

Carmencita sobs more loudly.

"See what you've done!" Pandora shrieks at Paco. "You've upset her."

"No, Mrs. . . ."

Carmencita climbs the steps slowly, Fidelito whimpering after her. The little one, now sleeping, is clutched in her arms.

Water is everywhere, and above her on the steps firemen in heavy raincoats are carrying axes and shouting back and forth. The crumbling tiles in the hallways are even looser than before. The graffiti APRIL FOOLS in red spray painted letters.

Heads poke out from behind every door to watch her trudge upstairs.

The firemen stop what they're doing as she goes to the door, looks, then bursts into tears. She turns away. She must sit down. Her legs have turned to jelly.


The cold must have kept the smell of fire out of the air, because DeJesus hears the murmur of the crowd first. Coming from the gym, he turns the corner and sees the fire trucks clotting the street.

"Carlos! Carlos! It's your house, man," yells one of the men in the crowd. "They got you this time, man."

On the front stoop Paco tries to stop him, talk to him.

"Out of my way, old man," he growls, pushing past. He kicks the front door open and everyone in the street stretches to see.

Now he can smell the fire. Water drips in the rear near the *cabrón* Dagmar's apartment.

When he turns to go up the stairs, Dagmar is standing there lighting up a cigar. "Tough break, Carl."

There is nothing to say to him. He pushes past him. DeJesus is a man with strength. All residents of the building know this. He is wearing a green beret with a rhinestone pin on it and a combat jacket. His hair is long and black, flecked with gray. He has a Zapata moustache, carefully trimmed to fall in sharp angles.

Even inside the cold makes smoke come from his mouth and nose as he runs up to the fifth floor.

At his landing he hears hammering, banging and people walking on the roof. He goes ahead without looking in his apartment, and there are the women, the old, fat Pandora and Delilah, her *puta* daughter, clucking, and their eyes all turn big for him, and they make room, and Delilah rubs his neck and says something like "Poor Carlos-baby," he doesn't know what, and they make room when he scowls at them. "Oh, he's mad!" the old bat of a mother shrieks, and the two of them step aside, muttering, "What's he gonna do?"

And there . . . there is his wife, Carmencita, and the baby, William Guillermo Morales DeJesus, crying, and little Fidelito, holding his head, and his oldest son, Segundo, the tough, angry one, making threats, "We're gonna get them for this! We're gonna get them! They'll pay for this!"

"What happened?"

"They burned us out! What's it look like?"

"Who did it?"

"The *maricones,* who do you think?"

"Did you see them do it?"

"Look around, man—one Puerto Rican family in the building, there's a fire, and we're the only ones to burn, and we're burnt out. Tell me what you think."

Carmencita cries harder. "Why would they do this to our family?"

"Look after your mother," DeJesus says to his son.

"She's no mother of mine!"

DeJesus slaps him. "Shut up, and do as I say."


The fire started when a person unknown climbed to the roof, cut a hole, poured gasoline into DeJesus's apartment and lit it. The firemen arrive in a hook and ladder, two pumpers, a red chief's car, and an Emergency Services ambulance from the station on Eldridge Street. With power saws they cut a four-by-eight-foot hole in the roof and blast away with water. That puts it out.

When DeJesus gets home the steel door into the apartment has been torn off its hinges. The apartment is a mire of black muck and charred furniture. "Motherfookers! What are you doing here?"

The chief has called the fire marshal, who steps forward. "You the gennelman who lives here?"

"*Claro,* I live here."

"What do you know about this?"

DeJesus shakes his head. He is a bull. His hair jumps about his neck. "I don't know nothing. A dog chewed a hole in the roof, poured gasoline into my apartment and lit it. What is there to know? Why don't you ask one of the *maricones* what happened?"

His English is only as bad as need be. "My home is ruined," DeJesus tells him. "My wife and children sit in the hallway and cry."

"I'm not crying," Segundo shouts from the door. "I'll get them."

"Silence!" DeJesus puts his hand up. His son stands propped in the doorway with a scowl on his face.


Carmencita doesn't want to see, can't bring herself to see. Fidelito runs down the hallway, then runs back to her and throws a tantrum. He wants to be held, but she already has the sickly little Willie in her arms. She pushes Fidelito away.

Her neighbor with the beard and the cats, Señor Cotton, comes out of his apartment. "Well, he's done it now," he says in his horrible, nasal voice. "Who set this fire, Carmencita?"

She cries into her hands, sobbing unintelligibly.

"Somebody set it!" Señor Cotton stomps back into his apartment where three or four firemen are milling around. He begins talking with them, gesturing toward her, toward her apartment. She hears him accuse her Carlos.

Another of the homesteaders clomps up the stairs like a donkey. Who is it? The woman from the other building. Carmencita can see into her apartment from across the well. She's new in the building, has only been here a few months. She has a new baby. Carmencita has seen the woman only a few times. Perhaps the woman had nodded or smiled. The baby is in her arms now.

The woman passes her, looks at her, says nothing, looks away. Then she peeks into Carmencita's apartment. "Oh, it's horrible," she says. The woman has an accent, but it is not Spanish, and Carmencita cannot imagine where she might be from.

Carmencita looks at the woman's red patent leather shoes, her white makeup, hennaed hair, the black eyeliner drawn thickly around her eyes, the thin scar running down her cheek to her rouged lips.

The woman looks down at her red patent leather shoes, then she looks back into the apartment, at the ashes and charred blackness mixing with water, coating the apartment floor like a black, glooey paste. "I should change my shoes," the woman says. But she doesn't move. From where she stands, just inside the door, she can see the whole apartment. "What a horrible mess!"

There are four small rooms. All the walls are burnt and the firemen have chopped through several of them. The rooms were once little boxes, squares inside a small box apartment with a little tail for a bathroom. The firemen have axed everything in sight. The windows are shattered, the doors smashed open, the furniture blackened. On the stove there is a pot of beans. Curiously, the pot is not scorched. The beans are warm, cooked by the blaze.

Carmencita's other neighbors trickle in to assess the damage, thanking God it wasn't them. Pandora, the crazy old half-breed Indian woman, who lives with the old Puerto Rican junkie who had the heart attack last year. They want to know what happened to the cat.

"Everything ruined, huh, honey," Pandora cries. "*Mira! Mira!* If you need anything . . . hear?"

Paco pushes past her, muttering, "*Mala suerte! Mala suerte!*" He looks inside the apartment, covers his eyes. He sees the woman from next door, the foreigner with the little baby. "Hello," he says. Then he discovers the pot of beans on the stove. He picks a spoon off the floor, wipes it on his pajama pants and helps himself from the pot.

Carmencita wonders if it is true what they say about Carlos, that he has set the fire to be rid of her. Welfare would get her a new apartment now, they would buy her new clothes, new furnishings. Carlos would help her and the kids get started, but he would never move in. She sees it all now. After they were all moved, she would ask him where he is staying. He would say the street or the gym or a friend or his cousin. Things like that happened, she knew. Eventually he would just disappear.

It is five o'clock on a winter night, already dark, everybody running up and down the stairs with flashlights when the front door to the building opens with a bang and slams shut. Carlos DeJesus stomps into the hall.

"Mother*fookers!*" he bellows, and mounts the stairs.

The group of them on the roof. Homesteaders, tenants, firemen, cops, city inspectors. Carlos stops, framed in the roof doorway, the smashed bulkhead skylight lying in rubble at his feet. The smell of fire overpowering.

They are standing around a ragged hole in the roof, a huge opening, four by six feet. The firemen cut this hole to allow the smoke to escape, chimney effect, the same reason they have pulverized the hall skylight with its triangular panes of filth stained, century-old glass.

"You motherfookers," DeJesus says, "who started this?"

"Who says it was started?"

"I am not blind, *hombre.* I see the hole. I smell the gasoline."

"It's interesting you're saying it's arson. I find no trace of accelerant here." This from the fire marshal.

"I smell it."

"Without the can, without someone standing here with a match . . ." The fire marshal shrugs.

"You could have burnt down the building!" the *maricón* from across the hall screeches in his face. "We all know what you've done. You've been threatening long enough. Admit it!"

"You accuse me, you cocksucker? I should throw you

off the roof!" DeJesus is enraged, outraged, hurt, insulted. He pounds his chest. "It was *you!*" he shouts, angrily pointing at Mewie. "You! All of you." He takes a deep breath to catch himself. "My son is right. One Puerto Rican family in the building. Then a fire. And who should burn? The Puerto Ricans. No one else."

The man looks like Che, and he knows it. He named his first son with Carmencita after Che Guevara's compadre Fidel Castro. He wears an army jacket and a military beret. On the front of the beret he wears a rhinestone pin of an elephant. In the summer he wears a straw Chinese coolie hat. He named their second child William Guillermo Morales, little Willie, after the Puerto Rican revolutionary hero who blew both his hands off while making bombs in Mexico, and still used the stumps to shoot his gun at the Federales when they came for him.

"Gennelman! Gennelman!" the fire marshal begs, taking DeJesus by the arm and walking him downstairs, saying something soothing to Carlos in Spanish as they pass into the stairwell. They stand together for a few moments, speaking in lowered tones.

Back in his apartment DeJesus finds the cat, Diablito, charred and growing stiff. He picks up the carcass, looks at it, mutters a benediction, and tosses it out the window where, five stories below, it lands with a thump.

# 20

# The Return of Benny

Benny shows up three days after Christmas, six days after the fire. He thinks everything is cool.

Once again replete in fatigues, sitting in Mewie's apartment, he brags to Mewie and me that he's AWOL from the army. This time the Ecuadorian National Service.

Benny's all excited about the fire, wants to know every detail, how everyone reacted, what DeJesus did, what he said, what about Segundo, Nubia, where was Mewie, who discovered the blaze, but can't sit still to listen, blurts out the questions rapid-fire, pacing Mewie's floor, looking out the window, scanning the street, his eyes aglow, going on before you can speak, not listening, hot words spilling from his mouth, spilling, spilling, does he know what he's saying, does he care?

"Cool out, dude."

"Serves him right. Burn the fucker *down.*"

Mewie touches his eye and adjusts the patch he wears

over it. Somebody helping him sweep the floor at the club, where he been rehired, caught him with a broomstick. He peels the patch back. "How does it look?"

Ugh. Nasty is how it looks.

Benny explains that he was stationed in Esmeraldas, in the northwest. "Biggest, strongest niggers you ever seen. Worked on the river as loggers. Muscles on muscles. It was impressive," he says. "Impressive."

Benny tells us his old man thinks it's a joke he's a soldier again.

While he was there in Ecuador, Benny says, he took a side trip to the village where Beneficio came from. Benny actually tracked down his ancient grandma, living in a hut in the mountains outside the village. She spit at him once she understood who he was. He laughs when he tells it. This old withered Indian lady hawking on his army boots.

Benny says it was nothing against him. His grandmother still held a grudge against his grandfather. When Benny's father was five his father took him to the U.S. and never brought him back. Beneficio's mother never saw her son again. And now, forty-five years later, a dude comes back, says he's her grandchild. She didn't want any part of it.

Benny says his mother's descended from Viking blood, but on his father's side they were Otavalan Indians from the mountains north of Quito. His grandfather was a merchant. He stood on norteamericano street corners and sold beads and blankets and weaving, while his wife and son waited for him in Ecuador. He was standing on Collins Avenue in Miami, a handsome tall Indian man in white pants, blue ruana, long silky black hair braided down his back, when a schoolteacher on vacation from Minnesota saw him and decided she'd like to have some of that. Benny's grandfather returned to his village, told his wife he wanted his son to learn the ways of the world early and brought him back to America with him, and Beneficio never returned home or saw his mother again. To this day doesn't want to. "Won't hear of it when I talk to him about it," Benny says. "Can't blame him, old lady probably spit on him too."

Benny's grandmother didn't speak any English or Spanish. She only spoke Quechua. "Six million Indians speak Quechua in Latin America," he tells me. "Dig it, the Russians actually broadcast radio propaganda in Quechua."

Benny asks if I know anything about the Incas. Did I know, for example, that Pizarro invaded with only twenty-six men? That he took Atahualpa, the Incan Sun King, prisoner on a day when the conquistadores killed till they couldn't lift their arms? They killed three thousand Indians and the Incas killed zip Spanish, didn't even wound anyone superficially. "Superior weaponry," Benny explains. Another thing: Did I know Pizarro kept Atahualpa in a room twenty-eight feet long, eighteen feet wide and eight feet high and he wasn't going to let him go until emissaries sent to every corner of the Incan empire had collected enough gold to fill the room? That the Spanish didn't just take the gold, but stomped every platter and chalice into the ground till they were flat as pancakes? That on the day the room was finally filled, Pizarro escorted Atahualpa into the courtyard and instead of letting him go with a grand celebration like he had promised, garroted him in front of the very people who thought of him as the sun?

Benny stands up, smirks, and, for Mewie's benefit, says, "I am Atahualpa with just the right amount of Erika the Red!"

"So let me get this straight, buddy." I say. "You joined up without your parents' permission. After they moved to Florida, you ran away and enlisted?"

"Correct."

"You trained in Georgia."

"Correct."

"You were crack military, but you didn't dig it."

"They busted my hump."

"So?"

"So, I tole 'em I'm sixteen. I say, fuck you guys. I got

double citizenship, dude. I'm Ecuadorian, I'm an American.
I'll go down South America and fight."

"Okay, so you're down in Ecuador—Quito, right?"

"Esmeraldas, on the coast. I told you, you don't listen."

"What were you doing?"

"My job was to guard the border Ecuador shares with
Colombia."

"What were you looking for?"

"We were looking for *base* or *pasta,* anything going up
to the coke labs in Colombia. We were looking for guerrillas,
man, *banditos.* "

"You liked that?"

"The coke was good. The *hierba* was good. *Punta roja.*
I liked that. The uniforms were pathetic. Everything mismatched. You can get better stuff at the war surplus outfit-
ters here in the city. Sometimes, man, you wouldn't believe
it, the pants had patches, big fucking black stitches on the
ass. I showed them my *Soldier of Fortune* magazines and
they grasped the style, but it didn't interest them. There's
soldiers who take themselves more seriously than these
Ecuadorians."

"Is that why you came home?"

"I walked away. So what?"

"You been in two armies now. The U.S. and now the
Ecuadorian, and you're not quite seventeen years of age, is
that correct?"

"That's right. I lied here, I lied there. I'm sixteen, bro.
How old are you?"

"Amazing."

"That's right. Listen, any sucker who's been brought
up on the street like I have is a survivor, no two ways about
it. Listen, you're talking about Segundo DeJesus all the
time, right, you and Mewie and Ike and all them dudes?
Segundo's nothing, bro. The DeJesuses are a thing of the
past. There's a modern warrior out there today. No conscience. Not a long future. One day soon you gonna feel the
whole world shudder, man."

He waits for my response. Mewie coughs.

"I don't have to tell you who that modern warrior is, do I, Mr. Peltz?"

"No, Benny, you don't."

"You know what's next for me? I'm gonna wait till I'm eighteen, then I'm going to navy flying school, fly one of them airplanes works like a video game. Shoot the shit out of somebody, haven't quite decided who!"

# 21

# A Dirty
# Rotten Copper
# on Every Corner

Unseasonably, miraculously warm. Southern winds blowing north, almost frightening in their heat. Dense cloud cover, and from the roof all we can see is the thick underside of the Empire State Building. Closer, the Mutual of New York Insurance Building, MONY, its lights illuminating the white underbelly of the sky. Annabelle and I sit on the deck chairs, the baby asleep in her wicker basket at our feet. She's outgrown it, she's growing fast, faster than I can imagine. We're sitting silently, watching the clouds momentarily break up, allowing the moon to show through the shredded haze, then the clouds clump back together and all is melded, nothing to see, only a thick clotted sky and dampness in the air. Annabelle sighs.

She stretches a little in her canvas deck chair, the feet of which I can see are eating through the tar-paper roof. If Yves came up here now, he'd have a fit to see this. He's on my mind when the bulkhead door opens and out step Spike and Mazie. They're arguing loudly, and seeing us doesn't deter them at all.

"How are you, dear?" Mazie says to Annabelle. "Wherever did you get that lovely tunic? And the baby!" She continues. "Such a beauty! How old is she now, sweet thing?"

Annabelle is about to tell her when Spike cuts in. "Enough of the small talk," he growls. "I'm not finished with you yet."

"Not finished with *me*," Mazie snorts. "That's a laugh. It's me who finishes with you, not the other way around."

If I were Spike, I wouldn't dispute that assessment. Seeing them in action was a laugh, all right. Those two could never agree on anything, and now that Spike was hitting it big in the art trade, his thinking was distorted.

But his style was unique, I'll say that for him, although personally I could take it or leave it. His influence, he said, was an Eastern European Jew who speed-painted in the Catskills using pieces of toilet paper instead of brushes. The guy's name was Morris Katz and he'd set the world record for the fastest canvas ever painted, completed in forty-four seconds flat. A waterfall and a deer drinking at a forest pool. Katz painted it in front of an audience at Kutsher's and sold it on the spot. According to Spike the guy had sold almost 140,000 canvases in his career, most of them priced at $19.95 or less.

Working in the delicatessen was another major influence on Spike's work. He said he had deli in the blood, his father being a waiter and him having worked in half-a-dozen New York delis throughout his youth. Instead of brushes or bathroom tissue, Spike had taken to painting with chunks of salami and corned beef. He also smeared pigment on kaiser rolls and wedges of rye bread. He attacked his canvases, using the sopping delicatessen to create weird textures, but everything was representational, Neo-Delicatessen, he called it, even though he said he didn't like labels. Having worked in some of Manhattan's most famous eateries, he did all the stars and ball players and the internationally known business big shots who lunched at the long formica tables, painted them all yapping away and stuffing their faces, all of them completely nude, their sandwiches hovering about six inches off the table, and somehow the stuff caught on, not only downtown in the trendy new galleries, but uptown as well, on Fifty-seventh Street and Madison Avenue. The big question, the one that intrigued the art world and culture mavins, being: Would the flanken and gefilte fish he glued to his canvas, would it rot away?

Spike swore it wouldn't, keeping secret the reason why, and I only found out later how he could make such a claim. Nothing was real, nothing was as it seemed, everything was resin and papier-mâché, made by a Japanese ersatz-sushi maker in SoHo. The pickles weren't actually pickles, although the pickle juice was, the essence caught with a sort of scratch-and-sniff mentality, and maybe this is what gave the works their charm. Their distinct odor was part of the package, part of the attraction. Anyway, the late Leo Steiner from the Carnegie and the other big deli men were Spike's biggest fans, and every show sold out, just like Julian Schnabel's show might, or LeRoy Neiman's, and people put their names on lists to buy his work and he wasn't making chopped liver either, they were going for ten or fifteen thousand a pop, major money in my book.

When I told Annabelle about it, she yukked it up. "How could that be?" she wanted to know. I took her down to Spike's studio and showed her around, stale bits of sandwiches on glass palettes, let her look and take it all in, but still she couldn't fathom it. "This culture!" she muttered. One day, she told me, she sat Mazie down and grilled her, wanted to know every little detail of Spike's professional life, just between us girls, because Spike seemed like such an inept fool at times, so self-centered, and I was bringing home the papers and she was seeing Spike's name in the gossip columns, not to mention the downtown trendy magazines and art glossies, but who was this Spike, besides our next-door neighbor, him saying he's the next Picasso, and justifiably taking a huge amount of flak for saying it?

"That's how it is," he complained. "Everybody's jealous."

"They won't be around the building long," Annabelle told me. "The kind of money he makes, I bet they move to SoHo or NoHo or LoBro, one of those places."

"AssHo," I told her. He's interested in the hot new area above Houston surrounding Astor Place.

Annabelle said she would wish them well, but wouldn't be sad to see them go. She could take Spike or leave him and felt the same about Mazie, whom she considered obnoxious and impossible to deal with, uninteresting and all the rest. But I suspect she might've softened up a bit if Mazie had offered to take the baby once or twice, but she never did, she never offered to do anything, she was not helpful in the least.

One day I'm sitting in my crib when a knock comes on the door. The baby's sleeping in her cradle, and I'm looking at the newspaper I brought home from the newsstand the night before. There's a long article written by Howard Cosell and he's explaining why he quit broadcasting boxing, that he'll never telecast another match because of what happened to Muhammad Ali, who slurs his words and is giving signs of brain injury, *dementia pugilistica*, although no one connected with the sport will admit it. I guess Howard never realized getting punched in the head repeatedly does that to you.

At the door I find a highly agitated Mewie. Segundo has been around the building while Mewie wasn't home, at the invitation of Benny, and has stolen more of Mewie's marijuana, this time harvesting the crop under the bathroom halogen lights, not a stalk left. Mewie swears he's going to kill Segundo, if not elicit some satisfactory retribution that will leave him crippled for life or insane. I tell

Mewie about the Cosell article, and suggest he might interest Segundo in a boxing career. Mewie could volunteer as
Segundo's trainer, overmatch him brutally and thus exact
his pound of flesh from the skinny little twerp. Mewie thinks
this is hysterically funny, but only for a second. Then he's
back into his tirade about what happened to his good grass,
from Afghani seeds, the leaves so broad and green . . . and
the baby stirs and begins to cry.

I pick her up, drape her over my shoulder and pat her
back. Why's she always crying? Something wrong? I ask
Mewie if he'd go to the freezer and get Annabelle's milk,
which she's expressed and frozen, and defrost it in the microwave (a thoughtful present from my parents, though
Annabelle loathes it) so we can feed the stuff to the baby
and she'll be quiet, and we can continue our ruminations
and decide how to take apart the DeJesuses, who remain our
sworn enemies, the ones we are pitted against, life and
death, and must dissect and defeat, keep them away once
and for all.

"Victory can be ours!" Mewie proclaims, "if only we
plan a final strategy, Joe. They're over with. They're history.
Finally they don't live here anymore, they're out. Now all
we have to do is keep them away, keep them on the run. Let
me tell you what happened to me, and what I should've
done in order to have won, instead of letting that little
bastard get the best of me, not to mention about three
ounces of very good marijuana which I was not prepared to
part with, not under any circumstances and certainly not
under these."

Mewie, always looking for support, threatening to take
things into his own hands if we don't do something immediately about DeJesus. No more negotiations, no more talks,
just get rid of him and every last one of his family, including
little Fidelito and little William Guillermo Morales, the two
childlike ones, whom Mewie now accuses of making pee-pee
and ca-ca outside his door on purpose, and wailing all night,
every night, "Didn't you hear them, Joe?" the washing

machine overflowing all the time, why you think, but those two little kids dirtying their clothes every day, making so much laundry, and don't you think Carmencita would do something to discourage them from messing themselves, or at least take it to the Peoples' Laundromat on Avenue D or the *laundería* on Seventh Street between B and C rather than do load after load, day after day in that tiny portable? And I tell him I have my doubts about that *laundería*, where I heard a woman was raped one Sunday morning, or maybe it was a girl. And Mewie says, "Good, maybe it will happen to them." He rubs his hands together. "Oh, I'd like to see that."

"Mewie," I say, "that's not a nice way to talk."


Led by Beer Can, the block association assembles in the basement of one of the apartment buildings across Avenue E to meet with community relations officers from the local precinct and map out strategy, how to keep drugs off the block.

The charge is the police let the narcotics business flourish. Asked why they allowed it, no answer is forthcoming, only a series of shrugs and I-don't-knows.

"Community Relations Officer O'Malley, what do you have to say? We have a problem here."

This is a family neighborhood. What is bad here is the drugs, the way they've been allowed to proliferate, and no one does a damn thing about it.

It's an outdoor drug supermarket. People marvel at it, they're actually mesmerized, fascinated. How else do you account for all those writers and artists running off at the mouth about it, and how does it get into all the literature and magazine articles and movies?

Beer Can introduces me. "Cultural Liaison Officer Sheeny, Jo-Jo Peltz."

"Glad to meet you, sir."

"Jo-Jo is president of EAT CO, the 310–312 E Avenue Tenants' Corp."

"Is that a fact?"

It's a crime really, the fascination, the preoccupation the culture has with C and D, and now this crack thing. What the fuck's that?

"Crack is whack, Joe. There's gonna be a purge, a real pogrom. Don't be down on the books as a drug abuser, Peltz!"

Myself, I have my doubts. Here's my confession (but this is for your eyes only, don't let O'Malley or Sheeny see it): Before I lived here, before I met Annabelle, I came down to the neighborhood to score. Man, I loved the drugs, I loved the action, I loved the street scene, so cool, so fine, pitting my wits against theirs. Of course, they knew who I was. I was the white boy. The white junkie. White on white, right? Papa, you reading this? Don't be angry, Dad, okay?

"We want to get rid of all this crap," Spike stands and addresses the gentrifiers. "This neighborhood is our neighborhood. We want it back. We demand it back!" (This draws applause.) He goes on. "Like what people did with the parks, right? Just a few short years ago, the parks were no-man's-land. No one would go into them. And at night, forget it. They were off-limits, home to only hoodlums and thieves. Then what happened? The country was swept by the fitness craze. The entire white middle class out jogging. Everyone of the absence-of-color persuasion and the fat-wallet contingent wanted to be in top shape, breathe deep, run, skate, bicycle. Obsessed."

Spike's right. A man can't exercise on the street of this city, competing with crazed taxicabs, trucks, car traffic, whathaveyou. Citizens need parks for that shit. Spike spoke to the point, told how it was, how we, the people, took the parks back. Sure, there was a skirmish. The turning point was when a black mugger walloped a white stockbroker on the head in Central Park and stole his eight-hundred-dollar ultralight alloy bicycle. The cyclist was clocked well enough to die. An outraged crowd gathered and chased the culprit down. They got the guy and he's off to the can, fifteen to twenty-five at Elmira even though he's only sixteen, and the New York population breathes a collective sigh of relief. One down, a few hundred thousand more bad apples to go.

Segundo DeJesus, could you step front and center, please? This land is our land, you little scumbag. Understand?

New York City's always had this problem with immigrant people. It's nothing new.

"The poor are not comrades-in-arms."

"Even if you love the poor, in a neighborhood on the way up, they're the enemy, pure and simple. . . ."

"What can we do, Officer Sheeny? Officer O'Malley, please. Help us!"

"Drug dealers are your main enemy. Crack is whack, as we said. You ever hear about the neighborhood crime watch? Help yourselves!"

"And you help us too!" a voice in the crowd shouts. I think it's Beer Can or Mewie.

"What do you want us to do?" Officer Sheeny asks, suddenly defensive. "We can't put a cop on every corner."

"Why the hell not?" Spike shouts. "Why the hell not? We need protection!"

# 22

# Have a Nice Day!

Seven o'clock in the morning, the day following the all-night block meeting, and one of the few days Constance is actually sleeping late, and now Pandora's calling Paco in the well. Her voice comes in my window and I say, "Shut the fuck up!" but probably not loud enough for her to hear, only loud enough for Annabelle, who moans and stretches and looks dreamy and sour.

I already told you what Mewie and the others say about Pandora, didn't I? That she killed her first husband. Shot him down. How many years ago was that? Maybe not that many. I asked Yves. He was the one who told me.

Twenty? Thirty? He didn't know. Ten?

Pandora came here more than thirty years ago. Did she kill her husband before or after?

Delilah's her daughter, but who's the daddy? Not Paco?

No, not Paco. Delilah's her daughter with the dead cowboy.

Delilah said her mother would kill again. Kill for love. And Paco's the man, bro.

Pandora's loud voice. Overweight physique. Big enough to kill.

"Shut up!"

So I'm not the only one she woke up. Sounds like Benny. Then another voice, Dagmar. "Shut up, you old bag."

Dagmar got Delilah to spread all kinds of stories about Pandora around the buildings, up and down the block. Dagmar, a gossip, a real troublemaker. He loves to get all the pill-selling stories going, all the detriment. And Delilah, poor dumb Delilah. She'll wind up sending her own mother back to the reservation. Dagmar set her against her own mother. What Delilah doesn't realize is that the more she hates Pandora, the more she grows to look like her every day. And sound like her.

"Shut up!" Delilah screeches.

See, you can't tell the difference.

Paco's supposed to go to the methadone clinic. A man drives up outside in a beat-up Chevy and sits in the car in front of the hydrant, sounding the horn. Beeeeeeeeeep. When Paco don't show, he yells up. "Paaacoooo!" Pandora comes to the window and screams down. "What you want?" Wakes up the whole neighborhood. The baby is crying now.

Paco's friend from the methadone, he says the very same thing I say, but louder. "Shut the fuck up, you old cow! When Paco coming down?"

"He ain't home!" Pandora screams. "He never coming down!"

After that, for whatever reason, I don't have any spirit, can't drag myself out of bed. The baby's still crying, Annabelle's grumbling.

I take the baby downstairs, give her some cereal and a bottle, then take her across the street to the daycare.

Velma's sitting there, her face ashen. It's eight o'clock.
She says, "Joe . . ."

"What's the matter?" I say.

"I don't know, something."

"Velma . . ."

"Some of these parents. Joe, I think there's a child
being sexually abused. . . ."

"The world's in a state," my uncle said when I got to work.
He had the papers spread in front of him and he was sucking
on his teeth. His upper plate was clicking inside his mouth.
I kidded him, said his teeth sounded like a metronome. He
didn't know what that was, thought it was the stadium
where the Twins played, but he knew he didn't like it.

"The world's always been in a state," I said. "It's no
worse now than it's ever been."

"Yes, it is," he said. "Joe, your generation's fucking up
—royally, and there's no two ways about it. Why don't you
people get responsible?"

My father stepped up. The two of them stood in their
newsstand, looking out on Broadway. Leonardo walked
down the block, nodded to them and strolled into the burlesque after telling me to quit slacking off and get to work.
The crowds were breaking from the Wednesday afternoon
matinees, and some of them started buying the afternoon
*Post*. The headlines were about a model whose face had
been sliced up by a razor. Couldn't help reminding me of
Annabelle, except the girl in the *Post* is cut up a lot worse,
and Annabelle didn't get no publicity. The guy who did it
was a Jewish kid from Queens. The story said the reason he
did it was because the girl had demanded he return her
security deposit after she had sublet his apartment. How
much does an apartment like that cost?

"Don't make no sense," the Yitz said. "What's it in-
volve, a few hundred bucks? Nobody does something like
that for that kind of money."

"People do it, all right," I said, "just not Jewish boys. That's what you're saying, right?"

"Watch your mouff, Joe. You know lately, you got this attitude like you know better than others. You don't know. You don't know shit."

"Maybe not."

"No maybes about it."

"It was two *shvartzers*," my father said, "working for this Jewish kid."

"I saw them on *Good Morning America* this morning," I told them. "The black kid's parents said he was a good kid. Told the reporter he went to the Jewish kid's bar mitzvah."

"When was that?"

"Drugs is what it is, Joe," my uncle said. "Your whole generation is hooked on drugs. Look at you."

"Me?" I looked at him. "I don't take drugs."

"Bullshit!"

"No more. I kicked."

"Yeah, you reformed."

"Leave off him," my father told my uncle. "He don't deserve it. He's doing all right."

My uncle grunted, muttered under his breath, "Man's a crack addict."

A few minutes later they had packed up their flight bags and were ready to head for the RR at Forty-ninth Street and head to Queens, pick up the car where they parked it near the subway and drive home. The pile of *Posts* with the model story was almost gone. A short stack of *Daily Newses* was still there from the morning, and quite a few *Timeses*. *New York Newsday* with its color front page was there too. Its headlines weren't about the girl, but about the nuclear disaster in Chernobyl. That wasn't my generation fucking up, but who cared. I looked up into the sky. The article said a million reindeer would have to be destroyed. The Lapps were "visibly upset." I could just see a strip of gray up there above the B'way. The flickering lights from the Gotham caught my eye. Then a guy said, "Hey, Mac, you carry *El Diario?*" I looked at him. It was Attila the bum, DeJesus's lawyer, leering crazily at me.

"Señor Peltz," he said, "I'd like to talk to you."

"To me?"

"Yes. About our common problem."

"Do we have a common problem?" I asked.

Here's something. Before I was gonna be a doctor, I was gonna be a cop, like my mother's cousin, Meyer. You know him? He was married to a reporter for the old *Journal-American*. Remember that newspaper? When I was a kid he used to bring me trucks. Drive up to the house, his beautiful wife riding shotgun. He'd get out, open the trunk and there was a toy truck. Fire truck, gasoline tanker, paddy wagon. A truck for me, a hot typewriter or stethoscope for my sister. "Meyer," I used to say, "one day I'm gonna be a policeman, just like you."

He'd say, "No, Jo-Jo, you be something else. Something smarter." Pinching my cheek. "You go to school, be a doctor like your sister wants to be."

"I don't want to be a doctor," I says. "A police officer's for me."

Poor Meyer. He went out not too long after that, when I was how old? Twelve. A month after Quai Dong, a month after my sister. A hell of a year. Old one nine six three. My mother said it shook him up, shook Meyer good, seeing that flag-draped casket.

Did he get shot down? No. Heart attack on the job? A young man cruising Bushwick Avenue, some guy grabs a gold chain or a purse? Cousin Meyer in plain clothes strolling by gives chase, a block later he's lying gasping on the sidewalk, clutching his heaving . . . That wasn't it. He pulled his car into the garage, closed the door, sucked fumes, didn't leave a message. My mother was beside herself, inconsolable. Another one who grew up on Avenue E, fucked by the promised land. The place was cursed. America. Maybe no one knew it yet, but they were going to find out. Maybe not in my lifetime, maybe not in yours, but in the lifetime of our kids—Constance, poor Constance. I hate to say it, but maybe that's why she's always weeping, always crying—because she knows. America could have been beautiful for her, for me, but it's cursed and my kid knows it, can smell it, taste it, sense it. How many from my family, those I know, struck down before their time? Meyer, my sister, still more . . .

Sitting at my kitchen table, my grandmother said the biggest indicator of what was to come was some cousins of ours, a poor immigrant family who arrived on this block from Rumania. My grandmother was only a little girl, maybe only three or four years in the country herself. They came, the immigrant cousins, and moved into the building next door. "Not your building, Joe, but the one across the well, 312, in that apartment right there."

She pointed to Paco and Pandora's open window.

"The first night ve all came to visit, velcome them to the promised land. They vere cousins of cousins, I don't remember the exact relationship," my grandma said. "Ve brought them kreplach, crocretzel, cholly, homentashen. They vere very nice people. After ve left, they blew out the lights, and vent to sleep. They never voke up. The next morning they vere all dead. They didn't understand America. The technology. How things vurked here. They didn't have such things in Europe. The gas from the vall lamp killed them. They didn't know any better, they didn't know from gas jets."

Welcome to America, neighbors.

"But you can't blame a whole country for vhat happens, Joe."


My mother said she walked the streets—Avenue E, Sixth Street, Seventh Street, Eighth Street—after I came back.

And had she, as a little girl, ever dreamt that one day she'd be walking these very streets where she grew up, wheeling her granddaughter in front of her?

Attila stands in front of me at the newsstand.

"Mr. Peltz," he says, "or perhaps I should call you Joe, or even José. More Spanish, more neighborhood. How you like it? José, we have something to speak of together, you and me. This fire," he says, "I don't like this fire."

Everything is settled, then it's not settled. DeJesus is satisfied, then he's not. He wants to know who did it, who set the fire, then he doesn't care.

"He says he's ready to make a deal, yes, but the money means nothing. He says his son no longer talks to him, calls him a *maricón,* for even speaking with you and your corporation. This hurts him."

I tell him I can't help that.

Attila says he thinks I can. He knows it. He wants me to fess up, tell him what I know.

I go, *"Señor . . ."*

"It's no good," Attila tells me. "No good. I have a list. Let me give it to you. It's inclusive. Only add a hundred dollars more for Carlos's mink coat."

I say, "Attila, I got this mouton coat. It's beautiful. Full length. When I wear it on the street, you can't believe the people who stop me. I want Carlos to have it, in partial recompense for what happened. . . ."

One day I'm thumbing through the *Village Voice* and there's Attila's face staring out at me at a painful angle, twisted and ungainly, chin tucked into neck, struggling to escape from the camera. The article said Attila had gained control over a city-run daycare located at the Consejo Community Center on Delancey Street. He'd hired his wife and all his cousins and paid them excessively. He himself worked for only a dollar a year, but his wife was earning more than a hundred thousand.

When I showed the article to Annabelle, she shrugged. "Fair is fair," she said. "Maybe he's the only counsel DeJesus can get. It's no wonder they caught him, though. They're probably looking for guys like him."

"Guys like him?"

"You know, third-world, white-collar," she said. "Didn't they get the chancellor of schools or something, another young Spanish guy, Alvarado? They put these token Puerto Ricans in, then can't wait to shout corruption. Welcome to America, land of opportunity."

"I guess so."

"So what did he want?" Annabelle inquires.

"Who?"

"Attila. Didn't you say he came to visit you at your job?"

I pulled out the list and showed it to her.

Carmencita's name was at the top. Attila explained it was a rundown of the DeJesuses' losses from the fire. He claimed Carlos didn't want no money for himself, but for his family, help them get settled, maybe return to Puerto Rico.

I don't want to say too much about this list, only that the ONE HUNDRED DOLLARS IN CASH category is valued at five hundred dollars. This might just be an oversight on Carlos's part, because all the figures add up, everything is worth eleven thousand dollars just as it's supposed to, or maybe it's a comment on the times, their inflationary aspect, who knows?

In Carlos's list there are more dollar figures than explanations. These extra "losses" are not described. Maybe he lumped some things together or simply ran out of space. For example, did Carmencita and Nubia really spend a thousand dollars on cosmetics, and was it all lost in the fire? Maybe Carl himself was buying expensive foundation. Very expensive.

Could be. Anything's possible.

What would you estimate the price of *TWO CANARIES IN THEIR GAGES* at? It's hard for me to believe the real cost is $210, but these might be rare birds or fabulous "gages."

Maybe it's *BOOKS* and *TROPHIES* or *FOOD STAMPS* all lumped together. I mean is little seven-year-old Fidelito's wardrobe worth $275 or $250 or $180 or $500 or what? The kid ain't a bad dresser. And maybe his clothes fit the canaries. Hand-me-downs for the birds. It might not be a bad act for Leonardo and the Gotham burlesque: *Fidelito DeJesus and his Dancing Canaries! First Time Out of the Neighborhood.* Have to mention it to him.

Did you hear the one about the cat?

After the fire, Carlos came home, right? The cat was dead, burnt up, so Carlos tossed it out the window. This is the cat he's supposed to love!

Do you have a picture of what the man is like? Then he says, "Poor kitty! *Pobre gato! Pobre gatito!*"

Up yours, Carlos. Eleven thousand bucks my sweet ass!

Now is there any confusion as to what has happened here?

I live in a building, actually two buildings (tenement twins, one-hundred-year-old sisters), where the landlord abandoned his property. Live to let die. In the dim past, one building, invaded by junkies, had a fire. The top two floors burn up and the last few straggling tenants vacate. In the other building, heat and hot water are memories, the window frames are rotted, the hall tiles cracked and broken, the plaster falling down. Most of the tenants are gone, but a few remain. Carlos DeJesus never paid his rent, even though welfare gave him money to do so. "Not on your life, mother-fooker." Claims that his apartment is not fit for human habitation. So when a group showed up and said, "Tenants in common, we are your new landlord, from now on you pay your rent to us," he said, as a matter of principle, "Screw you, I never paid rent to the old one."

Nothing good happened, and tremendous animosity developed in the building. Here were all these people trying to work together and get the building together, and the DeJesuses, Carlos and his son, Segundo, and his daughter, Nubia, were doing their best to sabotage everything. One month the front door was repaired on four separate occasions. Someone kept kicking it in. There was no buzzer. If you don't have a key or someone doesn't run down, you can't get in. Carlos or Segundo kicked it in, someone kicked it in, so their friends could stroll in anytime they pleased without disturbing the family above to run down and open the door. After the door was repaired for the fourth time, the person or persons who did it, they put Super Glue on the key and broke it off in the lock.

They stole Mewie Cotton's marijuana, not once, but twice. When Mewie's lover came off the roof where he'd been sunbathing, and walked naked in the hall, they threw their trash in front of Mewie's door and set it on fire.

Carlos said, What would his baby think seeing naked men walking in the hall? He said, What if the *maricones* tried to suck Fidelito's dick? Or William Morales's dick? He'd kill them.

You can't blame him really. You heard what Velma said, that she suspects one of the parents over at the daycare of being a short eyes. Sick!


In Yves's words: *Pussy bumbers over there* (across the street) *and a bunch of queers over here* (our building).

And Yves is one of them.

But that doesn't make him or any of the others sexual offenders.

It certainly does not! What people do behind closed doors is their own business. Listen, the gay guys in my building, I like them all. Even Mewie, as sick as he is, has his charm.

But Jesus, you want a stable place to live. Poor little Constance. What's she going to think? Seeing naked men walking in hallways.

At Leshko's, Carlos's cousin Shorty said, "There were times, *cabrón*, when a Puerto Rican didn't come in here, into this restaurant. This was Polish turf."

"I remember."

"You was around then?"

"I was around," I said.

"No Puerto Ricans here. No Polish east of B. No Italians south of Tenth. No Jews either. Fuck the Ukrainians. We eat them for breakfast." Shorty was enjoying himself, on a roll.

"Listen, Shorty, I don't want to fight you."

"That's good, asswipe. I'd sweep the street with you."

That's all right, mon, we have to stick together.

"You burnt down my cousin's apartment."

"Who did?"

"You did, motherfucker!"

"Hey, let's not fight." Attila's the voice of reason. "Let's cool it, ain't that our plan? Hey, Joe, you sit over here. You, Shorty, you sit over here."

"Hey, when I got my face on nobody messes with me," Shorty said. "Otherwise I got a baby face, and if I don't put my face on, everybody messes with me and thinks I'm easy. But when I got my face, I'm the toughest." He scowled.

Mean son of a bitch. Scare that impacted shit right out of me. Everybody trying to play the white boy nine ways from the middle.

Here, Shorty, sit down, boy. That's a good boy.

Dagmar just looked on. The man with the big mouth didn't say word one.

And DeJesus never paid his rent. He was a disruption in the building, you understand? When Mewie accused Segundo of stealing his pot, DeJesus wanted to take him outside and beat him to a pulp. No weapons, only fists.

Mewie became hysterical.

"No weapons!" he shouted. "No weapons? He's a weapon. I'll kill him."

But the truth is, Mewie would need a howitzer. DeJesus would make short work of him and love every minute of it. DeJesus is a mammoth weight lifter, an ex-professional wrestler. He snarls and the cave quivers.

What are we going to do with this man?

Burn him out?

Good suggestion, Joe. Very bright that you put it in print. Would the prosecutor please step forward?

"Mr. Peltz?" He glares at me. Title stamped on his forehead says ASSISTANT D.A., NEW YORK COUNTY. "Sir, are you ready to confess to the charge of arson in the first degree? Specifically to the spreading of gasoline and the torching of Mr. DeJesus's apartment? Stand up, Mr. DeJesus, so Mr. Peltz can have a good look at you. All right, Peltz, this is the final question I'm going to ask you! Are you a burnout, Mr. Peltz?"

Prime the firing squad! Peltz, stand up against that wall there.

Sir?

Stand up against the wall! Don't you hear? Can someone affix this paper heart to his chest? . . . Thank you. Ready on the left! Ready on the right!

It was justified.

What's that, convict?

It was justified, sir. I did the right thing.

What? You did what? It's too late for excuses, Mr. Peltz.

Ready . . . aim . . . *FIRE!*

\* \* \*

Carmencita seemed like a nice woman. I didn't really know her. And the kids, Fidelito and little Willie, they were cute.

It is only once they're grown that they seem to turn vicious.

There's no excuse. Not if you've burnt the son of a bitch out.

Not me, man. I told you already. What do I have to say? I didn't do it, I didn't do it, but I have my suspicions who did.

Ah, finally, some cooperation . . .

"I know who did it," DeJesus says. "And the guy, he hates Puerto Ricans."

Oh, man. Not that again. I don't hate anybody. It's not the way I was brought up. Ask my folks. Peace, love, *fleurs*, man. I've been in situations where people of different colors get together, bro. I got nothing against people of different color or different language or different inflection, religion, curiosity, whatever, I believe in humanity, don't this guy, why don't he buy my sincerity? It's genuine. It is.

I told Negrito, the Puerto Rican guy who lives below me, that if it was up to me, I'd've given DeJesus the god-damn apartment. I got nothing against him. What I don't understand in the first place is when this all started, this building, why weren't the people who lived here originally invited to join up? Why didn't they become part of the E Avenue Tenant's Corp. too?

"Joe!" Mewie protests. "If you only knew. We tried. We really did."

"White is might, right, Mewie?"

In a neighborhood like this, it's not so bad. This neighborhood's never been the melting pot, no matter what people lead you to believe. This is pre-melting pot where people maybe start to get used to each other, but mostly what they do is just boil over. Right now all we do is hate, and be scared, although the colored people ain't so intimidating in the neighborhood anymore, because they ain't so plentiful. We're learning to fight back. Most of the buildings are bombed out. There's fewer and fewer poor people left. We won't have to hear their language that much longer. Once this was the most densely populated area in the world. Now? Where all those people go? They're somewheres else, bro, maybe in your neighborhood. You see them coming, beware!

My mother's friend was asking me about Fifth Street, is the school still there? I said, "Sure, it's still there, but it's the only building standing on the block."

The only people left around here are bone pickers, New York City piranha. But these scavengers leave that dirty carcass, they don't pick them bones clean. Look about me, oh how nice, ticks and roaches, silverfish and lice.


Mewie tells me the government's giving cheese away down here. People line up all the way around the block, stretching from the church, for a big block of orange cheese. Federal government got more cheese and milk than they know what to do with. The starving people in Africa could use some, but Mewie says Howard Kumundga told him they're lactose intolerant. African people can't digest milk products.

Is that true? I never heard that shit.


The poor people in the neighborhood frighten me. I'm on the front line. I'm a soldier. Joey Peltz at your service! I went to Brooklyn to look for a house. This was before Annabelle and I found the digs on Avenue E. She's pregnant, we're desperate. The house we saw was in a neighborhood that once was white, went black, then wanted to be white again.

The real estate agent was very aggressive. She was black, but the old bloods hanging on the stoops told her: "What you doing with that white man, woman? What you doing bringing the white man around our neighborhood?"

Beats me. Neighborhood busting? I didn't want to be there. The old blood thought I wanted to be on those mean streets when the revolution showed up? He's dead wrong.

Easy question: Whose side do you think DeJesus is on? Their side or mine? Or his own?

Whose side am I on? Don't be too quick. Don't prejudge. I might fool you.

The party line is: Everybody should get what they deserve. The haves and the have-nots. Let's redistribute the wealth. The only problem is I want to be sure to at least keep what I got. It's not so much. No way I want to be throwing everything I got over for the revolution. Just put me right there in the middle, half the people above me, half the people below me. Fucked and fucking.

So we're at the newsstand and I ask Attila what he wants from me. He says, "Want from you?" He doesn't want anything from me. He only wants to do the right thing. "Look, we both know Carlos, we know who he is. Carlos is not an educated man. He's led by his blood. His hot Indian blood. His scalding *castellano* blood. It drips in his eyes. He cannot see. We must be his eyes. We must tell him what to do."

"Look, if it was up to me . . ."

"I know," Attila says. "You are a good man. We both are. We both have only the best interests of Carlos DeJesus on our minds. We want to do the right thing. I have worked very hard in the neighborhood, on behalf of the people who live there. You have worked very hard on your building. Neither of us wants anything to happen."

"It's already happened."

"Your building could have burnt down, but it didn't."

"Because the guy who lived next door was quick."

"Because the one who set the fire exercised restraint with the gasoline."

"Perhaps."

"*Claro.* We both know, *señor.*"

"Do we?"

"Carlos says he did not burn his apartment. I believe him. You say you did not burn his apartment. I believe you."

"I saw your picture in the newspaper," I tell him. "I know you're in trouble."

He shrugs. "Trouble? I've been in trouble before. I always land on my feet, *gracias a Dios.* You, *señor,* you are actually the one who is in trouble. So far we have only negotiated. You have paid a small cash stipend. Carlos might accept a larger cash settlement. He could be satisfied. At this time it seems very fair what he offers. But things may happen, and in the future I may wonder if, in fact, your corporation has treated Carlos fairly. Somehow I think not."

"Listen, Attila."

"No, you listen, *señor.* I've come uptown for only one reason—to see you. Now that I see you, I think only one thing."

"Yeah, what's that?"

"I got you."

I didn't start the fire. What do I got to tell you? I didn't start the fire. I have Yves in front of me, and I'm telling him how I deal with DeJesus and Attila, and I'm saying how I got to be smarter than them. "I give them their heads, make them think they got me. I don't want no trouble. I don't want them coming back seeking vengeance."

"No, these are rough men, Joe."

"You know, Yves," I tell him, "it's not that I think I'm smarter than these guys, but it's like they're so fucking transparent, the way they treat me, the way they try to play me, like I don't fucking see their game."

"Who do they say set the fire?"

"They say you. They say Ike, me, Mewie. They don't know. DeJesus has plenty of enemies. Every junkie in the neighborhood hates his guts. The drug dealers might have burnt him out. Espina, those boys. Remember, his apartment looked out directly on Eighth Street, on all the dealing that went on down there. How many times did he run down there, his baseball bat at the ready? You know what I mean? He saw a lot."

"Who do you think burnt him, Joe?"

"Ah shit, I don't know."

Mewie comes out of his apartment, rubbing his eyes, smoking a joint. He crosses the hall and picks his way through the debris to stand with Yves and me at the blackened window of what was once DeJesus's apartment, looking down on the vacant lot and abandoned buildings. Our view sweeps across Eighth Street to Ninth. A group of men are busy picking bricks and bedsprings off the neglected expanse between the two streets.

An aroma of cat piss wafts out of Mewie's apartment with him.

"P.U. to you too, Mewie," I say.

He doesn't appreciate me. "What are they doing down there?" Mewie asks.

Yves says they're building a baseball field.

Mewie snorts. "A baseball field? What do they need that for? Who gave them permission?"

"The city," Yves says. "That guy Juan from Avenue C, he's been trying to get it for years. The city finally rented it to him for a dollar a year."

"How do you know so much?" Mewie demands.

Yves says Ike told him. Ike knows everything happening in the neighborhood.

I ask Mewie how come he's so annoyed. Does he have something against baseball?

"I suppose it's your favorite game, Joe. The American pastime, no? I suppose you played? A big bruiser like yourself, I'm sure you did." He's trying to get me back, don't you know.

"I played once," I tell him. "I was scouted by the pros.

I almost got drafted. My dream was I was going to be a doctor and a professional baseball player."

"Oh Joe! Poor Joe! Obviously crushed. What happened? Do tell . . ."

"My best friend hit me in the eye with his bat during a sandlot game. He was a kid half–American Indian, half-Jewish. I began to lose the vision in my right eye until, finally, I went legally blind, lost the sight in that eye completely. After that they wouldn't let me play anymore. Said insurance wouldn't cover it."

What was it really? My grandfather dying. Then Quai Dong—my sister killed overseas. Meyer the detective goes down in a garage in a back alley. I don't know. Do you understand? I just lost it. The fates were against me.

*"Quiero más ayuda! Quiero más ayuda!"*

Juan and the guys down below on the once and future ballfield are raking and singing, raking and singing. *"Quiero más ayuda! Quiero más ayuda!"* The song says they need more help. Don't they know everyone does? Ourselves included. If I still played ball, I'd be down there myself.

I sigh. Still a good anthem. *Oh say can you see . . .*

"This place sucks," I say.

"What's the matter?" Mewie asks.

"What's the matter! What's the matter! What's always the matter?"

"DeJesus is at it again," Yves explains.

"We should just have him killed," says Mewie, offering the simplest solution possible. "I'm serious. People come to the club all the time, would like to do it. I swear to God I could arrange it. It would be so much easier. I mean, why bother with the man? I've said it before."

"Mewie, give me a break."

"I'm serious, I'm telling you."

"Yeah, just like you were serious about burning him out."

"He's gone, isn't he?"

"He is. You telling me you're the one who lit the match?"

"Joe, Joe, Joe. Would I admit that, even if it were true?"

"You used to brag about the firemen who came to the club and offered to do it for you. You could be the one, Mew."

"Yeah, so? They did come in, and they did offer. But I never took them up on it. Frankly, I wish I had. I wouldn't have had to wait so long. I could kiss the one who did it to him. Burned him out. Oh, Joe, it's so much better without him here, don't you think?"

"It's a drag, Mewie. The aftermath, so messy."

"It'll end. All these negotiations. You'll come to some kind of settlement with him, and we'll never see him again."

"No."

"Isn't that how you see it, Joe?"

"It's how I used to see it. I don't know how I see it now."

"Do what's best for you, Joe," Yves says. "We all trust you."

I tramp down the stairs. These buildings are so much trouble. I knew it way back when, I was a sucker to become the president, but I did it. As I saw it, as I had discussed with Annabelle, I was the only one who could do it. Sacrifice myself for the short run for the benefit of everyone in the long. I wouldn't have to do it forever. I was no king, though. No way. Martyr, that's what I was.

On the second floor landing, Paco and Pandora's door opens a hair. Someone's watching me. Paco steps out. "Hello, Mr. Ju-Ju."

"Yeah?"

Pandora peeks out. "Joe? His name is Jo-Jo, Paco, not Ju-Ju."

"That's right! That's it! I'm sorry, mister. Sorry. Can I get you a cup of coffee, Ju-Ju. Need anything from the store? Cigarettes?"

Pandora takes my hand—"C'mere, honey"—and pulls me inside. She offers me a plate of cabbage soup, wants to know if it's true we discussed her at the shareholders' meeting. She says she *knows* we discussed her. That someone accused her of selling drugs.

"Who told you that?"

"Don't tell me it's not true! I know it's true. I don't have to tell you who said it, honey. Just let me say I'm gonna kill that fat Jew who lives down there." She points down the landing to where Dagmar lives with her daughter Delilah.

"Dagmar doesn't even come to meetings, Pandora. Only when he wants something. He hasn't been to a meeting in months."

"I respect you, Joe, you know that, but don't lie to me. He puts my stupid daughter up to it, and she don't know any better. Sets my own flesh and blood against me so's he can get my apartment when I'm gone. I know his game. I told Delilah to first keep her knees together, don't be so eager to spread her legs. You know what she did to me the other day, Joe? I call her. Delilah, honey, I say, go down to the corner for me, and get me some of that powdered instant cream for my coffee, and then I'll give you a cup. You know what she says? Can I have my coffee first! Honey, the coffee's not even made yet! You see what I'm saying, Joe? And that little cunt, excuse my American, that little cunt goes to your meeting with her old man and accuses me of selling drugs! My own daughter! Her own mother, and it's not even true! Paco's finally doing good—ain't he doing good lately, Joe?—and she's trying to ruin it. Let me tell you something. I have eleven brothers and seven sisters. Every Sunday used to be we'd all meet here and I'd make a big dinner for the whole family. We'd laugh and joke and have a good time because we were a big family and knew how to have a good time. None of them come anymore, and I'll tell you why. I won't let them. And you know why, Joe? Because of that big, fat Jew! That's why. No offense."

# 23

# Picturebook Rates

Last night someone went down the street with a piece of pipe and broke the rear passenger-side windows on seven cars, mine included. I woke up and heard the shattering of glass, the clatter and ring of the pipe as it bounced off the sidewalk.

Earlier, coming home, I walked pass Tompkins Square. It was after two in the morning. A woman strode toward me carrying a screaming kid in her arms. I told her, "It's past the kid's bedtime. Put the kid to sleep, he won't be crying."

"Fuck you," she said. "Mind your own business."

Like the time Annabelle and I had Constance out. We wanted her to walk, and she wanted to be carried. She lay down in the street and started screaming, flailing her legs, pounding the cement.

When Annabelle asked what we should do, I said leave her. She'll pick herself up and follow.

But she didn't, and a crowd gathered around her. A

man bent down and said, "I don't blame you one bit, kid, stay right where you are."

Another guy shouted, "Hey, you oughtn't to do that, leave your kid. They steal kids in this neighborhood, you know."

So I went back for her. I was gonna leave her, but I go back and slap her bottom. "You will obey!" I tell her. "You will obey! You will obey! You will obey!"

Annabelle said to be careful. Don't break her spirit. She said it was already hard enough for a little girl in this world.


Here we go again. "You're just paranoid," Scarlet tells Delilah.

We're all sitting on the stoop in the sun, it's the morning after the episode with the broken windows. Annabelle has a piece of cardboard and a roll of duct tape and is trying to temporarily repair the window on our car.

"Listen, Scarlet, I'm not," says Delilah, her voice rich, imploring. "I know what's going down. I know how things are with the people who live here, what their feelings are toward me and Dagmar and my mother. My mother lives in confusion, scandal. Dagmar fans the flames, but really, it has nothing to do with me."

Not likely.

Isn't this the same Delilah who walked the street, enticing the boys, enticing me for that matter, muttering, "Wanna try me? I am assassin."

"Listen, Dee, every day's a new day."

"I know, God loves me."

"That's right, and he's gonna look after you and protect you," Scarlet says, "and don't you worry none about what your mama and your hubby's gone and done, because it ain't no reflection on you."

"Is that so?"

"Nope. No nevermind."

Pretty soon Dagmar comes out of 312 and stands on the stoop, puffing his cigar.

Across the street, Velma opens the door to her building and the kids come streaming out. She carries down a double stroller and a red wagon, ready to lead the kids to the park.

Constance stands tottering on the top step. "Hi, Daddy," she calls. Then she sidles over to the rail, carefully lowers herself down. When she hits the ground she waves, then climbs onto the wagon and waits for the others.

"Joe," Dagmar says, "that's a cute kid."

Delilah concurs.

Dagmar tells me he had a cousin was a minister in a Puerto Rican church up in the Bronx. "How you like that —a Jewish minister sermonizing to a congregation of Puerto Ricans!"

"Yeah, the man's fully committed," Delilah says. "So committed he had his foreskin glued back on."

Dagmar explodes. "I swear to God, where you get your mouth from?"

She grins. "Do you have to ask? Wanna meet my mother? C'mon, I'll introduce ya."

"Where you brought up, Dagmar?" I ask.

"Right here, the good ole Lower East Side."

Sitting on the stoop, Dagmar thinks for a moment. "I don't know what makes a man give up his religion. I don't personally have no religion, but you would think a man wouldn't want no religion at all, wouldn't believe in it today, just forget about it, let it ride."

"These are godless times," I agree.

"Let's hope so," says Annabelle.

"Bye, Mommy," Constance shouts and waves, as Velma wheels the kids off. Yolanda is pushing the stroller.

"Man is just trying to find himself today," Dagmar says, "that's all that can be expected."

"How'd your cousin become a priest?" I ask.

He shrugs. "Don't know."

"He should have become a rabbi," I suggest. "Could've taken over the temple across the street."

"Gimme a break, will ya, Joe. No Jew in his right mind would ever take my cousin for a man of God. You don't know him. You listen to his rap when he's preachin', you'd have pity on him."

"Count your blessings," Delilah says, "he's not here."

"Listen, Joe, me and Delilah been thinking. We don't want to start any trouble, but there's some things we got to talk to you about. This whole DeJesus thing. How you gonna deal with it?"

Scarlet gives Dagmar a withering look, then she glares at me like it's my fault and splits.

"Dagmar don't want to start no trouble?" Delilah says.

"Go molest your mother, would ya?" he snaps.

She purses her lips. Hate from the man she lives with. Her eyes are wild, and I'm not talking about sexy eye makeup.

Annabelle looks up to see the venom.

"I am assassin, dear," she reminds him sweetly.

Then Pandora starts screaming from the window above. "Deee-li-lah!"

Delilah slinks back out of sight into the foyer.

Pandora stretches out onto the fire escape. "Deee-li-lah!"

"Why don't you answer your mother?" Dagmar says.

"Paaa-cooooo!" Pandora don't care who she's screaming for, who she gets.

"Jeeez," Dagmar mutters, "give us some peace and quiet."

"Shhhh!" Delilah crawls deeper back into the vestibule. "You want to answer her," she tells Dagmar, "answer her."

"She ain't calling me."

"Daag-mar!"

He scurries back so fast that, trying to get away, he almost crushes his wife against the door.

Eventually those eyes settle on me. "Joe! Joe, you seen the mailman?"

"No, Pandora."

"That damn Edwin, got his ass fired, now this new one don't know junk mail from a welfare check. What time is it?"

"Eleven o'clock," I tell her.

"Oh, God! Oh, God! Paaaaaaaaco!" Her voice rolling along Avenue E like a street sweeper. Then she disappears back in her apartment.

Down the block a little yellow-skinned gypsy is banging on the side of a car with a ball-peen hammer.

Dagmar slinks back out onto the stoop, the coast clear, to watch the gypsy work. "Remember there used to be a bakery on Eighth Street? It was originally a firehouse, but then Continental Bakeries took it over and converted it. Continental makes Wonder Bread. You know, helps build strong bodies twelve ways! You believe that shit, you believe anything. I got a job there. A lot of neighborhood guys plugged right in. One guy in particular I remember, fellow named Big Mike. He had a partner, Walter, little pip-squeak, they ran together. I'm pretty sure they're both in jail now. Burned down some buildings over there on Ninth Street, and the jerks got caught.

"Mike, he worked as a mixer up on the third floor, making dough, and Walter worked on the slicing machine with me. One day, Big Mike, he's so big, he falls through the floor and was stuck hanging from the ceiling above our heads. I swear to God the guy weighed three-fifty, four hundred pounds. Big heavyset guy. There's a creak, boards give way, man falls right down through. Maybe the floorboards was rotted out, maybe all the dough on the wood rotted it. Mike goes through like a barbell through a wet paper towel, you ever see them television commercials? Anyway, Walter looks up and there's his main man dangling by his belly button. Didn't look so tough just then, the poor fat fuck. The look on Walter's face after he looked up—quite a scare, seeing Big Mike like that—that was the look worth a million dollars. Big Mike all exposed, every one of us thinking just then, if he falls, good. Walter was shitting bricks, the asshole, all the crap he pulled, hiding behind Mike's big belly. Walter had that trapped-rat look like he knew what we were thinking when we looked at him. We eyeballed him, eyeballed Mike dangling, and we got to thinking, you little fucking cockroach, your minutes are numbered, we get your rat ass right now! You see what I'm gettin' at, Joe? *Comprende?*

"I'm just looking up the block," Dagmar says, "and I see this gypsy, you see the gypsy I'm talking about, fixing the bodywork and broken window on that car, and I'm thinking, I remember this guy, sure, he fixed my car once. Yeah, Walter comes up to me, says, 'There's a gypsy outside on the street wants to fix your car. Let him do it. I had one do my car once. He was good. Very, very good. After he's done all you got to do is go get it painted. Go over to Earl Scheib.' "

"So, did you?"

Dagmar looks at me. "Fuckin' Walter. The gypsy fucked up everything. Ruined my car. He said oh, you got a poked in fender let me put it right. It was a joke. Fucking guy wanted thirty bucks, right? I talked him down to twenty-five. Thing is I already had the paint job appraised in Brooklyn, on Cropsy Avenue. It was going to cost me ninety-five bucks. After the gypsy got through, it wound up costing me one and a quarter. Yeah, I remember it like it was yesterday, and that was why I wanted to get Walter when Big Mike fell through the floor. It was so hot working at the bakery, I was at the water fountain eating salt tablets. I'm looking at Walter at the slicing machine, him yakking and laughing about some stupid thing. Then I hear a creak from the ceiling above, then a sound like wood tearing and a whoop that either make your skin crawl or make you laugh. Big Mike. Dangling there.

"Walter he was never the same after that. A cherry picker had to come and pluck Mike out. I caught up with

Walter, chased him all over the neighborhood, you know what I'm saying? Caught him on Avenue D and Fourth Street, hiding under a car, and I beat the shit out of him. I ain't lying. Anyone'll tell you. Dagmar ain't gonna take no shit. Now I'm looking at this gypsy, wonder if I should kill him or just twist his little yellow head off. You know why? Seems to me the day that other gypsy came around that day, all the car windows on the block got broke the night before. You see what I'm driving at . . . ?"

If Dagmar only knew so much about the plumbing stacks or the hot water return lines as he does about running at the mouth. Shows you how distorted some people's points of view are.

The Spanish guys from the corner come over to me as I stand in front of my car, the gypsy rapping about how he gonna fix the window for me, do some Indian red patch work where the rust is eating through on the fender. One of the Spanish guys says, "Why you let that guy take care of your car? You don't want a man like that taking care of your car. He don't know nothing about your car. We know about your car. We see it every day, we listen to it run. Gypsy man cheat you, and he don't know nothing about your car, but if you let us take care of your car then you get good service, and a good job, you know us from the block." Then they ask me to tell them what's wrong, what it's going to need. They're right about one thing, I know them. I see them work on cars on the block every day, morning to night. Dagmar agrees, tells me not to let the gypsy do the work these fellas do better, and because they live right here they can be held accountable, the gypsy I'll never see again.

I tell the Spanish guys I have a friend who's a mechanic, he tell me get myself a shovel and shovel my car right into the garbage. I tell them it's a junker, '62 Galaxie, I take it crosstown on moonless nights, but nothing more.

The up-the-block boys remain expressionless. They don't get the joke. "We do the job," they say. "We fix it good. First off we replace the broken window. Next we do whatever you want. We make the brakes work, we make the signals click on and off, we make the gas tank gauge work. We make the roof stop leaking, we make the lights bright. We do it all, bro."

"All right. How much?"

"Six hundred pesos."

"Six hundred? Forget it. I'll take it to Mr. Good-wrench."

"*Hombre,* look at your car. Be realistic."

Segundo DeJesus come strolling down the street. He stands and sneers, makes me think I know who walked down the block last night busting windows, and it wasn't no gypsy. He stops, stands there watching.

"I don't got that kind of money," I protest.

"Five hundred."

"Where you gonna get the parts from?" I ask. "Down by Chambers Street?"

Suddenly Dagmar's impatient. "They *steal* them. They don't get parts on no Chambers Street or no Four-teenth Street, man. They go to Queens, they find a car, spitting image of yours, and they'll steal it, park it around the corner or behind one of them vacant buildings, and they'll have a regular parts warehouse over there. Everything they need they'll take off that car, and if they need more, they'll go out and get another one. It's the way of the world down here. The scavenger and the scavenged."

When I look up, Segundo's still watching, smiling. I turn back to the car jockeys and say, "Okay, three hundred pesos."

Later, young DeJesus drifts away (to what new felony?) and the rest of the crowd is back on the stoop drinking beer.

"Now what about this DeJesus character?" Dagmar says. "You want me to take care of him for you, Joe? I can arrange to have him murdered where he sleeps, blown away on the street, you name it. I know just the guys who do that for me, just say the word."

He's serious and when Delilah blows on her nails, I see they are, in fact, blood red. Her face is pasty like the limestone of the temple where my grandparents married, its facade now adorned with Benny's and Segundo's tags, and Delilah whispers with a smirk on her face, in this hoary, husky voice, "I am assassin!"

"Watch what you say to my wife, Joe," Dagmar warns me. "What you insinuate."

"Dagmar and me, we're smart," Delilah tells me. "I grew up among these street types. I know them all, every one of them, if not personally, by types, the murderers and thieves, the killers and rapists, the niggards and cutthroats that dope brings. I know how to get along. I was here when no others were. I was here when I was alone, and there were no bar mitzvah boys around, let me tell you. It was only me and one day this Spanish family comes and the next day two more, then three, and then more and more, like locusts. You hear me?"

One day, shortly after the fire, Delilah came up to me, very serious, like she was letting me in on something.

"You know what DeJesus told me?" she said. "You know what he told me right before the fire? He said he was going to burn the building down to get rid of Carmencita. I swear to God, that's what he told me."

"You and only you."

"He told Dagmar the same thing."

Sure he did. Anyway, now Dagmar has wandered off with the boys from the corner to survey his Caddy. Maybe he'll sell it to them, he says when he saunters back. He pulls his dollar cigar from his mouth and checks out the chewed-on end. "Let me tell you something, Joe. Pandora now, she's Delilah's mother. I don't got nothing against Delilah. I don't got nothing against her mother. We get along well, we really do. But you can imagine having your mother-in-law living directly on top of you. It's too close for anybody's own good. I can imagine maybe going round the corner for a visit. Two blocks away—you know what I'm saying? I swear to God, I'd see her or Paco on the street then, I'd kiss them on the friggin' lips. If they moved to Bayonne, I swear to God, it's a trip, but I'd make it gladly once a week. You hear me! Out of duty! Out of loyalty! It would have to be better than this. Anything has to be better than this."

"Pandora's my mother," Delilah says, "and I love her for it. But everyone knows hell has no fury like a mother scorned."

"Nobody's scorning your mother," Dagmar says defensively.

"Oh no? That's not what she thinks, and it's not what I think neither."

"A big, heavyset woman like that, if she's scorned, she deserves it. Hell wants her ass."

"You know something, Dagmar?" I tell him. "It's a pleasure how you're always thinking. The smoke's always rising. Yup, you're a veritable stellar star in our tenement constellation. I've been sitting here on the stoop with you thinking, and I was wondering if you actually think you're getting over. Do you believe it? Do you really believe that anyone is actually buying this?"

"What?"

"This! Your routine, man. Your rap. I don't give a damn if you're the slickest fuck alive, all I want from you is for you to be slightly honest. If you're gonna go with me to deal with DeJesus, bro, you can't be spouting all this bullshit."

"Hey, blood, I'm with you. I ain't gonna let you die. All of us people who live here, we all want the same thing —a decent place to live. We're all in it together, Joe. Don't worry, I won't let you down. I won't screw you."

"Right."

"Joe, I do something for you, you do something for me. It's as simple as that. A solid for a solid."

# 24

## Trouble Comes to a Head

Joe walks the street with his arm around the thin shoulder of his mother. They walk down Avenue E, cut onto Seventh Street where the cocaine and crack gang hang outside the evil little grocery store, shooting baskets at a makeshift net. The rim stands only about six and a half feet off the ground and everybody slam-dunks.

The Avenue E Boys stop their game when Joe and his mama come near, and silently allow them to pass.

"It's nice of them not to tell me to hurry," Sarah says. "They're gentlemen." She looks right at them and says, "You're all gentlemen."

Then leaning toward Joe, she whispers. "They don't look it, but they are."

"Sure, Mom, they're all swell."

Joe remembers last night, when he's coming home. A drug deal's going down on the street. But everyone's not happy. Two dusty black guys are standing off by themselves, down the block, glaring. The Avenue E Boys are glaring back.

"Move it off," someone shouts.

Joe sees the confrontation about to happen. Little Bit, strong-arm man and leader of the E Boys, steps onto the sidewalk, a gleaming aluminum baseball bat in his hand. "Move along," he orders, and starts down the street toward the black guys.

Somewhere a radio's on, or a tv. Joe recognizes the music, seen the advertisement, a jeans commercial. Willie Nelson warbling, "So you think you're a cowboy? . . ." A picture of Willie's butt, swathed in blue denim.

The black guys are backing off. Joe moving forward. Little Bit, the baseball bat held at his side, is standing pat.

Joe wonders what's going down exactly. The black guys probably don't have enough cash for the dope. Joe's holding two bags of groceries from the Korean greengrocer on Avenue A. Apples, a cantaloupe, peaches, green seedless grapes, a pint of ice cream, half gallon of milk, cookies, a Boston lettuce, Jersey tomatoes and a container of the plain yogurt Constance likes. Both his hands are full.

The black guys retreat as Little Bit steps forward, dragging the rest of the E Boys with him in his wake, and Joe crosses the street. The black guys are short of money, they're going to look for more. They're gonna see Joe, Joe the white guy, and pounce on him. Joe is money.

His adrenaline is pumping. Joe's ready for action. He transfers one bag to the other hand. Now his right hand is free. Joe relishes action. If these guys attack him, what will he do? He'll swing the bags. He'll throw the bags at them. "Here! Catch!" Then, while they're preoccupied with the groceries, he'll hit them, he'll kick them, he'll run, he'll swoop low for his Gerber knife, uncoil with the sharp double-edge blade. He'll come up hard with it. Slash. Swing. Slash. He walks on.

The black guys are standing off a distance, menaced, ready, inching away, eyeing Little Bit. Joe skirts around them, around their terrible energy that shakes the street. They cross to Joe's side of the street. "How do you do?" Joe's going to have to fight, he knows it. Then he knows he won't have to fight.

Joe won't have to fight because a cop is standing on the corner swinging his baton.

"Why, Officer Krupke," Joe says, a big grin on his face. "Peltz," the officer murmurs.

The officer nods and the black guys disappear—where? Joe won't ever know. He never looks back. At the door to his building Annabelle is waiting, Constance in her arms. Joe kisses her on the cheek, Constance reaches for him.

The Yitz tells Joe that Jewish gangs proliferated in the neighborhood when he was growing up. Says they fought every son-of-a-bitch immigrant nationality there was. "When we were in our early twenties," he says, "there was one connected guy interested in your mother. She was scared to death of him, wouldn't go out or have nothing to do with him. Then your father came along."

Joe's paternal grandmother died when she was only forty-one years old. Yakov was four. She had given birth to six children in a little more than ten years. One day she went into the bathroom and she never came out. A heart attack on the john. After that, Yakov says his father couldn't bear up under the pressure to take care of all the children. He said his old man had a history of never being able to make any money, he was just one of those people. He did have a job in the temple for a little while, but less than a year after his wife died, the rabbi caught him chasing the cleaning woman around the pulpit. She was naked as the torah is long, and that was that. The rabbi fired him. Yakov's sisters were taken in by two aunts, but the boys were left on their own. His older brother ran the streets, but Yakov, the next oldest, was a responsible little boy who worked on the streets trying to make a living, help support his father and brothers. He sold light bulbs on street corners, bringing the money home to his dad. He wasn't quite five years old. Eventually he was able to manage to put away some Indian-head pennies and some buffalo-head nickels for himself. These he kept his whole life long, never spent them, and gave them to Joe when he was a little boy.

Joe's mother's older brother, Yitzhak, once peed in his father's eye. As an infant the Yitz slept in a bureau drawer because the family couldn't afford a crib. Joe's grandfather was resting on his bed after work. This might have been one of the days Louie Lefkowitz had stopped in. Perhaps Joe's grandfather had dozed off. The stream of piss from the baby hit him right in the eye and woke him. The baby was cooing when Joe's grandfather went for him. At first he didn't realize what the baby had done. A steady stream had rainbowed through the air, crossing the edge of the bureau drawer in a golden arc.

Out of reflex, Joe's grandfather almost backhanded the kid into the middle of next week, according to family legend as related by Joe's mother. But then he caught himself and laughed, and called everyone into the room and told them the story and what a strong wanger the baby had, and the family repeated it, and repeated it, and Joe had heard it twenty times or more, and Sarah had already sat Constance down and told her, wiping the tears out of her eyes as she remembered that day, one she had never known in the first place, her brother being firstborn, the day Uncle Yitz peed in Grandpa's eye.

One day at the newsstand Joe read a similar story in the papers. The same thing happened, a baby pissing in his father's eye. Only this time the father was a Czechoslovakian, his wife holding the naked kid out to him, show him his son's first tooth or a rash on his belly, and he hadn't caught the humor, hadn't laughed. This time the father grabbed the kid and threw him through the bedroom window, shattering glass. Thank God, someone was walking past on the sidewalk and was able to catch the plummeting baby. Joe read how the person looked up and saw something falling. The father fled, but was later apprehended in a subway station in the Morisania section of the Bronx. The man claimed he was under a lot of pressure. "I'll bet," Joe says. In today's climate they blame it on drugs, but who knows? Maybe the father just didn't like his own kid. Maybe he wanted to see time fly. Maybe his handcuffs didn't fit.

Joe's great-grandfather on his mother's side died of a heart attack while counting his money in the back of his cleaning store on Avenue E, shortly after he came to America. Joe's great-grandmother was sitting on the stoop while dinner was cooking. Seeing the shop door open she'd gone inside, and there was her husband thumbing through the day's receipts.

"Do you have to count it there?" she said. "With the door open, anybody can walk in."

"Who's going to come in?"

"You've been robbed three times before."

He shrugged. Dark, bearded, old world, he took the money, and went into the toilet, to count there. He never came out.

You see what it is in Joe's family? People all the time dying on toilets. He's scared of it. Wonders if this is symbolic, or if he'll die the same way. Recently, Joe went to a Chinese fortune-teller who believes in natural law, that the world is divided into five elements: fire, metal, water, wood and earth. He could read Joe's face, he said, and Joe was all wood. Because Joe was wood, water was a danger to him, it could rot him, and he saw how sitting on something like a toilet with the water underneath him might strike Joe as dangerous. But the fortune-teller said not to worry so much, only to be cautious, that he thought Joe would live a long life but not, perhaps, a happy one. Since Joe's ears were too far below his eye line, he probably wouldn't ever be rich. But he would gain some renown, and instead of always selling newspapers he might one day be in them.

"A headline?" Joe inquired. "Featured commentary?"

"Perhaps," the fortune-teller answered. He spoke no English, the cashier at the take-out place on Avenue D, the one with bulletproof glass, translated. The fortune-teller had recently arrived from Taiwan where he was a very successful businessman doing his Zen exercises until one day he'd become enlightened. Suddenly he was able to read people's fates in their faces. He looked into the mirror, saw a shadow across his own face and understood that it was bad. To try to escape he ran away to America where he worked as a dishwasher.

Joe's grandmother always warned him to be careful in the bathroom. "Don't strain yourself on the toilet," she'd say. Joe reminds her that her father didn't actually die *on* the toilet, he wasn't straining, he was counting his money. He went into the bathroom only so no thieves would see the day's receipts.

"That too . . . ," Joe's grandmother says.

Spike asks Annabelle if she ever heard the story of his old man and Madonna at the deli.

One night this chick sits down with a couple of guys on Spike's father's station. Typically, his old man is trying to look down her blouse, Spike says. He doesn't know who she is.

The Spiker's grizzled dad, he tells Madonna she's a very pretty girl, could go far. He has no idea she's already gone, far gone. He says he knows an agent comes in all the time, might be very interested in her. Does she want to meet somebody up at William Morris?

Spike says he's got to laugh when his father comes into the kitchen and tells him. Spike takes one look through the little round window in the swinging kitchen door and he knows. "Pop," he says, "that girl don't need you."

"No?" Spike's pop says. "Why not?"

"That girl's already made it, Dad. Don't you know who she is?"

He doesn't, so Spike tells him.

"Is that right!" Spike's pop says. He whistles to himself. "So that's Madonna!" Then he bustles off to his station to tell her how he didn't realize who she was, *Madonna!* A glamorous girl like her, but his son told him back in the kitchen who she was, and now he knows. Does she want to meet his son? "Steve! Steve, come out here. Steve, this is Madonna. Say how do you do. Steve's an artist, only works as a waiter to make ends meet, keep me company, his poor old dad. He's a nice boy despite his looks."

"Just call me Spike," Steve tells Madonna.


Spike complains his father's always bugging him to bring Mazie around, she lives in the neighborhood, she could drop in for a sandwich. Spike's dad hasn't met Mazie. He thinks maybe there's something wrong with her, something Spike doesn't want him to see. Maybe she's not Jewish, or worse —black.

"She ain't black," Spike told him, "but she is Jewish, only not religious."

"Then why don't you bring her?"

"She shaves her head."

The old man didn't like that, being made fun of, he demanded to know if Spike was telling the truth or pulling his leg.

"Fathers can be annoying," Spike explains to Annabelle.

Spike's pop didn't give up. "I don't care if she don't have a hair on her head," he insisted. "Have her drop by for something nice to eat."

Joe's listening to all this from upstairs in bed.

"We're doomed," he hears Annabelle say. "Have you noticed major aberrations in the society today?"

The baby wakes up and shouts for her mommy. Annabelle gets up from the kitchen table. Joe hears her chair scrape. He listens to her climb the stairs, hears her talking with Constance in the next room. "Ready to go to school?" she says. "Velma's?"

He stumbles down the stairs. "Coffee," he groans. "Coffee."

Spike's talking to Mewie. No one's been to bed except for Joe. The four of them sitting in his kitchen. He left them there how many hours ago, and they're still sitting.

"My old man never knew what I'm into," Joe is saying. "Harry, the president of Metro-Goldwyn-Mayer, came over to the newsstand. They know each other for more than thirty years from Harry buying his newspapers at the stand whenever he's in New York. 'Yakov,' he says to my old man, 'I got a stock for you.' He's busy whispering in my father's ear. The old man nods, like he knows what the fuck's going on, like he hasn't lost half the money he ever earned in the market, on tips just like this."

Mazie ain't bad. Scarlet and Spike used to do the downtown run during their heyday, when they both worked with their fathers at the Delancey Street deli. Every night after work, scoot down to Chinatown, a steaming Hung Shu fish awaiting them at the Nu Wah Dor, corner of Bayard and Bowery. Meanwhile, Mazie's been out copping. They meet, get high in a back room, enjoy their meal.

So Mazie offers go out cop today, Spike's treat. We all

wait for her. She stashes clean gimmicks she swipes from her father, who's diabetic, in a book. She's cut out the center of each page with a razor blade. "Who has time to read anymore?" she says when she catches me staring.

"I never read," I agree.

*Don't do those drugs, Zho. Please.* Somewhere in my brain Annabelle's voice is echoing. No matter.

Scarlet says she never reads either. Not ever. Reading's for faggots, bookworms, nerds and turds. We all dig tv and the movies, bro.

"Joe?" I hear Mazie saying. "Didn't you ever go to college? I thought you told me you went to college," and this is while we're cooking up.

"Nope," I tells her. "Never. Nursery school maybe, but after that it was a no-win situation. Anyway, I got expelled."

"From where—college?"

"I told you I *didn't* go to college. I quit school in the ninth grade. From nursery school."

"Expelled from nursery school?"

"Symptomatic of my entire educational experience, babe. Put me on the wrong track from the outset. My first day this little dude was coming down the slide, and I clocked him on the bean with my lunch box. For that, they expelled me."

"Why'd you do that?"

"Kid was an asshole."

They all look at me. I stick the needle in my arm, and that's that.

# 25

# A Building Falls Down on Eighth Street

DeJesus begins to come around again. Mewie saw him visit Scarlet and look in on the burnt ruins of his apartment. Mewie's hysterical now that DeJesus is back, but Benny says we should let the big man come, see what he's made of. Yves has been nosing around what's left of DeJesus's apartment and claims Beneficia promised it to him when she was president. He wants to start work on it, but won't as long as DeJesus is around. Yves is a man who never stops working. If Yves stops working, he dies. It's that simple.

Scarlet calls me over to her apartment, says there's somebody she wants me to see.

When I come in, DeJesus is sitting at her table, smiling. He stands up, shakes my hand, nods hello.

\* \* \*

Mazie asks me what I think of Scarlet, and what am I supposed to say? "I don't know—Scarlet? What should I think?"

Annabelle at the stove, patting the baby on the back, four gas jets on, trying to keep warm. A pipe broke in the basement and we're waiting for the boiler man. Waiting and waiting and waiting. "Cold nights breed cold hearts," Spike says, and looks at me and then at Mazie to see what impression his words of wisdom have on me, on her.

Nothing, no impression. We're waiting.

I tell Annabelle we can go to my parents, their warm house on Long Island, until the heat is fixed.

Annabelle says, "Not on your life."

"Ain't that the way it always is," comments Mazie. "Nobody likes the in-laws."

"Thanks for the insight, Maz." I look right at her.

She purses her lips, makes a kissing sound. "I don't like you either," she says.

*Dear Abby,* I begin. *I live in a building. I am at the center of every conflict. What do I do? Signed: The Arbiter of Avenue E.*

"You handle the corporation so well, Joe."

"Do I?"

"You run such a smooth meeting."

Mazie is one snide bitch. What, she feels competitive with me or something? I turn, laugh in her face. Why can't Spike keep her under control? I told him once. "This might be the 1980s," I said, "but Mazie oughta be bound and gagged. Can't you tell her to calm down, take a breather once in a while? She's a troublemaker. A bad influence on Annabelle. What's the matter—she hate men?"

"Mazie's a free woman. I don't own her. You got a problem, you tell her."

I will. Don't think I won't. I should've told her from the git-go.

So we're at an impasse. Four of us rich landowners just

sitting around the table, sparks flying, checking if we have the votes to control the corporation.

"Maybe," I say to Annabelle, "just maybe, it would be a good idea if you started to do a few things around here too, worked for the corporation, you know. Take some responsibility for this place."

"Oh, Zho, you must be *fatigué!*"

She said she really wanted to meet me halfway, she really did, but it wasn't her language, wasn't her culture. She felt self-conscious. "Can you imagine if it were you in Paris, for example? How much would you handle? Go see the *concierge.* I don't think so."

The camera snaps, a flash. I look into the lens. Who do I see behind it? Her.

Under his breath, Spike tells me he does everything. Mazie does nothing but fuck and gossip, stir up trouble.

"You know what I should do?" Spike says loudly. "I'm a successful artist. I should make enough paintings so what I make pays for having the rest of my apartment finished." He looks at Mazie for approval. "I mean, frankly, I'm never gonna finish it myself. Have the sheetrock done, the windows framed, the floors sanded. All in one shot. I ever tell you about this guy paints a painting in forty seconds, Joe? He doesn't use brushes, he uses toilet paper. He spends more than eighty thousand dollars a year in materials alone. Can you imagaine what Scott tissue is raking in from him?" He slaps me on the thigh. "What do you say, Mr. Prez, that's an aces idea, right?"

"Annabelle's family, her friends come to visit, they don't know what to make of this country," I tell Spike.

Spike asks me if I speak French.

"No, I don't."

"You speak Spanish?"

"Spike," I tell him. "I don't speak anything. I barely speak English."

Spike says it's the same for him. His European collectors have no idea whatsoever where he's coming from. "It's the hard edge of my work that confuses them," he tells me. "Once one of my collectors come from Paris brought this French guidebook. You know how they symbolized our neighborhood? With a skull and crossbones, that's how. DANGER! KEEP AWAY! stenciled over the street grid. No wonder I paint the way I do, right? Skull and crossbones."

"Get off it, Spike," Mazie says. "You're lucky to be here. For an artist like you, this is the place to be. You shouldn't complain about good luck."

"I'm not." His glance slides over her, back to me. "I tell Mazie, she should paint like me, take her example from the tried and true, but she don't listen."

"I'd rather stay true to my vision," she says. "At least I have some integrity."

"Get whatever you can, ain't that your philosophy, Spike?" I say.

"Life's ephemeral, bro, that's what they say in the streets."

"Ain't that the truth!"

Spike explains that DeJesus is working himself into a state. That's what Mewie told him. Carlos is becoming a very dangerous guy, a big problem for everyone in our building.

"He don't bother with Butch like he used to," Spike says. "DeJesus never swallowed none of his neighborhood-activist crap. You know what I'm saying, Joe?"

"DeJesus don't bother with Butch anymore because he knows Scarlet ain't fucking him anymore," I tell Spike.

"Carlos thinks Scarlet's fucking you, Joe. He's gonna be on your ass next."

"I'm not fucking Scarlet." Annabelle stares at me. I grin sheepishly. "I'm not."

"Scarlet don't give a shit about anybody else," Spike says. "The girl has no morality. If it suits her purposes, she'll tell DeJesus anything, just to see him hop."

When I first came here, I was sitting on the stoop during that first work party, the sun beating down, feeling good, and Butch came out to sit in the warmth with me. "You know," he said, "you seem like a nice guy. Do you know what you walked into here?"

Did I know what I walked into? "No. What have I walked into? You tell me."

"Some of the original tenants are getting a royal screw job. If you ain't part of the solution, you're part of the problem."

"I don't see it that way."

"C'mon, man, don't be blind. You're in the middle of a class struggle."

"Am I?" Tell me, Butch, c'mon, what's going on here?

"I'm telling you. Listen! Use your brain!"

Spike says, "You're a creative thinker, Joe, make something creative of the presidency, straighten out this mess."

He turns to Mazie. She's getting up from the table, says she's going to meet Beer Can downstairs on the street, walk over to Vazac's, have a beer, discuss block politics.

"Scarlet's our route to DeJesus," Spike says. "If we're gonna come out of this alive, we need Scarlet in our pocket."

"Let's not exaggerate," I say.

"DeJesus is a man, just like any other," Spike continues. "The only difference is he wears his Achilles' heel between his legs. Imagine the discomfort, poor thing."

Meanwhile, Spike states it's his responsibility to make dinner. He claims he's a great cook. Mazie cooks worth shit, but he brags that he was born with delectable nutriments in his blood, vibrant acrylics in his mind. Spike uses a cookbook, but that doesn't make his cooking any less tasty. He says he's inherited his culinary skills from his father, DNA from all those years in the restaurant business.

Spike's sharp, no argument, making money hand over fist. Maybe he ain't the second coming of Picasso, but then again maybe he is. Who can tell? Man paints the same image over and over, the food hovering six inches off the table, his slightly green subjects, stark naked, sucking up their pastrami and tongue sandwiches, blintzes and kreplach, their eerie bodies slumped forward, bellies distended.

I know dollar for dollar how Spike's doing from his father. I love that old deli magic down there on Delancey. Can't keep away, scoot over every chance I get. Go in, shoot the breeze with the Spiker's old man, he can't help talk about his son, his pride and joy. I hear what every canvas sells for, six thousand, eight thousand, he told me Spike stands to make a hundred thousand this year. "Never ceases to amaze me, my son comes in he looks like a complete degenerate, and what anybody sees in that crap he paints. Do you understand that stuff, Joe?"

I don't.

Spike's father says he doesn't understand it either. Or care for it. "But who can argue with success?"

I shrug. "Not me."

"We'd both like to have that money, right?"

"You don't like your own son's paintings?"

"I don't see anything in it," the old man says. "You can't fault me for that, for being honest."

What's Spike say? "Pickles are my life. Or at least they once were. They're the same green as money. You ever notice? Pickles are my tag, bud," he tells me. "Always put one big fat green one in my painting. First the critics thought it was a fat green prick, but now they understand what it is."

"I thought your tag was a hypo with a trail of blood?"

"Yeah, that too, but that was before the pickles. I used to tack my favorite syringe on the canvas, but you know what I'm saying, you move down to this neighborhood, you need to be more subtle, you grow up quick, you mature, the drugs lose their mystique."

"Your mama, they do. I don't buy that, not coming from you."

"Yeah, well, maybe I don't either, but it sounds good."

As I say, Spikey's old man works in a Chinese-Roumanian restaurant on Delancey Street. A place called Goodman's, known for its spicy pastrami, matzoh brei lo mein, and its kosher Peking duck. Half the waiters wear yarmulkes, the other half wear pigtails. Spike's old man wears a gun, Spike uses a needle. The restaurant has been there ninety-seven years. Howe and Hummel used to eat there when they were the sharpest pair of criminal lawyers in the city. Maybe Spike would need a high-priced pair of mouthpieces like them one day. Maybe I would. Spike learned a thing or two about cole slaw and potato salad at the deli, and then translated it into other things. When his career finally flourished, he was ready for it.

Yves came to him with a proposition. "Want to sink all your money in a building, Spike? I hear one just fell down last night on Eighth Street. The roof and the whole west wall collapsed. I'll bet we can get it dirt cheap."

Spike wasn't interested. "Hey, I already bought five apartments in this building," he told Yves. "Now I'm going to have a contractor come in, renovate them. Nothing wrong with that, Joe," he says, turning to me, "not if I can afford it. I'm a loyal member of the corporation. I want these buildings better, not worse. DeJesus, he's the type of guy do anything he can to bring the buildings down all around him. I'm not into that. I paid my money, now I want to see it grow, grow, grow. That's capitalism."

"You mystify me, Spike."

"Yeah, when Beneficia said she was selling out, I never was happier, end all this crap going down between her and Ike, those two, they really didn't like each other."

"What you pay for your apartment, Spike?"

"Twelve-five. How much you pay for yours?"

"Thirty grand, but it was all Annabelle's dough."

"Didn't you have any money, Joe?"

"Me? You kidding? From selling newspapers? Not even two thin dimes. I'll tell you what the economics are. We sell as many as three hundred *Daily News*es a day. We used to sell as many as four hundred and fifty *Posts*, but not anymore. When the *Challenger* astronauts got killed we sold three hundred and fifty-two *Time* magazines in a week, that's our record."

"Is that enough for the three of you to live?"

"Get real! Who lives?"


Imagine this. They're leading me up there to the witness stand. Attila the bum's prosecuting. "Why'd you do it?" he asks.

"I didn't do it," I tell him. "DeJesus did it. He did it to himself. He burnt himself out. How many times I have to tell you that before it gets through your thick skull, before you understand?"

With that DeJesus explodes out of his chair at the prosecution table and tries to get me.


Mazie, the cynic, walks into my apartment and plops herself down at the kitchen table and starts lecturing me. The end-up is she says, "Joe, you're too easy."

"Okay, why don't you take charge, Mazie, instead of just running your mouth all day long? You be president."

"Me?"

"See! Nobody wants to do the dirty work. I understand. It's my duty—I'm gonna get him. I made the promise, I'll keep my word. I'll clean up the building, once and for all. But then I'm out, I'm out of corporate politics forever. Is that a deal?"

Later on Spike tells me I'm a good thinker. "That's why you're president, Joe. 'Cause you got that solid way of reasoning. You'll always be one step ahead of DeJesus. He'll never be able to catch up to you."

"I wouldn't wish this on my worst enemy," I say.

"Welcome to the legacy of Beneficia."

"Why did they ever have rental units in this building?"

"Money, Joey, pure and simple. Money."

\* \* \*

"Since Benny moved into Mewie's, he's had virtually no contact with the outside world," Spike marvels. "It's like Mewie's keeping him under lock and key. Everyone goes on about Beneficia's power over Mewie. When she lived here, he practically lived under her thumb. But now that her little boy's staying with him, Mewie's having fun exercising his own power."

"It's like Muhammad Ali used to say," I tell him, " 'Ain't life strange!' "

"Yeah, what goes around comes around."

When Annabelle told me Mazie was leaving Spike, I couldn't believe it. Then she told me Mazie was leaving him for Beer Can, queen of the pussy bumpers, actually moving in across the street with her. It shocked me. It truly did. I couldn't believe it. I thought Mazie was straight as the day is long.

"Those damn pussy bumpers," Yves scoffs. "Always stirring up trouble. Did I tell you, Joe, about the time they called the cops on me for throwing boxes of plaster off the roof into the backyard? I gave the cops twenty bucks, and you know what they said . . . ?"

The other day Yves was working on the storm drain in the basement, digging out a trap so the rain water wouldn't flood the foundation, and Mewie comes down and says you can't do that.

"Can't do what? This is the way it's done, Joe. He don't know nothing, but Beer Can and her mob tells him Yves is doing it wrong, you got to do it this way. They know nothing, and he believes them."

Ike loved his father. Ike's father wasn't always a woodrobber. Once upon a time he had been a successful lawyer, but his mind snapped when the girl he was engaged to marry died in a tenement fire.

My mother told me Ike was from a very good family, but after his fiancée's death, he lived on the street and held his pants up with a long, frayed length of rope. If someone stepped on the end, Ike's pants fell down. The neighborhood kids thought that was a grand game.

Ike was a lisper. He reveled in telling stories about kissing the prettiest girl in the neighborhood. He would tell anybody who would listen that she would let him do *it* to her on the couch in her living room.

Ike warned the kids who relentlessly teased him that if he ever caught one of them he'd stick his crutch up their asshole.

One day the man who owned the local pickle factory, the father of newly born twins, chased away the Yitz and a bunch of other kids who were teasing Ike. Ike turned on the samaritan, lisping venomously that he doubted the man was capable of making twins by himself, that he had undoubtedly needed his brother's help to do the job.

Our Ike claims when he was growing up, he witnessed the neighborhood children tormenting his father, says he can see the action in his mind's eye to this day.

When they found Ike the Woodrobber's corpse in the winter of 1944, frozen to death under the stoop of 314 Avenue E, no one mourned, not even Ike junior, who was with the navy in the South Pacific, but everyone came out on the street and watched the police stand around stomping their feet, waiting for the meat wagon to pick the body up, take it to the morgue at Bellevue. . . .

I'm sorry to say, the same fate awaits John Plastic Hat. John lives on East Seventh Street between Avenue A and First. John's got more than a semblance of pride. He won't take handouts from just anybody, only from people he knows. John wears about a dozen green and black plastic garbage bags piled on his head, covering a skullcap he made out of a brown paper sack. On the coldest day of the year the mayor came around and tried to pick John up in his limousine, take him to a shelter. John refused to go, staring at the mayor, but not budging. He got his picture in the paper, centerfold of the *Daily News*. The caption read, "I like it right where I am, thank you," but that couldn't be John Plastic Hat talking. John don't talk. He makes noises in his throat, but it ain't talking, it's not speech. John comes from the Ukraine. Supposedly he was in love with a girl, followed her to America, but when he got here she was married to some Pole, had a bunch of kids already. His mind snapped like the mind of Ike the Woodrobber before him. John's been on Seventh Street ever since, picking cigarette butts off the street, eating out of garbage cans, taking occasional handouts from people he knows from years ago, when his mind was lucid, from the old country. He sleeps on the steps of the Ukrainian church. He wears an overcoat and a ragged-ass pair of pants, lately split from crotch to ankle. When the winter winds come whipping off the river, man must freeze his butt.

"Them damn pussy bumpers," Yves grumbles. "It's really something, Joe, Mazie running off with Beer Can. Is Spike all broke up?"

Yves remembers his own loss years before, his wife, his little girls. He can't believe Mazie deserted Spike for Beer Can, who got her name from traipsing the streets with a can of Bud clutched in her fist, looking for someplace to stick her nose.

"I don't know about you, Peltz, how your mother feels, but if my father were alive today," Ike mutters, "if he were here to see what's happening to this neighborhood, he would die."

## Cornblatt
## the Mensch

It wasn't a party, but it must have struck Mewie as one because he began to rap excitedly on the window.

"What's going on over there?" he says.

I tell him to come around if he wants to, he says Benny's with him, I say bring him too.

They climb across the ledge, even though I'd told him ten times to cut that shit out.

Mewie says "Hiiiy" to Annabelle. He indicates Benny and says, "You two know each other, right?"

Benny nods, Annabelle says, "Sure, sure, Benny."

"You know who Benny saw the other day?" Mewie asks, a real conversation launcher. "Segundo. Says he's gonna burn our ass right down to the ground if it's the last thing he ever does. Right, Ben?"

But then Mewie's attention is diverted by pop eyes and annoyed expressions. "Hey, Joe, who you got over here? Scarlet! The one and only. My favorite."

"You know, Joe," Mewie goes on, "she looks so dramatic, don't you think? Lovely girl, dear, lovely."

Mewie shakes distasteful hands with Spike, then looks at his palm. "Charmed, I'm sure. So sorry to hear about your personal loss, desperate, unhappy Mazie." He makes himself at home, waiting to be let in on what's happening, "Anybody got a beer or a glass of wine?"

Doctor, I'm calling because my little girl is sick. Really sick.

Can you bring her over, Joe?

Sure, Doc, but . . . I'd rather not. I'm telling you, she's *really* sick. In this weather, I don't want to take her out, make things worse. You see what I'm saying? . . .

All right, I'll stop over at the end of work.

Thanks, Doc. Thanks a lot. But really, I don't want to be insistent, but can't you come now?

By the time the doc comes, Segundo lies gasping on the blood-soaked floorboards.

I thought you told me your daughter was sick, Joe?

I needed a way to get you over here, Doc. Hurry, Doc! Bandage his wound!

Segundo gulps. He's spitting up blood. Waves of it are welling in his mouth, and he's gagging.

The bayonet is attached to the end of Benny's M16 rifle, Vietnam issue. "The better to kill you with, my dear," he leers. "See, Peltz, I've learned my lesson well."

Oh, boy.

Is the kid dead, Doc? Is he dying? Is this a dream?

"Zho, there's some cheese and crackers, you know, and I thought I could open a bottle of wine."

There's a lot of people here. Everybody's scared.

Annabelle's mother came over from France. She looks around, her face hollow from the terrible tragedy that has befallen her. Her husband dead, killed by a terrorist bomb

planted in a restaurant on the rue des Rosiers in the Jewish
quarter of Paris. Damn Zho-Zho turned Jean-Jacques on to
corned beef and pastrami, and the man couldn't stay away.

"King Zho? So this is your empire. I don't understand
completely why my daughter calls you that. To me you are
lumpen proletariat. *Rien de plus.*" She waits for an explanation, any explanation. A rebuttle.

Annabelle says her mother is bitter because she refused
to return to France for her father's funeral.

I ignore her, my mother-in-law. Repeat to myself the
universal cowboy motto: Die with your boots on! Ride herd!
How deep is my valley? How far is my field?


"Sure, I coulda come back dead," Benny says, "but I didn't.
The Ecuadorian National Service, the U.S. Army, they're all
the same to me. Life on the edge, that's what I dig. Life
worth living. I woulda liked Vietnam, chewed up some of
that gook ass, but I missed it, I'm a different generation.
Now I got to roll my own."

Annabelle looks at him. He thinks he's getting the
once-over and caresses his balls casually and smiles at her.

"Look, it's simple. I deliver Segundo DeJesus here to
you folks, put him right in your hands. You take it from
there. I'm telling you, I know him, he's the hot sauce,
he's the trouble. Take care of him, take him out, and it's
over."

"And how exactly do you propose that we *take care* of
this *hot sauce?*" I ask.

"Simple. Eradicate him, blood."

"Eradi— what?"

"Eradicate him. Erase him. Put an end to him. Exter-
minate him. You get the drift?"

"Yeah, I get the drift, but we're not doing that."

"Okay, look, you don't have to, I'll do it. It's cool.
Leave him to me."

"You got to be kidding!"

"Mr. Peltz, you ever see on the streets here, people got dogs? These pit bulls, you know 'em?"

I'm not answering. I know what's coming. Same dog attacked Scarlet, chewed up her purse. Probably the same fuck that ate Fausteen's Great Dane that last day when Butch was walking the huge son of a bitch. It was horrible, bits of paws, tail, snout and dog ears all over the sidewalk, but Butch thought it was a great thing, a fantastic social phenomenon, not to mention a tremendous relief to be delivered so completely from his canine responsibility. Matchsticks to marmalade, Benny's been talking to Mewie, and Mewie's been putting ideas in his head, even if he denies it from here to Canarsie.

"Mr. Peltz?"

"English pit bulls, yeah. Unbelievably macho animal. A killing machine."

"Avenue E Boys got 'em," Benny says. "Seventh Street Boys got 'em. Better than a knife, better than a gun. You say, 'Gee, Lieutenant Kojak, I'm sorry, dog just got away from me. All this time I thought he was well trained.' See what I'm saying? I could borrow one."

One day when my mother was a girl the neighborhood ragpicker came to her door and asked my grandmother for any old clothes that might be lying around. She offered a few odds and ends, but the ragpicker cried and begged, pleaded that he needed to earn enough money to send for his wife back in Budapest. A wave of sympathy welled up in my grandmother and she scoured the house for a few spare garments the poor man might be able to sell on the street. While she was looking, he emptied the front closet, where my mother and aunts kept their clothes.

"Not a stitch left," my grandmother says, her eyes twinkling.

"Jo-Jo," my mother says, she's standing at the stove listening. "Remember the dress I told you I bought from babysitting and Aunt Dorie borrowed before I even had a chance to wear it?"

"That dress too?"

"Everything," she laughs. "The ragpicker took everything."

My grandmother ran downstairs and eventually caught up to him on the corner of Avenue C and Sixth Street, but he'd already sold all the clothes. He cried. He said he had no choice.

"God vill get you," my grandmother said.

And God did.

His wife finally arrived in New York, and they had four children. But after the last was born, she got cancer and died.

Needing a mother for his children, he married again, this time to a Russian woman from Third Street who refused to feed the children anything but stale bread. She died too, and the children were left on their own.

"One son moved in vhere you live, Joe," my grandmother says. "Vhere you eat, he ate. Vherc you sleep, he slept. His name vas Herman Cornblatt, but everyone called him Hermie. In spite of his father, he vas a hard vorker, an honest boy.

"Everyone loved Hermie. He had a lovely girlfriend who vurked in our house. She helped vith the cooking, the cleaning, vhat to do. Hermie vurked on Avenue C at the appetizer store. He vas in charge of the herring, and if you vent by and said you vere hungry, he vould fry you a nice piece of herring. In 1942 vhat vith the war, he vas drafted. He vent to France. Vun day he vas in a farmhouse and the Germans came. His friends they stopped eating and raised their hands and nothing happened to them, the Germans took them prisoner and six months later they vere home, but Hermie vent for his gun and they shot him dead."

The family heard of Hermie's death from a G.I. who came to the block to tell his fiancée what had happened. But Hermie wasn't the only one no longer living. His girlfriend was dead too, having succumbed in the terrible flu epidemic of 1945.

Both my grandmother and mother shake their heads in wonder.

"Still, Hermie Cornblatt vas a *mensch*," my grandmother says. "God should rest his soul."

Life. Life and war. Me, a little boy, playing in my father's dresser drawer, my father reaching for his medals. There were some beautiful Nazi medals and swastikas he pulled off dead Germans, and even the Bronze Star for carrying one of his wounded buddies back through enemy lines after they'd been shelled by a tank.

"Same case," my father said, after I remind him of the sad and tragic case of Hermie Cornblatt. "We'd holed up in this farmhouse, so how'd the krauts know we were in there? Who do you think? The farmer's wife. Fucking farmhouses, give me the city anytime. Right, Joe?

"Those cocksucker Germans. My friend lost a leg. I tell you what I said when I seen him? This is after thirty years. I didn't know if the guy's living or dead. All I know was he had his leg blown off, I take my belt off, tied it around the stump like a tourniquet, carry him back three miles to our lines. Lieutenant says, we'll take it from here, soldier. Last I hear of the man. Then I get this letter from Minneapolis inviting us out there all expenses paid. Me and your mother, we go out to Minnesota see the guy. He's a jeweler, very successful. I get off the plane, there he is. He grabs me, hugs me. I owe you my life, he says. You know what I say?"

"No, what?"

"Where's my belt?"


My sister's last letter came two days after her funeral. There was a special part for me: "Jo-Jo, I wish you were finished with your education and a doctor already so that you could be here to help me, because so many are sick, so many are wounded, so many need us." This a few weeks after my mother and father had been notified by the army that she'd been killed attending the wounded near Quai Dong. The first American female to die in the Vietnam conflict. October 23, 1963. Medals to follow. I woke up to hear the crying, the sobbing. I was twelve years old. She'd bet me that I couldn't stop sucking my thumb before my bar mitzvah. Wanna bet now, Sis? I stopped right after the telegram.

I went downstairs to the kitchen. My mother, my aunt, my four girl cousins, all sitting around the table sobbing. The men not home yet from the newsstand, but on their way.

"What's the matter?" I asked. "Why's everybody crying?"

When they told me, I screamed my sister's name. "Maddie! Maddie!"

My mother thought I'd heard wrong. My mother wailing, tears spilling from her puffy red eyes. "Not Daddy—Maddie! Not Daddy—Maddie!"

"He knows!" my aunt said. "He knows!"

"Maddie!"

"Not Daddy—Maddie!" My mother still didn't understand. "Not Daddy—Maddie!"

Me hearing those words now, today, this very minute . . . Not Daddy—Maddie! Not Daddy—Maddie! Not Daddy—Maddie!

# 27

## No One Knew Me Then, No One Wanted To

"Vhat explanation vas there?"

As poor as he was, my great-grandfather, after he came to America, had silk shirts custom made on Houston Street. After temple on Saturdays he ran home, donned his top hat and rushed to Madison Square to the Hippodrome to watch the half-naked girls dance.

"It's in our blood, Joe," my father says. "My own father the rabbi kicked out of the temple for chasing a naked woman around the ark."

I remember when the newsstand wasn't in that little kiosk, didn't even have a roof. When my old man and the Yitz sold the papers off the standpipe in front of the Knickerbocker Building, and if it rained they got wet.

"We come up in the world since then, Joe."

"Ja-voh, Pop."

"Don't bring me down, Joe, no worse than you already

have. Don't bring your family down. Improve yourself. Make them proud of you."

"I'm trying."

He looks around him. "Listen to what I say. Just keep it up, keep it in mind."

"I'll try, Dad, and thanks for saying what's on your mind, because sometimes I think you think that I think . . ."

Annabelle says I look like I got the weight of the world on my shoulders. She says why don't I stand up straight?

I say I thought I was standing up straight.

Ike tells me he met DeJesus on the bus. Everything's straightened out, DeJesus seemed happy as a lark. It must've been Benny's intervention.

"He was wearing your fur coat, Joe. Makes the man look like a pimp."

Dagmar comes over, knocks on my door. Pounds on it. I'm sleeping after a night of work. Annabelle's out with the baby. I put on my sweatpants and go downstairs to open the door. There's Dagmar puffing on a big cigar.

"I got a meet arranged," he says. "Finally got all the details ironed out."

"Glad to hear it."

"Sorry about the other night. Who knew they wouldn't show? This time Attila swears both him and Carlos'll be there."

I don't want to invite him in, but I do. I need coffee. Did he apologize for waking me up? Not a chance. What time is it anyway? Ten o'clock. I think I just went to bed.

"You want some coffee, Dagwood?"

He grins. "Mar," he corrects me. "Dag-mar."

The other night while we were waiting he told me how his son was killed by a bunch of muggers in Brooklyn.

I said I didn't know he and Delilah had any kids, but he says it wasn't with her, it was with someone else, a first wife.

Dagmar's son was fifteen years old, same age as Segundo, lived in Williamsburg with his mother. He was walking over the Williamsburg Bridge to the Lower East Side—"You know they used to call that the Jewish Highway, Joe?"—and ten or eleven black kids were coming from the opposite direction. Dagmar's kid was with a friend. The black kids demanded money. Dagmar's boy didn't have any, mouthed off, and they threw him off the outer roadway into the river.

"Yeah, I remember seeing the headlines. That was your kid? When was that? Not so long ago."

"Never caught the black bastards who did it."

"That's strange. I remember they made some arrests."

"Yeah, his friend identified some skinny little bastards, but they weren't the same ones. Those kids they arrested didn't have the strength to throw a marshmallow over the railing, much less my kid. It don't matter, justice was served, one creep's as good as the next. You know this guy Goetz, the subway gunman? He did the right thing. Shoot first, ask questions later. I always carry a gun. You want to see it?" He pulls a weapon out of his waistband. "Thirty-eight snubnose," he tells me.

I hear a key in the lock. The door opens.

"Zho, are you home?" Annabelle comes in, huffing and puffing. She's got the baby in one arm, the stroller in the other. "What are you doing up?" she says when I run to help.

"Dagwood's here."

She looks sour. She doesn't like him. He always wants something, she says. Rightfully so.

"How's your wife?" she asks him. "Your mother-in-law?" Annabelle blanches. "To each her own," she whispers to me in private, "but those two . . . I can't stand them."

He smirks, leers.

What's with Delilah? Was she really such a loose woman or did she just like pretending? Acts like she's working the Third Avenue street trade. Mewie says she is.

Mewie knows everything. Oh yeah. "I seen her," he says. "She came into the club with a john."

Yeah, high-class club Mewie works at, the art crowd frequenting the establishment these days, writing themselves up in the downtown gossip columns, impressing each other and nobody else, the hoi polloi pissing out front on the sidewalk.

Dagmar says he's got things worked out with DeJesus. We're to meet him at Consejo, the community center Attila runs on Delancey Street, the same one Annabelle and I went to for birthing classes, the same one the city's trying to put out of business thanks to the business acumen of our friend Señor Attila and the power of investigative journalism.

"This is the last meet," Dagmar says. "We're going to settle things once and for all."

"I thought everything *was* settled already. I don't understand. We come to an agreement, papers are signed, money exchanges hands, the man's wearing my fur coat . . ."

The phone had rung maybe a month earlier. A voice on the other end said, "Mr. Peltz, this is the Avenue D Check Cash, we have a Carlos DeJesus here, he has a check for two thousand three hundred dollars signed by you under the title of EAT CO. Is that right?—E Avenue Tenants' Corporation? Did you cut such a check?"

"It's good," I told the voice.

"That's all we wanted to know. Thank you."

My grandma wants to go see what the inside of the synagogue across the street looks like. The place is trashed and abandoned, but someone just bought it. A young man from

Pakistan, name of Hamed. Yves knows him, he's done a lot of work around the neighborhood, repointing, laying sidewalk, repairing cornices, stuff like that. Hamed says he's going to build luxury condominiums. When people question him—I mean, after all, he looks like an Arab, doesn't he? —he says it's all right, he's Christian not Muslim.

Oh, okay.

He'll respect the temple, he says. He really will.

He asks my grandmother if she remembers any trouble with the east wall, there seems to be some structural damage.

No, she doesn't remember.

"Your grandfather helped establish this temple," my grandmother tells me. "He vas vun of the founders. Before it vas the house of the Lord, it vas a vacant lot. I don't understand. An Arab's going to renovate it? For vhat? It's none of his business."

The temple board made stipulations, requisite to sale: any male who ever sets foot into the building must wear a yarmulke or at least keep his head covered, and the food served must be kosher, but you don't really expect Hamed to adhere to that, do you?

My aunt Dorie, my mother's oldest sister, the one who borrowed her dress that Cornblatt the Ragpicker eventually stole, says she hated the temple when she was a little girl, hated going there. The bitter old men who worshiped there drove her away from Judaism. She never saw a place so pretentious, she explains, so strict. The women and girls cloistered upstairs behind a curtain so the men wouldn't have to see them. And when the boys came in off the street, the old men would kick them out, "No *bummerkehs* allowed inside, thank you very much," and the boys would go out and play ball. Stoop ball at the Democratic Club.

We're all Americans, right, Joe?

"Vhat did they turn the yeshiva into again?" my grandmother wants to know. "Is it standing still? Vhat is it?"

"Pentecostal church," I say, but she's obviously already seen.

"*Vaiz mier!* They should be ashamed of themselves."

I should be as sharp as my grandmother is when I'm her age, but somehow I don't think I'm going to live that long. I'll die young. Tragically. ("Cut the bullshit, Zho.")

DeJesus worships there. I see him attending services every Sunday and occasionally on Wednesday nights. That must be bingo or something, I can't imagine him talking to God biweekly.

Is the Pentecostal church the same as the Church of the Neon Cross, the church of the electric street preacher who talks to the junkies?

What do they say again? "Come back to God! Come back to God!"

If they only could. . . . Who'd heard of crack? What's that? Heroin and cocaine, okay, but crack? Did they mean *base? Pasta?*

Annabelle says when she was in South America . . .

"There was one drug dealer, Zho, in Copacabana. His idea of a joke was he'd come up to you, say, 'Que pasta!' "

This is what I heard: I heard the Young Lords and the Black Panthers had set up offices once in the synagogue.

"No, not true," Ike corrects. "DeJesus's gym was once a bank, believe it or not. The youth gangs were in there, not in the temple, but they were the ones who trashed DeJesus's building, no lie. It was a bank, then a nursing home, and then the city government, the bureaucracy, turned it over to the community. The gangs got in a dispute and turned the emergency fire hoses on the power boxes, then stopped up the drains, let the water run and flooded the building from the top floor down. Dealt the building the death blow."

"Peek-a-boo, I see you!" Constance smiling, laughing, behind her spread fingers.

Just the other day I saw an ex–Lower East Side gang

member on *Live at Five* reacting to the U.S. government claims that Hispanics were making the least economic progress of any ethnic group in America. The guy had been Master of War for the Young Lords, now he's working for the local broadcast affiliate.

My grandmother says she still had the deed for the family's seat. "Joe, you take it. You assume your grandfather's position. Vurship vhere he vurshiped. Take your daughter too, and your vife."

"Grandma, I'm married to a Catholic."

"There's only vun God, Joe."

*She-ma Y'Isroael, Adonoi Elohaynu, Adonoi Eh-chud!* Hear, O Israel: The Lord our God, the Lord is One! The Shema, watchword of my people.

I remember the day I came home from playing Little League baseball over by the park near the highway. My team had just won, the first time that season after losing fourteen in a row.

Where was everybody?

"Your grandfather had a heart attack. Your mother rode with him in the ambulance."

"I'm sure everything's going to work out," Dagwood says.

Death stalking us.

"I remember vunce," my grandmother says, "my sister Lena, her husband run avay vith a loose vuman from the Yiddish theater on Second Avenue. She took him avay, this actress, to Detroit. Years later your aunt Lena heard vhere he vas and vent to bring him back.

"She found out he had five children vith the actress, the same as he had vith my sister, and he named them all the same: Mendy, Moishe, Mathilda, Melchi and Mandelbaum. Lena caught up to him and brought him home. She tied him up, a prisoner in his own house. But Harlem, vhere they lived, vas changing. The real estate people vere offering the houses to the *shvartzers* for cheap to get them out of midtown. They vere moving in by the bushel load. So Aunt

Lena is moving downtown vhere they still knew from Jews. Somehow ven they move, her no-goodt husband escaped.

"I used to bring home my vurk. I vurked on Vooster Street, Grand Street and then on Spring Street, in the sveatshops. If I brought home the collars, I could turn them out at night, and then in the morning the next day, I sew them on the dresses and get ahead. Piecevurk.

"Vun night, now this is many years later, I hear someone rapping on my vindow. It vas a man, a bum from the Bowery.

" 'Does Mandelbaum Vhimmer live here?' he asked.

" 'Yes, he does,' I said. 'Jacob? Jake, is that you?'

"It vas. But his son vasn't home. I told him he vould return, but he didn't vaut to stay. I said come around the next day.

"Mandelbaum had a fur shop on the second floor of our building, at two-ninety-nine. Is that standing yet, Joe?"

She looked at me, her watery blue eyes knowing the answer. She went on, not waiting for my reply. "He stitched the skins together. Your grandfather had his cleaning store on the ground floor. Mandelbaum and his brothers vould sort through the skins and throw the bad vuns out the vindow. Your grandfather vould pick them up at the end of the day and ve vould try to piece the scraps, make a nice cape or a coat of a nice quality that still ve could sell. I told Mandelbaum that his father had come looking for him. He hadn't seen him since he vas a small boy, and he stood the whole day at the vindow, his nose pressed against the glass, vaiting for his father.

" 'Is that him? Is that him?' he vould ask after every bum, street peddler and ragpicker who valked by.

"Finally he came.

"They vent for a valk together. Mandelbaum gave him fifty dollars and he vent to the Bowery vith him, and gave his bummy friends fifty dollars too, to look after him, because he knew if he gave him a hundred dollars he vould just drink it all up, and this vay, maybe it vould last a little longer.

"He never came back. The family never heard from him again. Vun day ve heard he vas dead. Mandelbaum vent to claim the body, and give it a proper burial. That vas the end."

"What about the actress, Grandma?"

"Vhat about her? I told you. She had five children vith the bum, just like my poor sister Lena. The children all had the same names—Two Mendys, two Moishes, two Mathildas, two Melchis, two Mandelbaums. But who ever heard from them? No vun. Not a soul in the family. I'm telling you, they vas all no goodt. And as far as I know, the vife, she never appeared on stage again, but who knew from such a person? . . ."

# 28

## Annabelle's Mom

In the aftermath following the tragedy of her husband's death, Annabelle's mom says she wants to sell her apartment in Paris, move to North America, be near us.

The grief. Tears well in her eyes.

"Even if Jean-Jacques were alive today," she says, "he would not have come to visit Annabelle and Constance with me. *Jamais*. Never. He had had enough of America." She looks at me. "No offense to you, Zho."

What do I care? I didn't care for him either.

She tells us everyone was very sad for her, very sad indeed, and shocked! Many of her friends asked for an explanation ("They're all so provincial," she says to me) of why her husband was frequenting this particular restaurant on the rue des Rosiers, especially with the recent wave of terrorist activity and bombing. *Un restaurant de Juifs à Paris!* It must be a target. How foolish! And he paid with his life, poor man. *Pauvre homme*.

Annabelle's mother said she tried to explain how, thanks to me, the sour, little man had become enamored of the spicy delicatessen food in America. That her daughter's husband, Zho, *le sauvage Commanche*, had taken him to a restaurant in New York unlike any he'd ever known. That back in Paris, no matter what she prepared for him, he had to seek out this other type food. It was on his mind all the time, she said, like a brain fever, the spiced meat, the cole slaw, he could taste it, that brown tangy *moutarde*, the rye bread with caraway seeds. Her friends listened with wide eyes, their noses twitching, their shrugged shoulders uncomprehending.

Annabelle's mom sits at our kitchen table quizzing everyone as to their nationality. For some reason this has become her favorite subject of conversation.

Yves comes. "I'm so sorry," he says, "I just heard."

"*Monsieur*, what is your ancestory if you don't mind me asking?"

Yves explains he is Quebecois, but that his family came to North America in the seventeenth century from the Basque region of Spain.

"Isn't that interesting!" she exclaims. "So you're not really French?"

Ike comes up for a plate of cucumber soup, says his father was full-blooded Rumanian, but that he never knew his mother, didn't even know who she was.

Over a Benson and Hedges cigarette, Scarlet says her father was Russian, her mother Dominican.

Spike is a hundred percent Polish.

Mazie, when she comes to pay her respects, claims she forgot where her grandparents came from—Miami, she thinks.

Pandora, down screeching on the street, is half-Irish, half–American Indian.

Paco's Puerto Rican.

Negrito knocks on the door and asks for an onion, another Puerto Rican.

DeJesus, whom she hears a lot about, saw once on the street, but never really meets, a Puerto Rican.

Lethal little Benny, who tags along with Mewie, is Viking and Quechua. The Otavalan aspect mixed with the cold Nordic blood seems to interest her.

Mewie, Sephardic Jew, family emigrated from Palestine.

"And you, sweet thing," turning to me, "have you ever been to Israel?"

"Never, and I don't intend to go."

"Why not?" She seems personally affronted. "There are your roots."

"No. My roots are here. In New York. I'm an American."

She snorts. "An American? What's that? You are a Jew!"

She wanted to know if Annabelle was keeping up with her picture taking, and if she wasn't, why not?

"And if I'm not?" Annabelle countered.

"Annabelle, I'm not so sure your father was wrong. Why are you here? Why have you come to America? Don't you love me? Your own mother!"

Now it was Annabelle's turn, but Annabelle only sat and stared. So her mother began again, took up the thread, went on.

"Those pictures are very important. They record your life. One day someone will look at this incredible record, see how you changed day by day. It will be the story of human transition. Not only for you, but for me, your daughter, your grandmother. No? Don't you agree?"

Annabelle walked away.

"And have you started with the baby?" her mother called after her. "You haven't, have you? You must!"

But Annabelle was gone. Her mother looked from where she had retreated. I sat at the table and inspected the blue enamel teapot on a silver tray in front of me. The honeypot was dripping, so I ran my finger over the lip, brought the honey to my mouth. Her mother looked at me. She must have thought me gauche. I did it again.

Annabelle's mother addressed me. Her eyes crinkled, her earnestness imploring. "Every day of her life," she said. "First Annabelle, now Constance. Do you see how important it is, Zho? A photograph every day of each of their lives. A registry like this does not come easy. Thirty-two years now. A third of a century! And who is to say what will come of it? Since the first day Annabelle was born. To start such a life work, it was inspiration, a stroke of genius. You know who inspired it, Zho-Zho? The baker! Now after all these years, don't you see, the brilliance of the idea shines through!"

At first, Arabs were suspected in the bombing on the rue des Rosiers. Six people besides Annabelle's father were killed; thirteen wounded, two seriously.

Palestinian liberationists, however, denied all knowledge of the attack. And shortly thereafter the world press reported that it hadn't been Arabs at all but disenchanted Jews who had performed the horrible deed.

They were said to be an Orthodox militant group, according to the *International Herald Tribune*, upset that this restaurant in the old Jewish quarter had abandoned strict dietary codes and were now serving kosher food and *trayf* on the same plate.

# 29

## Only the Fit Survive

Consejo, Dagmar said, the meet was definitely on for to-night. Him, me, DeJesus, Attila. They'd already not shown three times, so who knows? Attila had given Dagmar his home phone number, Dagmar had called to confirm, and what will be, will be.

"I'm not afraid of him, Joey," Dagmar boasted. "Not Carlos, not Attila, not nobody. DeJesus, shit, I'm gonna bust him, bust his hump good. The nerve of the man, right? Pulling our string. Pulling it. Pulling it till it's ready to break."

"It don't matter."

"It's survival of the fittest, Jack. Listen I lived in this neighborhood a lot longer than that Puerto Rican bastard, no matter what he thinks. Guys like me, we've been here from time immemorial. You got me? And as far as knowing Spanish people goes—I know 'em. I know 'em as well as I know myself. Shit, my cousin's a Puerto Rican preacher, he

works right up there in the South Bronx next to Carmelo
Estofado. So don't talk to me about Puerto Ricans. DeJesus
is a bad actor and he's not doing the right thing. I'm your
man, Joe. I'm the one."

He took one last puff on his cigar and the smoke rose,
whirling around our heads.

"Consejo!" he said. "We shall overcome or at least beat
ass! Whatever you say, Joe. See you tonight."


Once more for posterity, they were no-shows. We waited for
an hour, left them a note, went to get a cup of coffee at
Leshko's, returned. Nothing. Nobody. Dagmar tried every
phone number he had for Attila and no one answered anywhere.

Later that night at the newsstand, the headlines on
next morning's *News* finally proclaimed BASEBALL RIDS IT-
SELF OF DRUGS. The commissioner swore up and down how
drugs were a thing of the past, no more scandals, no more
faltering, no more players fucking up.

I was overjoyed to hear it. Baseball, after all, is the
national pastime, and I care about it. A lot. A neighborhood
like mine, it suddenly dawned on me, was like a big baseball
team, a big athletic venture, and drugs had come in and
dominated, proliferated and destroyed, rent its destruction,
knocked those good young men with the high batting aver-
ages out of the box. Sitting there on the stoop watching
those beat-up old Chevys cruise by, bad dudes in slouch hats
eyeballing you from the shotgun seat, or the ones parked
right in front of the building, you see them draw out their
needles, come with a Coke bottle of water, fold over the
matches, put in the cotton, cook up, draw, find a vein, a cop
strolls past and doesn't even stop.

"You see anything, O'Malley?"

"Not a thing, Sheeny."

Cops. *Les flics*, Annabelle calls them. *Les poulets*. The
chickens.

Not so long ago, they had public executions down here on the Lower East Side. Wouldn't be a bad idea these days, now would it? You in favor of capital punishment or against it? Listen: Reinstate the death penalty, one or two per weekend in Tompkins Square Park just like they used to have, nothing like a public hanging to keep behavior within certain prescribed limits, better than this antidrug campaign they got brewing, drop a dime on your buddy, drop a dime on your pal, drop a dime on your landlord, drop a dime on your gal. It was catchy. I caught Constance singing it. But did it work?

Suddenly the police are everywhere. The neighborhood is full of them, a cop for every junkie. A junkie in every pot.

Benny comes scrambling across the window ledge from Mewie's. "Dig this!" he says, the excitement making his eyes glisten. "I love it."

"What's going down out there?" I ask.

"An antidrug thing," he says. "You don't barely hear anyone shouting *'Bajando!'* do you, Mr. Peltz? Not a one."

It is a sad thing. Everything so quiet. All that local color gone. No guitars, no maracas, everything silent, only the click of the dominoes and the proprietor of the Kool Man ice cream truck crying, *"Helado!"*

"Hey, Benny, if you're heading up Avenue A, want to do me a favor?"

"Sure, bro."

"Pick up some of that Paul Newman salad dressing."

"He makes a mean popcorn too. You want some of that shit?"

"Popcorn?"

"All the money goes to charity. Not a penny for Paul."

"That so? I like it. *Popcorn,* you say? Didn't know he made that stuff. I heard about this industrial-strength spaghetti sauce. Yeah, I like it. Popcorn! Sorta like finger food. Perfect to lighten up the festivities." Mewie and I are going to sit on the roof and watch the drug busts over on Eighth Street. The mayor is promising twelve hundred to two thousand busts a night. Says he's going to clean up the heroin, cocaine, crack trade down here once and for all. Make the neighborhood safe for decent people.

"What do you hear from your parents?" I ask Benny. "Do they like Florida?"

"Florida?" he says. "They left that shit. They're living in Alabama now. They miss the Lower East Side. Everybody down there in the South, they all think my sister is black. She hates it. Her dark skin. They think she's a Negro and no one will talk to her."

"Your sister Gloria?"

"Yeah! Can you beat that?"

"Listen, Benny, you need any money? Let me give you some. What's Paul Newman get for that salad dressing and popcorn?"

I told Ben how Paul was up on Avenue B filming that film a couple of years ago, and now Steven Spielberg, the *E.T.* guy, he's starting to clear the vacant lot in the back across the street from our buildings. Rumor says he's going to build a tenement back there, a set for a movie. After it's built they'll torch the thing, burn it down. Ike was talking to those dudes, those production people. They said the script's about an old couple living in a crumbling tenement building, the last one standing on a block. The neighborhood's changing, a ruthless developer has eyes on the building, wants to put in a huge luxury condo. He harasses Jessica Tandy and Hume Cronyn, who portray the old-timers, and eventually his henchmen torch the building. But not before a family of aliens, cute little living flying saucers, crash-land on the tenement windowsill. One of the tenants, a battered old boxer, takes the aliens up to the roof and makes them a home in his pigeon coop, feeding them nuts and bolts and frying pans. The aliens wind up giving birth to three little adorable baby flying saucers, all with the magic power to make everything like it was, only better. So right after the developer sets the fire, the aliens rebuild the building, the real estate tycoon is thwarted, and everything turns out happy in the end. So good riddance to bad rubbish, I say. We all know how we feel about gentrifiers and developers, people who push us out of our homes, off our property . . .

"Is that really the story?" Benny asks in dismay.

"That's what Ike told me."

"Gee, I think I'll really like that," Benny says. "I can't wait."

Every time I turn around lately, some dude's standing on the corner, one of those big white umbrellas cutting the glare, a dozen recreational vehicles parked on the street. Besides Paul Newman that time, I seen Robert De Niro, Jodie Foster, Mickey Rourke, even Lucille Ball and Jackie Gleason, all these types jawing it up with the neighborhood junkies, and then they excavate the lot, pull down the building, and there's half a dozen bodies buried in the rubble.

"Yeah, hard times."

"Hard times."

"Don't forget the salad dressing, Ben."

"I won't," Benny says. "Not to mention the popcorn, right, Mr. Peltz?"

# 30

# He's the Invisible Man, Bro

The man in claims finally called me. "All right, Peltz," he said. "The insurance company is ready to pay. How much are you into money? How much you want to make?"

"Well," I said, "money's money. I like it as much as the next guy."

He told me we can get ten, maybe twelve, but if we settle for nine, we'll get it right now, no questions asked.

I asked his advice.

"Take it," he said. "Frankly, Peltz, you got a fire under mysterious circumstances. If you push too hard with the company, they send their investigator there, you're up the creek without a paddle."

I told him I didn't do anything. Is he inferring I set this fire?

"You? Why should you set it? Why should I infer that? Not feeling guilty, are ya? Nah, not you, but somebody."

Somebody, sure, but not me and not somebody from

the corporation. He'd met DeJesus when he was at the building taking photographs, recording information, trying to figure out how much would it cost to rebuild the apartment? He was wading through that black muck when we heard footsteps on the stairway, and DeJesus came up with his cousin, Shorty. DeJesus had that extraordinary knack for knowing when stuff was going down. Like he had a inner ear or a listening device on the premises. Yeah, something like that.

"What are you doing here, *amigo?*" he says. "Do I know you?"

"Do you know me?" I says. "Sure you know me."

"We know you, but we wish we didn't," Cousin Shorty says.

"You can't be here." DeJesus glares at the insurance man and then at me. "Nothing's been settled between us."

Shorty expands his chest. "This is still Carlos's apartment. Right, man?"

Who's arguing?

They want to know who the man is I'm with.

I'm not about to tell them it's the insurance adjuster. As far as they're concerned we don't have insurance. Never heard of it. As far as they know, this district's redlined. Can't get insurance here. They don't know we're planning to collect. So I'm gonna tell them he's the builder, but then he does. A quick thinker. He says he's the builder, figuring out how much it's going to cost to rebuild the apartment.

"It's my apartment," DeJesus says. "When it's rebuilt, I move back in."

I say, "Yeah. Hey, you know, we oughta finally have this little get-together, settle this once and for all."

"Bullshit!" he says. "*Cabrón,* I'm tired of you. You pretend to be one thing, but you're another."

"Who do I pretend to be?"

"You're one of them," he says. "You're their leader. This homeowner—it's you!"

"No way, dude. I only live here. I got a kid, a wife, my

roots are here. I'm a family man. My mother, my grand-mother, my whole family's from here. My history's here. I could live with you, you don't bother me, you're the man. Everything's cool. I want to be here. I want you to be here if you want to be. I was telling Negrito, I says—you know him?—the Puerto Rican fellow lives next door to me, next building, I asked him, I says, how come an apartment was never offered to Carlos DeJesus, how come Carlos never got a deal? You know what he says? He shrugs. He says, 'I'm the token spic. The corporation don't need another.' We don't need you, Carlos. You're problems, you know what I'm saying? But I'm on your side, blood. Let's just work out the details. What you say?"

Fucking Mewie. He's still got Benny living in his digs. "My crib's his crib," he says. Douche bag's still devoted to that fucking Beneficia. Even from afar, even from Alabama, she controls him. Her son's in trouble, she sends him north. Stay with Mewie, she says, or does she even know he's here? She didn't know when he enlisted, when he was at Fort Benning. She didn't know when he split, when he deserted. She didn't know when he slunk off to Ecuador and joined up down there. Now he's back, home sweet home. He's living with Mewie right here. And on Avenue D, he finds his old run-ning mate Segundo and they're back in action.

"You know, Joe, the fire coincides with Benny's com-ing to town," Spike says. "I don't want to say anything. Benny claims he arrived a few days after Christmas, but I saw him on the street three days before."

Benny and Segundo are standing on the roof and Steven Spielberg's across the street building his set. Hundreds of workers. The bulldozers arrive driven by huge, bearded men.

Clear that field, boys. These are Steve's workers, his

shitkickers. These guys snap to like an army. Spielberg's army.

Now what was here?

This was a neighborhood, Steve. It still is.

Sure, I recognize it. This is what I been looking for. This is what I want. A neighborhood. Right.

Steve, that there, that huge lot, that was a baseball field, man. Let me tell you what we got now. Back there we had the building where my friend Ike took me to get the bannister for my apartment. Remember, we went at dawn, with crowbars and duffel bags and we pried up the newel-posts and removed the balustrades while the neighbor lady screamed through the wall. And the cops came, she must've called them, and I hid in the closet and peeked out the front window and I saw them sitting in their car, looking at the building, but eventually they drove away, and I searched the floors, kicking the coke foils, seeing if anybody lost a little rock or blow on the floor, or some heroin, find a little, who knows, I might take it, what the fuck, the cops come back, they say what's your name, white boy? I say, hey, babe, take a walk on the wild side, it's me, Jo-Jo from Kokomo. Then they recognize me, right as rain, say, hey, dude, that's right, take a walk on the wild side.

A bunch of neighborhood guys built a baseball field right next door on Eighth Street. Had a real short porch, the Boston Red Sox's Fenway Park's Green Monster had nothing on that left field brick-and-mortar tenement wall. Steve, it loomed a minuscule two-oh-nine down the line, and the ball went out, bro, the ball went out. I can't tell you how many homers were smacked there. But you know what happened? Dude in charge, Juan from Avenue C, says, everybody pay twenty *pesos* an hombre. Your team joins the league, right? I hold the money. At the end of the season, winner takes all. See?

Yeah, sure, end of season, winner take all.

Right, except end of season, the dude is gone. Steve, *peso* equals a buck if you haven't figured it out yet.

So Segundo is standing there with Benny at the parapet and I'm standing there next to them, wall coming to my thigh, hands on the camelbacks, and we're looking down and Segundo says, "What the fuck that asshole think he's doing down there. He don't belong down there? This ain't Hollywood, this is the Lower East Side."

That it is.

"My old man's going to be in that movie," he says. "My old man's an actor, bro. He act with Paul Newman, Woody Allen, all those dudes. Rodney Dangerfield, Dustin Hoffman, Walter Beatty."

"Warren," I tell him. "Warren Beatty."

"Walter Beatty."

"I'm going down there, b. I'm going to be in that movie."

"Hey," I say, "bring Benny with you. You guys make a perfect team."

The baseball field's gone, the apartment building's gone. Spielberg sends one of his assistants across the street, they knock on the back gate and Ike comes out with his dogs.

The guy says, "Look, Mr. Spielberg needs something. You know Spielberg? He's a powerful guy. He's a movie-maker. We're making a movie here. This is how he sees it: See, he's gonna build a replica of a tenement building right here." And his hand flutters out and it includes all of Eighth Street and all the vacancies and decayed tenements the eye can see, and he indicates the building where the punkers lived, where they burned candles at night and we saw them flickering by night, me and Annabelle, reclining on the deck chairs, and one evening we sat up there on the roof in moonlight and suddenly the candles are bigger, it was the night we've got binoculars searching out the cosmic phe-nomenon, Halley's Comet, it's not there, not in our sky, was it in yours?, and the candle grows bigger and bigger still and then the building is up like a Roman candle, and the punk-ers, their voices pierce the darkness, "Help! Help!" and the fire department is coming, wind whipping, and they all get out, save one poor fuck.

"It's remarkable," Spielberg's man says. "There's nothing here."

"It's according to how much you're into money, Mr. Peltz," says the insurance adjuster. "Now I can get you nine thousand right off the bat, no sweat."

I say, "Nine thousand?" and then I think, okay, because in our wildest imaginings what we'll have to fork over to DeJesus is only a couple of Gs or maybe three at the outside, so that leaves us with six, and then with DeJesus gone, it's new-system time, we put the money into all sleek, new, no-hub risers, BX, and breaker panels, all us corporate members are gloating, feeling really good, really fine. Like I say, personally, I already kicked in my fur coat, the pimp's mouton, to make Carlos look sharp, put him in a mood to bargain, a mood to deal.

"That apartment, you know," Yves says, "that apartment was promised to me. Beneficia said if we ever got DeJesus out, that apartment belongs to me."

"On the open market, Yves, that apartment is worth fifteen grand."

"No! Not for me it isn't. Beneficia said fifteen hundred, twenty-five hundred at the most."

"It's happening this time!" Dagmar says. "I'm going with you, Joe. Wouldn't miss it for the world. Can't do enough for you or the corporation. Did I ever tell you what a great job you did with Butch, man, taking him to court that way, pay his ass out of here? Hey, by the way, since Fausteen's been evicted her apartment's available now, so I won't have to kick Paco and Pandora out. What you say I take Fausteen's place over, open up the walls, it becomes mine, me and Delilah, we make it into our little kingdom, our living arrangement? Hey, Joe, you hear Fausteen's out of the can, living over on Thirteenth Street with guess who—Butch!

"I know them Puerto Ricans," he tells me, "I can be a help at the meet."

"Sure," I say. One more time, me and Dagmar will go together. "You do the talking, I do the listening. In the end it'll all come out okay. I hope."

I'm thinking maybe Dagmar will keep the evil eye off me. So no one knows I exist, not in the Latino community, not in the corporate community. Somebody mentions my name, they say, "Jo-Jo Peltz," and DeJesus don't remember *who* I am.

I'm the invisible man, bro.

# 31

## Payment in Full

Dagmar calls me up about seven-thirty, ready to leave, and tells me meet him in the street in front of the building. We walk down the block to where he keeps his car in Phil the Pisher's lot. He takes out a key and opens the padlock. I help him pull back the chain link fence, and he backs the Caddy out into the street. I lock up and get in the car. There's no heater and our breath is showing. He makes a right off of Avenue E onto Eighth Street, pulls around the block onto Seventh and guns it west. Beer Can is walking down the street with a Bud in her hand and we almost nail her, cut down Avenue C to Delancey and park two cars in from the corner.

The Consejo offices are under the bridge, where the ramp goes up. We park and walk over. First we think, here we go again. The place is locked up, the steel gate down, nobody home, but then a door opens and a young woman comes out, slides up the gate so we can slip under, says to come in.

With the gate down and all, I tell her, I didn't think anybody was around. No, she says, they just do that for their privacy.

Nothing much happening inside. Attila isn't there and neither is DeJesus. In a back room about fifteen women are working on industrial sewing machines, looks like a sweatshop, and one room I can't help noticing is stacked full of cleaning supplies, about eight feet high, reminds me of Benny's story about Atahualpa, though this time someone's paying the ransom in scouring powder and pine oil and not gold.

Eventually Attila shows up, sorry he's late, and gives us a quick tour. Introduces us to the seamstresses, busy as little beavers at their sewing machines, tells us these are neighborhood women learning a trade, shows us the Bureau of Janitorial Supply, says somebody's got to do it, we keep this building spic and span. Sniff the pine disinfectant. "We got a daycare here," he says proudly.

I say, "Yeah, I know. I been here, took birthing classes here with my wife. Came in handy when our daughter was born. That good rhythmic breathing. I liked that."

Attila smiles, slaps me on the back. "Glad to have been of assistance, José."

He leads us into his office. Dagmar and I sit down opposite the desk. Attila says he spoke with Carlos, and he's happy. Very happy, and satisfied. He will agree to twenty-nine hundred dollars more, bringing the grand total to fifty-one hundred for the rights to his apartment, but there will be no reference to the first twenty-two hundred lest the income tax people, Social Services, the welfare, et cetera, should find out. Carlos feels that's a fair price, and a small consideration for all he's lost.

We agree.

Carlos never shows. His cousin Shorty arrives with the

papers, and says Carlos signed them and sent him over here and told him to pick up the dough.

"Hey," Dagmar says, "there's no money before we see the papers."

Shorty hands them to Attila, who opens them, makes sure they're signed and hands them across his desk to me.

I look over the agreement, duly notarized. "It all seems in order, but doesn't Carlos have to sign in front of us?"

"No, it's not necessary," Attila says. "As long as he did it in front of the notary, it's all legal and binding."

"Is that true?"

"Sure," Dagmar chimes in. "He's right."

So I slid the papers over, and he signed, and we signed, and we all signed and co-signed. . . .

Attila shook my hand, I gave him the check, and the next time I saw him, his face was in the *Village Voice* under the subhead INDICTED.

Sorry, bro.

# 32

## This Is a Stickup!

Segundo DeJesus comes up behind me. I hear him coming, but I'm not quick enough. "All right," the shrill Spanish voice says. "Hands up! *Arriba!* Hands up, motherfucker! What do you think I'm doing—fooling around?"

The mother of a kid like this will tell you he's not a bad kid. Sure, he gets in trouble sometimes, writes his tag all over the place. But that don't make a boy bad, does it?

A boy like that looks at the neighborhood. The changing neighborhood. No job for him. Doesn't see much hope. To his mind it doesn't leave him a big place.

"No one's kicking the poor out," the politician man says. "There's room for the poor in America too. The only thing is, no one's waiting for poor people to do their thing. Poor people have to grab just like everybody else in this country. That's the American way, after all."

"Survival of the fittest," we all volunteer unsteadily.

That's right. America—an equal opportunity employer!

So Segundo's on the roof with Benny, and they come up behind me and say, "Hands up! *Arriba, señor!*" and dance off cackling with laughter when I almost end my life, jump off the roof.

"Cut the shit!" I tell them. "I'm trying to watch Mr. Spielberg down there burn down his building."

Mewie is furious. I've heard his conversations with Benny. He can't understand why Benny would want to hang with Segundo DeJesus after their years of feuding and fighting, back when they were living in these buildings together. Now that Segundo's gone, living in the projects, the two of them are almost inseparable. Mewie's threatening sending Benny back to his parents.

"Do what you want," Benny tells him. "What the fuck do I care? Send me back, but I got my motives."

Word was Segundo had been giving Benny a hard time, teasing him about letting Mewie fuck him for money. Mewie was livid when he found out, but a few days later, he tells me he was just talking, he didn't mean it, says he trusts Benny implicitly.

We're all standing on the roof at the parapet wall, maybe ten or twelve rows of brick high, thigh high, with a protective clay camelback on top. Not much, and looking down five stories makes me nervous.

I asked Annabelle, you want to come up there, see what's happening, she said maybe later, call her when the fire starts.

"I'm not coming down here once the fire starts to tell you it's starting. I'll miss the best part. Come up in fifteen, twenty minutes, it should be starting then."

I told her I'd take Constance. She said be careful. The low wall scared her. Ike's dog, Miguelito, had already gone over the edge, chasing Negrito's little pup Tony, whoosh, right over Tony's head. I saw the dog's expression as he went out into space—not happy, confused. He was asking himself, where's the floor? Somehow the dog survived. Five stories straight down. Boom off the chain link fence, luckily the fence gave, the dog's alive, only it set Ike back twelve hundred bucks at the Animal Medical Center. "What the fuck," he says, "I like animals better than people."

I'm sure.

Ike and Steve seem to get along pretty well down there. The art director came by to ask who owned the lot and got steered to Ike, even though Ike doesn't really own it. The city owns it. They lease it to Ike for a buck a year to build a garden, part of an operation to beautify the neighborhood. They give Ike soil, trees, flowers, bushes, shrubs, a wheelbarrow, a garden hoe. He busts his hump raking the lot, removing the bricks and broken glass. There were three buildings back there once, but now they're gone like all the rest, and that's probably what Mr. Spielberg picked up on back here, the devastation, the nothingness, the wilderness, the desolate prairie. We're in a dream, bro. Mass decay has come, nothing will save us, except perhaps neighborhood real estate speculation or aliens.

The first day Ike talked with Steve, I listened in. Steve spoke in reverential tones. He said, *"I had a dream . . . ,"* and he described how in his dream these two old people living in a neighborhood just like our neighborhood came together. "Maybe they were immigrants. Maybe their building was the last one left standing on a block and a wicked developer had designs on it because he wanted to build a huge complex. But meanwhile these two old people, maybe one's from Poland and the other from the Ukraine, both grizzled but lovable, maybe they'd started a restaurant, a half century before, featuring coffee, blintzes, pirogies. They'd scrimped and saved over the years, hard times had come and gone, and come again . . ."

So Steve had the vision, and the vision was good, and a scriptwriter put it together for him, replete with Steve's requisite beings from another planet, and he hired his stars and he said, "I'm directing this one myself, 'cause this story's on the cutting edge, and that's where I'm at, and that's the new direction for America, we're not complacent anymore, everything's changing."

"I couldn't agree more!" I say. Leave it to a filmmaker to put the six-year-old kid back in all us Americans.

And he looks at me and says, "Who's this?"

"This is Joe," Ike says. "This is our corporation president."

"President for life!" I tell him. "Talk is they want to make me king."

Steve shakes my hand absently, he doesn't respond to my sense of humor. So I squeeze him.

"Ouch!" he yelps. Now looks at me good.

He wants Ike to cut down the trees along the fence, or rather he'll cut them down for him. He'll replace them, no problem. "What are they, anyway?"

"Ailanthus palms. No better than weeds. City weeds."

"Well, you tell my assistant what you want in their stead," Steve says. "Name your poison. Hemlocks, sycamores, pine trees. Whatever you want, Ike, because you're the main man. Today's your day."

Ike settles on poplars. There used to be a line of them at the back of our building but one night somebody came along under cover of darkness and cut them down. Who could that have been?

And Ike wants a cupola out in the middle of the lot. He says he wants to have a party and invite the mayor, all the city dignitaries, show them what a great job the people of the neighborhood are doing to bring it back alive.

"Hey, great, what an idea! Let me help." Steve says he's already contracted to build a playground over on Fifth Street at the public elementary school to show his appreciation for the city letting him use these vacant lots. He'll build the cupola for free. He wants to help.

Ike's really tickled and draws up plans of what he wants. "It's not really a cupola," Steve tells him, studying the

blueprints, "it's more like a gazebo," but then he confers
with his chief carpenter and comes back and says, look, if
Ike doesn't mind they'll pay him three thousand bucks extra
and he can find his own contractor. Steve explains, "You
don't want my guys anyway. It's like the time Harold Lloyd
had his crew build him a three-million-dollar mansion out in
Beverly Hills. But those guys were only used to building
movie sets, so even though the house looked fantastic, the
whole thing fell down after three years. You don't want
problems like that," Steve concludes, all smiles.

Ike says he understands. He'll talk to his friend Yves.
Yves can build it for him.

"That's the ticket." Steve slaps Ike on the back, tells
him, "We're in business!" He cuts down the trees. From a
construction site on Sixth Street he buys sheets of pre-
graffitied plywood. Benny's tag. Segundo's tag. He wants to
hook those up to our back fence so it looks like the real
enchilada, the real ghetto. *"Barrio,"* he corrects himself.
*"Barrio."* But ghetto was right in the first place. Barrio is
California. Ghetto or *shtetl* or neighborhood, now that's
New York.

He tells Ike he's building an identical tenement out in
California so he can complete the shooting there. Then he
looks at me, "What do you mean *for life?*"

Steve says there's only one problem remaining and
that's to hire an actor for the heavy in the movie. He wants
a neighborhood dude. Someone says, "Hey, Miguel Piñero,
the playwright and actor, he lives right around the corner.
He'd be perfect," and Steve's eyes light up and he says yeah,
go get him. And pretty soon Piñero's there and Steve rushes
up to him, and says he's glad to meet him, he's admired his
work for such a long time, he's seen him in Paul Newman's
*Fort Apache: The Bronx,* and *Miami Vice,* and *Short Eyes*
was absolutely first-rate, is it true he wrote it in Sing Sing?
Jeez, what a terrible set of circumstances, and he says he's
got this part in this movie he's shooting, a Puerto Rican
heavy, and Miguel would be perfect except for one thing.

Steve was looking for a little more breadth, width, meat on the bone, the guy's supposed to be scary, "But you don't look scary, Mikey, you look sick, you feeling all right?" And at this point Carlos DeJesus steps out of the crowd and growls, "I'm your man, *hombre!* I play the part."

So Piñero stuck around as Spielberg's script doctor, giving the dialogue that real neighborhood zing, and DeJesus landed the part as the neighborhood heavy and after a month of shooting we're all up on the roof, ready to watch Steve and his crew burn their tenement down.

"Hey," Scarlet exclaims, "this is fun!"

"Look down there! Look down there!"

We've already witnessed dozens of experiments, doo-wops and trial runs. Flexible pipes, six inches wide, running from fifty-gallon drums, containing what? Some liquid that makes the smoke waft out in thick clouds, and the flames lick the window frames, and Segundo's face lights up as his father stalks across the set, a kid watching his daddy, so proud.

*"Papi!"* he cries. *"Papi!"*

He waves his arms—little skinny appendages, and this dude's supposed to be lifting?—back and forth, up and down, semaphores in the wind, and Carlos looks up, sees his son on the roof of the building where they used to live, must think it's weird, all of us homeowners up there with his boy, Mewie looking down on him, Scarlet, Yves, Ike, Negrito, Spike, me, Dagmar, his cigar smoldering, only Paco and Pandora missing, they're having problems, Paco threatening to take a powder on her, Pandora threatening to help him pack, still somewhere deep in my subconscious I hear him singing now, "Baby, I love you! Baby, I love you . . ." even if they're not up on the roof, Paco and Pandora, or on such good terms, and DeJesus looks up and he gives us the finger.

# 33

# On with the Show

The arc lights are on. Eighth Street is jammed with curious onlookers. Spielberg's assistants are trying to quiet the crowd, keep them back. The cops are out in force, helping with control. The red fire trucks gleaming in the kliegs. Spielberg has a bullhorn, but he doesn't use it.

Yves laments the lumber. It kills him that all that beautiful wood's not being put to better use, only to be exploded and burned. He tells me how one night, after they had dropped off the first supplies of two-by-fours, a bunch of kids from Avenue D came over and swiped a whole mess of them to build a pigeon coop on the roof of an abandoned building. They also ripped Ike's chicken wire fence right out of his garden. "There were guards there too," Yves says. "The cocksuckers, they didn't do a thing! Just let the kids cart it away."

Steve's tenement looks absolutely real, more real than

any of the honest-to-goodness tenements around the neighborhood. At one point sixty artists were up on the scaffolding, painting the facade brick by brick. The detail is fantastic. You gotta admire it.

Somebody's shouting up at us. Maybe it's the cops, maybe it's the production assistant, nobody seems to care.

Spike comes out on the roof with his new girlfriend, talking to her in expansive tones about the *faux marbre* in Steve's tenement's hallway.

Very impressive, Spike. How you know all that technical shit?

Constance is running around, thinks it's really cute to make breakneck runs for the edge, so I scoop her up. If Annabelle were up here she'd die.

I tell Constance, "No, no, no!" but she figures it's a big joke. Fine sense of humor this little girl has, here in heart-seizure city.

Benny and Segundo are whooping it up.

Mewie looks around in disgust.

"What's happened to Benito?" he says. "He used to be such a nice boy."

They have some sort of sticks. Nunchaku. Another army game.

"Calm down, you two."

"Fuck off, douche bag."

Then somebody swings, and somebody else swings, and Benny leaps over the wall, over the parapet, into space, to the next roof, and Segundo follows. . . .

The story was that after the fire the whole neighborhood came around and were astonished to discover that the tiny aliens had rebuilt Hume and Jessica's building overnight, even better than it was before, and the real estate tycoon got his in the end, just what he deserved, financial ruin, probably more, something more cinematic, but none of us have gotten to see the payoff yet, it must be scheduled to be filmed out in Hollywood. To tell you the truth, I saw something along the same lines on television, so why were they making a movie out of it? Just look on any block—there's the aliens, there's the buildings.

Mewie says, "You don't know what the special effects are, Joe."

That's true. I don't know what the special effects are, Mewie. Granted, they could be anything. E.T. coming to Avenue D, finding out there's a brand of top-drawer heroin named after him, suing for infringement of copyright, whatever, using his name without his permission, a whole shakeup in the downtown structure, the Brooklyn Bridge flies off to Vermont, the Statue of Liberty on her hundredth birthday bends over and somebody tries to shove it up her aethhole. . . .


I shielded Constance's eyes.

Benny had made it. Leapt from one building to the other, but Segundo proved not to be the soldier his compadre was, had missed, and his plunge became a lot longer than twelve feet to the next roof, but down, deep, those five stories, the same Miguelito the dog had fallen, only when Segundo hit the fence, he didn't bounce, but became impaled and only quivered unto death.


I was standing in front of the building, and the sun was shining, the air hot and thick with humidity, closing in on a hundred degrees, and Butch came walking down the street with Fausteen, fat, pasty, bloated Fausteen. Dagmar said she'd been released from the penitentiary, and evidently it was true.

I'd already telephoned Butchie-boy, asked him what had happened to the refrigerator from Fausteen's apartment. When he had moved her stuff out, after the eviction, the brand new refrigerator, which belonged to the corporation and not her, suddenly disappeared. When I called the two-faced asshole, he denied everything. What ever became of his high and mighty neighborhood political rap, his big-deal morality, his Ph.D. thesis project, maybe he felt justified stealing a hundred-and-seventy-five-dollar refrigerator, not to mention grabbing the money we settled on him in court? No, he denied it, said he hadn't even seen a fridge in Fausteen's apartment.

I told my mother and grandmother about the pettiness, my grandmother repeated the story how Ike the Woodrobber used to carry ice in from the street for all the neighbor ladies for a nickel a block. The time my grandfather didn't want to pay the five cents, dropped the ice, broke the marble slab, the landlord made him pay to replace it. "Ike could've carried in a lot of blocks of ice for vhat it cost Pop to pay for that vun piece of marble."

Reminds me of when I used to come down here to the synagogue with my sister when we were kids. I'd dare her to sneak into the men's section, taunt her. "For a nickel you would!" I'd chant and she'd slug me.

I mumble it at Butch now. "For a nickel you would, you son of a bitch!"

He says, "What?"

"Where you going, scumbag?" I ask him.

"None of your business," he says. "You're in trouble, deep trouble, Big Joe. Segundo DeJesus dead. City gonna make an example of you, brother. Living in this unsafe building here, vacate order on your ass, you're out of here, you hear me? You don't belong here. You're losing the building. How many violations you got here anyway? I checked the computer. I know you got more than a hundred. And I'll tell you another thing, hot shot, Mr. Jo-Jo *Prez-eee-dent* Peltz. Fausteen here says she has proof you set the fire that burnt Carlos DeJesus and his family out! Not

JOEL ROSE

to mention poor Segundo! What's that—negligence? Man-
slaughter? Murder? Where I come from we got an expression to cover a guy in your position, Joe."
    "Yeah, what's that, motherfucker?"
    "Scrotum to the wall!"


Nothing to think about. I see Attila's picture again in the
*Village Voice*. This'll be the last time. The article says he
wasn't really a lawyer after all, just as I suspected. It said he
used Consejo to funnel two hundred thousand dollars of city
and federal monies into his own pocket. The corruption
extended into many other city agencies and the mayor's got
his back against it. I half expected to find His Honor in my
cell when they brought me into the holding tank down at
the Fifth Precinct. I asked them where I was going. If the
bull pen wasn't far enough, they said, there was always the
Tombs.
    When they brought me into the cell, a couple of the
guys looked pretty scruffy, pretty beat. One of them actually
recognized me from the street, from my block, and came
over to offer me a cigarette. A dude from the Avenue E
Boys, the guy with the pit bull. "Oh, yeah," he said, "I
remember you, the white dude, always pushing the baby
stroller, used to walk around sometimes with your kid in one
of those pouches, sleeping on your chest. That's cute," he
said. "I like that."
    Grandma? Grandma! Where are you? Mom? Dad? I
need you! Annabelle? Annabelle, say something! Something
in my defense. Please!
    "What you in for, bro?" the E boy asks me.
    I say it doesn't matter. "Don't ask, I'm innocent."
    "Ain't we all, blood," he says. "Ain't we motherfuckin'
all."

Joel Rose is the publisher and co-editor with Catherine Texier of the literary magazine *Between C&D*. He lives in New York City, where he is at work on a second novel.

Rose, J.

Kill the poor